# JUDI FENNELL

*She lost her shoe. He's on one knee. The little old man with the sparkling green eyes is suspiciously smug about it.*

Bella Casteleoni doesn't have time for Prince Charming. She's got a wicked stepmother, a little sister to protect, and a catering business held together with borrowed time and sheer stubbornness. The last thing she needs is a distraction in the form of tall, dark, and devastatingly dimpled.

Reese Charmant doesn't do entanglements. He does platinum convertibles, clean exit strategies, and definitely not kneeling on courthouse steps returning shoes to gorgeous blondes who look at him like he's the last thing they need.

Neither of them planned this.

Jonathan did.

*Because some fairy godmothers wear tweed.*

# Books By Judi Fennell

**Royally Sunk**
*In Over Her Head*
*Wild Blue Under*
*Catch of a Lifetime*
*Love on the Rocks*
*~Making Waves ~ outtakes*

**Bottled Magic**
*I Dream of Genies*
*Genie Knows Best*
*My Fair Genie*
*~Your Wish Is His Command ~ outtake*

**Once Upon A Time Romance**
*Beauty and The Best*
*If The Shoe Fits*
*Through The Leaded Glass ~ prequel*

**BeefCake, Inc.**
*Beefcake & Cupcakes*
*Beefcake & Mistakes*
*Beefcake & Retakes*
*Beefcake & Snowflakes*

**Manley Maids**
*What a Woman Wants*
*What a Woman Needs*
*What a Woman Gets*
*What a Woman*
*What A Guy Wants*

*Once upon a time...*

a long time ago
in a land far, far away,
there lived a girl by the name of Cinderella.

This is not her story.

*This* is the story of Lucinda Isabella Casteleoni,
who, like her namesake,
has a wicked stepmother, two tacky stepsisters,
and countless hours of hard work to (not) look forward to.
But unlike that fairy tale princess,
Bella's Prince Charming is nowhere to be found.

*Until* a little old man with sparkling green eyes
opens a shoe store down the street.

Then the magic begins...

# Chapter One

There was a fairy godmother when she needed one?

Bella Casteleoni gripped the railing on the steps outside the law office. Her stepmother was *not* going to send her little sister to boarding school if Bella had anything to say about it. Unfortunately however, the language she needed to speak was Cash since a custody battle required lots of it. And while Bella had been saving for one, she hadn't counted on it happening just yet. But Madeleine's latest threats had upped the stakes.

That witch had been using Sophia—as well as the family business—as a pawn for years. And now the woman wasn't just threatening to sell off the family restaurant, but to also send the fourth-grader away merely because, in the months since Dad's death, she'd found single parenthood counterproductive to the life she'd become accustomed to since marrying their father.

Bella would show her counterproductive…

She picked up her pace, her pumps clicking on the stone steps. If only she'd won that contract to cater the hospital charity auction dinner, she'd have a good chunk of her arsenal. But she hadn't. Which meant she'd have to find some other way to knock Madeleine's feet out from under her.

Like the dove that flew in her face did to her…

Bella missed the next step, stumbled down the last one, and found her skirt ripped up the middle when she landed butt-first on the pavement with one of her pumps flying off to God-knew-where.

Two seconds later, something—make that some*one*—ended up sprawled across her lap.

"*Ooomph!*"

A very large, very male someone.

Bella groaned as the big hunk of maleness hefted himself off her and got to his feet while she yanked the torn edges of her skirt together. Great. Add *mending* to her To-Do list. As if she needed more on it.

A hand appeared in front of her. "Here, I'm sorry. Let me help you up." The deep, husky voice resonated down her spine.

She looked up. Standing above her with broadly sculpted shoulders outlined against the afternoon sky, was one of the most gorgeous men she'd ever seen. Coffee-colored eyes, perfectly molded lips, sleek mahogany hair that showed just a hint of wave as it blew in the afternoon breeze, and those cheekbones. Good Lord. This guy could've been the model for Michelangelo's David, but with a much stronger jaw line.

And clothing.

"Miss? Are you okay?"

"Um, yes. I think I am. Are you?"

"Yeah, I'm good."

He certainly was.

Praying her blush didn't give away her thoughts, Bella looked around and spied her shoe on the next section of sidewalk. "Great," she muttered, taking the proffered hand.

"I said I was sorry."

At five-six, Bella wasn't exactly short, but he dwarfed her by a good eight inches. Tall, dark, and handsome. Like something from a fairy tale. Too bad she'd stopped believing in those ten years ago when a drunk driver had killed her mother and put Dad in a wheelchair, and the downward spiral of depression that had led to her and Sophia's current situation had begun.

No. She couldn't go there. Fighting Madeleine was going to take every bit of strength she had. And some she didn't.

This guy looked to have strength to spare.

She shook her head. Bad idea. There was no reason to drag someone else into her mess.

Speaking of mess… She brushed away a strand of blonde hair that had escaped the ponytail she'd scraped it into earlier. "I wasn't talking about you. My shoe." She nodded toward it.

"Oh. Hang on, I'll get it for you." Tall, Dark, and Handsome crossed the three feet of concrete with the grace and speed of an athlete. Filled out those slacks pretty nicely, too.

Bella bit back a smile. Good to know Madeleine and her machinations hadn't sucked all the beauty from her world.

Then he rocked it with one hell of a sexy smile when he returned with her shoe.

Tall, Dark, and *Potent.*

Bella teetered on her one pump as she tried to put the other back on, the teetering having more to do with balancing on one thin heel than his potency. At least, that's what she told herself.

The hand he put on her waist to steady her, however, made her a liar.

"Here, let me," he said, slipping the shoe from her suddenly boneless fingers, then sinking to one knee and slipping it on her foot.

Charming, too. *Prince* Charming, maybe?

As his light blue dress shirt stretched across those strong shoulders and the unbuttoned collar gapped open to reveal a strong, corded neck, she took a deep breath. If only he really *were* Prince Charming…

She glanced heavenward with a silent plea, only to have to duck as the dove circled back around and nearly poked her in the eye with a wing as it headed toward one of the ornamental cherry trees lining the sidewalk.

Prince Charming stood and put his hands on his hips. "There. Shoe's in place. How 'bout everything else?"

"Everything else?"

His eyes skimmed her. "Yeah. Anything else broken? Missing?"

"Well, if you don't count the skirt, I guess I'm in good shape."

He quirked his eyebrows and she blushed at the double entendre she hadn't intended. Oh, God. He thought she was flirting with him.

She so wasn't. She didn't have time to flirt now, much less date, Prince Charming or not. Sophia's fifth grade year started in a few months and Bella had to ensure that her sister stayed in that school. With all she needed to accomplish in such a short period of time, she'd be lucky to have time to sleep *alone*, never mind *with* anyone. And if Madeleine ever got wind of her having a relationship, forget it. Sophia would be shipped off on the next flight.

"I mean, yes, I'm fine. Thank you. Have a nice day." She spun on that heel, willing the stupid tingle his interest had sparked to go away, and headed toward her car.

"Hey, wait a minute." Prince Charming caught up to her and grabbed an arm. Awareness sizzled through her.

She took a deep breath and glanced over her shoulder. "Yes?"

"I'm Reese." His hand hadn't left her arm and his fingers were doing all sorts of wonderful twirly moves on her skin.

She tugged. She did *not* have time for this. Not now, not in the next five minutes, nor the next five years.

"And I'm late. Thank you for your assistance. Have a nice day." She gave him a slim smile and walked away. Another life, maybe.

"Hey, Cindabella!" called a nasal-y voice from behind her.

*Drew.* Bella missed a step, groaning while she tried to regain her balance. That stupid nickname. Her stepsisters found it funny. Bella did not.

But Drew would keep calling her until she turned around, so, resigning herself to three minutes of torture, Bella took another deep breath and turned around—

To find Prince Charming, er, Reese, with his arms folded, one shoe crossed over the other, and that mocking eyebrow almost touching his hair. "Cinda*bella*?"

"Don't ask."

He uncrossed everything and sauntered toward her. "On one condition."

"Huh?"

"I won't ask on one condition."

Drew was at the top of the courthouse steps and, even from there, the speculative gleam in her eyes was visible. Bella didn't have much time.

"Fine. What's the condition?"

"Your name. Unless it really is Cindabella?"

She laughed in spite of herself. "No. It's Bella. Bella Casteleoni. As in the restaurant."

For a moment she thought she'd seen disappointment on his face, but it was replaced quickly with a smile.

"Now that wasn't so bad, was it?" he asked, a dimple winking in his left cheek.

She was a sucker for dimples. And he wasn't making it any easier to forget about him. "I guess not."

"Bella! Wait up!" Drew was a third of the way down the steps. "I need you to do something for me."

Of course she did. Both of her stepsisters took that stupid nickname to heart.

Bella looked between Drew and Reese. "I'm sorry. I have to see what she wants. Thanks, again."

Reese glanced at Drew, then nodded toward the platinum convertible sportscar by the curb. Cool car, complete with rearing stallion logo. Not one of those souped-up muscle-bound cars, but elegant, classy, and sexy as all get out. Just like him. "I could give you a ride somewhere if you need an escape."

She could use the escape, but that would leave Sophia in Madeleine's clutches. "Thanks, but I can handle it, er, her."

"You're sure?"

They looked at Drew who was now extremely interested in Reese. Bella wouldn't sic Drew on her worst enemy.

Unless that enemy was Madeleine, then, yes, she definitely would. "I'm sure. Thank you again."

Reese took one last glance at Drew who had changed the angle of her descent to head right toward him. "Okay. Right." In half a dozen steps, he reached the car and jumped into the driver's seat. "Good luck. It looks like you'll need it. See you around." The engine gunned to life and he peeled into traffic with a wave just as Drew reached her side.

"Who's the hunk?" she asked.

"Oh, just someone I bumped into."

"Hmmmm." Drew flipped her hair back in that annoying affectation she thought made her look sophisticated. It didn't. "Listen, I need you to cater a party this Saturday."

Of course she did. Five days' advance notice was nothing to Drew. Matter of fact, Bella should probably be grateful for that much.

"What kind of party?" She'd love to tell Drew to take a hike, but the fact of the matter was, she needed the money. Even Drew's. And there was a certain irony in her stepsister contributing to the fight against Madeleine.

"Jimmy's mom is having a dinner party and her caterer cut out on her. I told her you'd do it." Drew had learned social climbing at Madeleine's knee; Jimmy DeLeo's mom was not only one of the wealthiest women in town, but also on every social committee there was—*including* the Arts board Madeleine was desperately trying to finagle her way onto.

Hmmm, this might just help her beat Madeleine at her own game.

# Chapter Two

R eese Charmant made a U-turn at the next traffic light instead of turning right to head back to the office so he could get another glimpse of Bella. Yeah, it was probably sexist in someone's book, but it'd been a while since he'd been that up close and personal with such an attractive woman and he wasn't ready for it to be over. And since the light was red, it didn't have to be.

So *that* was Bella Casteleoni. He should have looked more closely at her bid for the auction before going with Conlon's.

She crossed the street and that tear in her skirt teased him with flashes of shapely thigh.

Then again, maybe it was a good thing he hadn't contracted her for the auction—it was never a good idea to get involved with someone you worked with. God knows, he knew that first-hand.

And he definitely wouldn't mind getting involved with her. The woman was gorgeous. With long blonde hair that had felt so silky against his cheek, and breasts he'd only experienced for a mere second before he'd gentlemanly pulled himself off of her on the sidewalk. Hell, he was a saint. Someone ought to give him a medal for not taking full advantage of that situation.

*Give it up, Charmant. You've got a business to run.*

Too true. He didn't have time to hang around, ogling her.

His altruism earned him that medal when Bella got into an older model Honda and her skirt hiked up, giving him a generous flash of thigh.

He smiled before pulling into traffic. His good deed for the day. Hopefully the karma from that would carry over to the mess his so-called buddy, Luke, had created by pulling a no-show at both this morning's meeting and last night's Meet-and-Greet.

Promotional Sports, the sports-celebrity appearance and event-management company that he and his childhood friend Jake had launched six months ago didn't need any bad publicity. It was supposed to be a win-win situation for them and his former teammates, not temporary help for down-on-luck friends or their own personal dating agency-slash-ATM—all of which Luke apparently thought it was.

He'd known Luke was having a hard time with the forced retirement thing, and since his old teammate had run interference for him so many times in his career, saving him from countless injuries, he'd gone out of his way to help the guy out. But he'd never thought he'd have to run interference *because of* Luke. *Especially* when Luke had then taken the money and run.

Reese gripped the steering wheel tighter. His first clue should have been Luke's insistence on getting the fee up front. The second should have been his gut. Something had felt more *off* about Luke lately, but, God knew, Reese had had enough of those days himself. It wasn't easy going from superstar celebrity sports figure to has-been in a few months. Especially if you hadn't planned to retire. Career-ending injuries, as he knew first-hand, were a bitch. Luke's had only compounded a recent string of bad shit in the guy's life.

So Reese had gone against past history and common sense, given Luke the money, then had to field calls from an irate client. And not only had he had to refund the money, but he'd had to show up at the event himself. And could probably kiss any referral business goodbye, too. And that couldn't happen. Promotional Sports was now his life. Football had been—until it wasn't—and this was the only thing left of the game for him. He wasn't going to let Luke or anyone mess it up for him.

Again.

***

"You're giving me another chance, sir?" Jonathan Griff landed next to his supervisor on the street sign and blew the feathers out of his face as he tried to figure out how to resettle his own wings across his back. They weren't the ones typically associated with Guardians, but since Jonathan had yet to earn angel wings, any type of feathered appendage was appreciated—though he wasn't so sure how appreciative Bella and Reese had been of his prolonged aerodynamic learning curve, given that he'd caused them both to take a tumble.

"Of course you'll have another chance, Jonathan," said Raphael. "After all, you *were* responsible for that glitch in Bella's father's will."

It was because of that "glitch" (among other things) that Jonathan had yet to earn his wings—and what was a Guardian without wings?

He folded the pristine dove wings across his back, the question plaguing him yet again. "If I'd known both Anna and Salvatore were going to die within a year of each other, Sir, I would have made sure to include all the proper names in the will." The *wife* reference in the documents now referred to Madeleine, an oversight Jonathan deeply regretted. "I never thought he'd remarry so quickly. And then there was his fall…"

"That's the thing, Jonathan. As their Guardian, you're supposed to prepare for any eventuality. We'll work on it. Not to worry." Raphael's smile took the admonition from the words, but didn't lessen the guilt.

Guilt was one of the toughest emotions to overcome and, sadly, Jonathan had felt it far too often in his lackluster career. He just couldn't seem to get a handle on this Guardian business and had no idea why the archangel kept him on.

Oh, he always had all the best intentions, but it seemed as if he somehow managed to miss one tiny detail and ended up throwing everything into disarray. He hated being Jumbling Jonathan, the oldest and only one in his initiate class who hadn't yet graduated.

"So, what's the plan?" he asked Raphael, no longer willing to trust his own judgment.

"That's going to be up to you, Jonathan. You need to fix this for those girls. Bella needs to find a way to keep Sophia at home and it's your job to see that that happens."

"But how?"

Raphael took him under his wing. Literally. "I have faith in you, Jonathan. You'll think of a way. Look how you helped their parents find happiness."

Yet they'd died a year apart.

With those questionable words of encouragement, the head of the Celestial Guardians spread his wings and soared up to the heavens in a breathtaking display of finesse and beauty, leaving Jonathan to figure out how to clean up his mess here on earth.

Again.

# Chapter Three

Y"ou're late."

The words hit Bella the moment she stepped over the threshold of the Casteleoni home, her grandfather's pride and joy. An Italian immigrant with little command of English, he'd parlayed his family's old-country meals into a cornerstone restaurant in town, enabling him to build this stone mansion for his family. He was probably rolling over in his grave with her stepmother now calling the shots.

Bella glanced at the heirloom cherry clock in the living room. Eight minutes to spare. Then she turned to face the wicked witch. *Not* that she called Madeleine that. Well, at least, not to her face. No need to annoy the woman any more than her being alive already did. "I'm never late for Sophia's bus." She kicked off her pumps and dug her toes into the hand-tufted rug on the marble foyer floor.

"Sophia's bus? I'm talking about the ladies' tea. They'll be here soon and you have yet to prepare the food."

Bella rolled her eyes as Madeleine descended the foyer staircase, trailing a manicured hand down the curved railing. The woman thought she was royalty. Always had, ever since she'd finagled her way into the family. She'd been Dad's homecare nurse after the accident, and when his depression had set in, she'd used the opportunity to slide into Mom's place almost without anyone noticing.

Bella had noticed. But at seventeen, there'd been little she could do. As she'd found out, to her chagrin. Ten years later, she still didn't have many options.

"The food will be ready, Madeleine. It always is." Though she'd truly love to succumb to the temptation to just skip the whole affair. But Sophia would end up suffering. A cancelled horseback riding lesson, a dance class inexplicably filled, no friends able to make it for a play date… It wouldn't be the first time.

She *had* to get Sophia out of Madeleine's clutches.

"And what happened to your skirt? I will not have you serving the women of the Ladies' Auxiliary looking like something the cat dragged in. Honestly, Lucinda, I'd think you'd try to rise above your peasant upbringing. We are in the new world, you know, no matter how much you try to remain in the past with that restaurant."

"*That restaurant* is responsible for everything around you, Madeleine. I wouldn't speak so disparagingly about it if I were you."

"Well you're not me. That's the problem, isn't it? You loathe the idea that I control your sister's life and your father's estate." Madeleine's eyes narrowed to make her pinched face look like the weasel she was. "And if you don't want her sent half a continent away or the restaurant sold to the highest bidder, I'd suggest you march your self-righteous attitude into the kitchen and get the food ready. The Board will be announcing their selection soon so I need to make a good impression—"

"I get it, Madeleine." It just wasn't worth the energy to go down this road again. If only Dad had changed his will, *she'd* be Sophia's legal guardian and own the restaurant outright. But he hadn't, which pitted her against Madeleine when it came to the business, the house, *and* her sister. If she hadn't seen the fall that had put her father in the coma herself, she would have sworn Madeleine had had a hand in it. "You'll be asked to join the Arts Center Board, *the* most prestigious group in town."

Madeleine hissed. "You needn't make it sound so mercenary. The Arts Center holds many charitable events for our community and—"

"And will put you in the limelight and get you invited to all the social events of the year." Where she hoped to snag a rich husband. Again. "I *know*."

Madeleine's bony fingers gripped the pewter skirt hugging her anorexic hips. "You know, I'd think you'd thank me for trying to raise our station in this town so that sister of yours can aspire to be something other than a busboy."

Bella so wanted to unload on the woman, but with legal custody of Sophia, Madeleine held all the cards. And the witch knew it.

Bella was amazed she didn't have an ulcer from keeping her mouth shut for the past ten years. If only she'd won that catering contract, she'd be able to put her money where her mouth wanted to be.

The grandfather clock chimed and Bella turned back to the door just as Sophia's bus pulled up outside.

"Sophia's home." It was all she needed to say to get Madeleine to leave the foyer. The woman had as little interaction with Sophia as possible. For all intents and purposes, *Bella* been Sophia's guardian while their stepmother had played at being the put-upon wife whose husband lay unresponsive in a hospital bed for years.

But suddenly none of it mattered as a tornado of energy bustled through the door. A tangle of arms, legs, schoolbags, and long blonde ponytail, all eagerly wrapped themselves around Bella's waist.

"Bella!" the tangle shrieked.

"Sprite," the tangle's sister returned. "Welcome home, honey." She unwound the gangly appendages, pushing the ponytail out of the face of her ten-year old sister. "How was school?"

"It was great! Me and Cara got to take extra long turns on the swings because Nicoletta got a time out for pushing Joseph. Then Marco's mom brought in cupcakes for his birthday, so I won't be hungry for dinner. Maybe I'll just have dessert." She looked up, eyes wide.

"Nice try." Bella tweaked her nose. "But if you're going to eat anything, it'll be something good for you rather than more sweets." She bent down to kiss Sophia's cheek. "Besides, you're sweet enough as it is."

Bella wrapped her arms around her sister and hugged her tightly, her last link to their parents. Parents Sophia didn't remember. It was up to her to make sure Sophia never lacked for love since Madeleine had about as much capability in that department as, well, Cinderella's stepmother. The woman did love to play to type. "Want to help me set up for a tea party?" She touched Sophia's nose with her own.

"A real live tea party?"

"A real live tea party."

"Okay!" Sophia shrieked and raced to the kitchen.

"You *will* keep her under control while the guests are here." The order was dictated from the landing above, accompanied by the tapping of one pointy Prada.

Bella looked at her stepmother as she rose. "Don't worry. Sophia and I will be nowhere near your precious tea party."

Or anywhere else around her if only dreams could come true.

***

"You're a miracle worker. How do you do it?"

Reese smiled at Jake, his business partner, on the other side of his desk. "I simply pointed out the positive publicity she'd get for her career as she comes out of retirement."

11

Jake arched an eyebrow. "Sure it didn't have anything to do with a dinner invitation, oh royal prince?"

"Not you, too, Jake," Reese tossed the dossier onto his desk and stood up. "I'd like to think it was my sparkling wit and charming personality that won her over."

"Well, there's that I guess, but I'd put my money on the HRH thing. It always gets their attention."

Reese walked to the floor-to-ceiling glass window overlooking the river. Ever since The Injury, this view had always soothed him, but even the view couldn't make the "royal prince" thing any better.

HRH—Henry Reese Hapsburg Charmant. He shook his head. His mother, star of stage and screen, had given him one hell of a moniker. His dad's, his own, and that of some obscure long-lost great-great-something-uncle of the famed European royal family. The press had picked up on it, dubbed him *Prince Charmant,* and he'd been dealing with the jokes about fairy tales and lost shoes ever since.

Ironic that he'd actually put Bella's shoe back on her foot. He'd made a point of *never* doing that for any woman just so he *wouldn't* fuel the stories.

*But Bella wasn't just any woman.*

Reese grimaced. Great. Now *he* was the one buying into the fairy tale. At thirty-four, he ought to know better.

He watched a pair of speedboats race down the smooth-as-glass surface of the river, their wakes splitting the water like a sharp knife through freshly-baked bread, then stuck his hands into his pockets and rocked back on his heels. "Well, whatever did the trick for her, Bella McIntyre said she'd be able to make—"

"Bella?" Jake joined him. "I thought her name was Belinda McIntyre." He grinned at Reese in the window. "Or is Bella a nickname only a select few know about?"

Hell. He had to get his mind back on the job—or there'd *be* no job. "No, you're right, it's Belinda." Reese walked back to his desk and picked up the dossier with the papers he'd gotten the golfer to sign earlier. "She's agreed to participate in Community Hospital's 'Auction for Action.' I got her to promise nine holes to the winning bid, with full press coverage from ESPN."

"And that came through...?"

"An old buddy in the high-ups who owed me a favor." Reese set the contract papers down. The auction was the first big contract Promotional Sports had won. His name and celebrity status would only carry him so far; he had to deliver. He was determined to make his mark with the event, so he'd called in as many favors as he could. "But business is business. ESPN gets an exclusive, Belinda gets her publicity, the bidder gets the chance to golf with a pro, Community gets its donations, and the kids in the foster system get their programs." He tapped his knuckles on the stack of paper. "Everyone wins."

"And we'll get our fee and make a name for ourselves."

Reese nodded. "As I said, everyone wins." He picked up a pencil and tapped the eraser on the file. Everything was falling into place with this event. "So what else do we need to go over?"

"Well, you need to pull out your miracle-making stops again. There's a problem. With Conlon's Catering."

He'd spoken too soon. "What problem? I talked to Marisa last month. She was good to go for the event."

Jake slapped a file on his desk. "But did you know that she and Luke went away together recently?"

"Don't tell me." The pencil tapping picked up speed. "He dumped her with all the panache he's always had."

Jake didn't even need to nod. His silence said it all.

"Damn it!" Reese threw the pencil onto the desk and the graphite tip slid across the outside of Belinda's folder in an angry black slash. *The Midnight Maiden*'s top chef would be at his annual culinary conference during the auction; he *needed* Conlon's for this event. "I've told him to stay away from my personnel! There aren't enough women in the world for him to blow off? Now he's got to pick someone I need? God, you'd think he would have *gotten it* after my fiasco with Devin."

Reese rubbed the back of his neck, the old tension headache starting at the thought of that nightmare. Coach's daughter had been the one to seek him out. She'd been around pro sports all of her life, had known the score. Reese had figured he'd been just another hotshot for her to date.

He winced. That made her sound callous and shallow, when she really wasn't. Devin was a nice girl. Too nice in fact. They'd started dating and she'd started thinking *forever*. He never saw it coming.

The breakup had been horrible. And public. The team's owner hadn't liked the negative publicity. And Coach just plain hadn't liked it—to the point where the bad feelings began affecting their interactions. The fact they won the Super Bowl that year was due more to the team's competency than him as a shining star or to Coach's management. Reese knew the man had hated him for "using" his daughter. Not that he had, but perception was nine-tenths reality.

There'd been talk after the win of either trading him or letting Coach go. The team couldn't manage the tension. However unprecedented it would have been, there were serious discussions of breaking up the championship-winning pair.

Reese could never allow that. His talent and his reputation; they were who he was. He'd refused to be traded to another team in shame and refused to let Coach leave in the same manner. So he'd ignored the stories, learned how to evade the questions, wore his game face 24/7, and toughed it out. But when he'd ruptured his Achilles tendon the following season, he'd opted out. Went out on a high note. Blaze of glory. All the banner stuff.

And then found himself at a loss when it came to employment. Retirement had always been in the future. It'd taken him a while to regroup, figure out what he wanted to do with the rest of his life. Slowly but surely Promotional Sports was panning out. Yet now his "good buddy" Luke was about to bring it down with his Casanova crap.

"That explains why he decided not to show for our appointment today." Reese leaned back in his chair and steepled his fingers. "But how can Marisa do this? It's business."

"I tried that with her," said Jake, "but he must have done a hell of a number on her. Her exact words were 'I want nothing to do with anything that weasely maggot touches.' I tried to explain that he wasn't involved with this, but she wasn't buying it." Jake tossed his own pencil onto the file and sank into one of the chairs in front of the desk. "We're tainted by association in her eyes."

Reese bit back the foul words he wanted to say. He'd been counting on Conlon's. "How the hell are we supposed to find another caterer at this late date—"

Another caterer. Bella. And she'd already bid on the contract; was she still available?

*In more ways than one—*

Reese shook his head. It figured. The one woman to affect him in a long time was one who could make or break his business.

# Chapter Four

Bella opened the glass door to Casteleoni's the next morning and ducked as a flour-laden something whirled past her head, exploding into a vast cloud of white mist when it hit the front counter.

"You are a madman!"

Not again.

Bella waved through the powder and closed the door, then flipped over the OPEN sign and flicked on the dining area lights. The scent of freshly baked bread and muffins wafted toward her as Giacomo, a tall toothpick of a man with a dyed black handlebar mustache, swished angrily from the kitchen, his gangly arms flying about his head.

When he reached the break in the counter, he flung back the hinged top and pirouetted through, sputtering, "You simply *cannot* make spinach-filled donuts. We work hard to make the name Casteleoni a proud one and you produce this... this,"—his tongue tripped over itself— "abomination."

Twirling, he pranced to a booth, shot a look of pure misery at Bella, then collapsed onto the vinyl-covered cushion in an exaggerated heap, his long, thin fingers massaging his temples as he shook his head, muttering to himself.

It was a familiar sight.

A booming voice bellowed from the kitchen. "Pah!" The superior inflection of disgust spoke volumes. "You! You know nothing! You are afraid to reach for the heavens, you provincial, bourgeois peasant!"

Bella winced at the tinny sound of copper pots clanging against the steel prep table.

"Only I have the vision, the desire, the *ability* to reach for the stars while you..." A rag came sailing through the swinging doors. "You settle for mediocrity!"

Bella held her breath as the short, rotund Giuseppe, a ring of graying hair encircling his bald head like a coronet, strode through the saloon-style doors between the counter area and the kitchen, turning awkwardly to shovel his girth through the small space.

"You!" His stubby finger pointed at Giac heaped in the booth. "You—go! I cannot work under these conditions. I will not." As he squeezed out of the counter, he flung another flour-covered rag at the foot of the booth.

He looked at her, red-faced, with his fists clenched, and his native Italian accent made heavier by emotion. "It is Giacomo or Giuseppe—not both."

Bella advanced further into the war zone, ponytail bobbing over her shoulder as she skidded to a halt at the too-familiar site.

"Okay, Giac." She leaned across the booth to plant a kiss on the bald patch at the back of the heap's head. "What is it today? Zucchini torte, cucumber flan, or cream cheese chocolate chips?"

Giac leaned back against the booth's blue vinyl and crossed his arms. "This idiot..." He nodded at the idiot in question. "Thinks our patrons are salivating for spinach donuts." He shook his head. "Incredible."

"If they try them, they will like them." Giuseppe, who went by Gus in his calmer, less Italian-accent-laced moments, gave Giac the Evil Eye before looking at Bella. "Everyone, they want healthy food. I try to give our customers what they want and he—"

"Healthy donuts?" Giac shot to his feet. "Are you out of your mind, man? You simply cannot make *healthy* donuts. The term itself is an oxymoron." He approached the counter, planting his hands on the floured surface. "Just like the person inventing them."

Gus turned purple, the veins on the sides of his head above his hairline threatening to pop. His knuckles turned white. "Why... why... you..."

"Now, Gus." Bella ran over to them and put her hands on his. "You know Perla and Harry always love to try out your newest creations. You go right ahead and keep making them." She winked over her shoulder at Giac. Usually, he was the calmer of the two. "We need Gus's creativity for our more adventurous guests and your artistry, Giac, for the regulars." She kissed Gus's bald head and squeezed his hand. "I couldn't have done this without both of you since the accident. You've kept Dad's soul alive in this place."

Mention of her father's passing bound them all in a moment of silence before Giac hastily cleared his throat and leaned in to give her a quick peck on her cheek. "And you are our sunshine."

Gus shot a disgruntled look at Giac, then, with a heavy sigh, wiped his hands on his apron. He tweaked Bella's chin. "For *you*, I work." One more disdainful look toward Giac, then Gus waddled through to the back, letting the hinged countertop fall into place, the resulting crash saying exactly what he did not.

Bella slipped beneath the counter, arranging items on the other side of it. She placed a metallic napkin container on the countertop and slid a salt and pepper holder next to it. A glass shaker of crushed pepper followed.

Giac and Gus, they were like family—definitely more of one than Madeleine and her daughters that was for sure—but their arguments were happening much too frequently. With the Madeleine nightmare, Bella didn't know how much more stress she could take.

Giac bent down to retrieve the rag at his feet then sighed, absently pushing the flour around on the countertop. "I don't understand why he insists on such… such…"

"Creations?"

"Actually I'd call them creatures—and monstrous ones at that." Giac shook his head. "Why must I put up with this?"

Bella reached out to take the ineffectual rag. "Because you love him. And when you love someone you do whatever it takes to make it work, no matter how much you hate it." That included dealing with wicked stepmothers.

Giac raised an eyebrow. "Even if he makes me crazy?"

"Would he be Gus any other way?"

He sighed. "You're right. But you should hear him at home. He's getting worse—always trying more adventurous combinations. No one will eat them."

"Perla and Harry will." Bella swallowed her chuckle.

Giac laughed outright, their little conspiracy out in the open. "Even though you pay them to eat the food, it amazes me that those two keep coming back. They're our best customers. But I wonder how much this newest batch is going to cost you. You know you keep Perla in all her newest sandals with the money you pay her, don't you?"

"I'll do whatever it takes to make him happy."

He chucked her under the chin. "You are too good." His face

hardened. "And *that* woman takes advantage of your good nature. You really should—"

Bella held up her hand. "Giac, as long as Madeleine has custody of Sophia and, therefore, control of this business, I'll do whatever it takes to make sure my sister grows up in our family's house, knowing she's loved. With a family business for her future."

"What about the boarding school threat?"

She exhaled. "I have a plan."

"Does it involve cement shoes?" Giac twirled his handlebar mustache.

Bella couldn't help laugh. "Me ending up in jail won't do us any good, Giac, so no, it doesn't. It does, however, involve you and Gus."

"Us? Madeleine's not exactly our type, sweetheart, but if you want one of us to marry her to get control of the place, I guess we can take one for the team."

"No, not that. I want to fight for custody of Sophia."

"Oh, honey, that'd be wonderful, but that witch isn't going to give up her meal ticket."

"I know. That's why we have to *make* meals. A lot of them." She brushed a hair from her face. "I didn't tell you, but I put in a bid to cater the hospital auction."

"We're catering *that*? More work sounds exhausting, Bella, love," said Giac.

"Unfortunately I didn't win the contract. But I'm going to pursue other events. Sophia's worth it. But, you're right. It's going to be a lot of work, so if you'd rather not get involved—"

"Now I didn't say that. You know Gus and I will do whatever you need, but if only there was some way to challenge Madeleine's claim on Sal's estate—"

"Don't go there, Giac. It's fruitless. And hopeless. Trust me, I've tried to come up with a way, but Uncle Vinny's lawyer said it's iron-clad."

"Well, maybe your prince will finally come."

Yeah. Wouldn't it be great for Prince Charming to ride in on his white horse and slay the dragon that was Madeleine? That would be the only time that the similarity between her and the fictional princess would be welcome.

Thoughts of Mr. Art Sculpture from yesterday danced in her head.

She made them waltz right out again; fairy tales could break your heart if you tried to apply them to real life.

## Chapter Five

The merry jingle of bells rippled through Casteleoni's as the early morning regulars streamed in. Bella quickly donned her apron and set about pouring coffee. Plates of eggs, muffins, croissants, and donuts—though not spinach ones—appeared as if by magic from the back, so Bella knew Gus had calmed himself down and was fully engaged in his creativity.

Bella loved being in the thick of the community, loved hearing the latest news of everyone's families. This place, this business, was her sanctuary. It was the home she didn't have in the house she *should* call home.

Father DiGennaro stopped by after morning mass. The Napoli brothers hopped in for a cup of coffee and their regular cannolies, while the Donatelli twins played hooky from third period to flirt with the construction workers on a break from their job site. Bella was wiping down a table and admonishing the girls on the merits of English lit when a shiver flashed over her skin.

She recognized it immediately; Mr. Art Sculpture had entered the building.

"So what's Gus's special of the day?" The voice behind her played like the slow, sensuous melody of a violin up her spine.

She turned slowly. Six foot plus of gorgeous with a strong, sculpted face, that smile—Lord, that smile—and those eyes... It was as if the air came alive, the sunshine brighter, sounds crisper.

"Hi." He smiled at her.

She gulped. She honest-to-God gulped. "Um, hi."

His smile deepened. Ah, those dimples. She could do nothing but stare at them.

"So… the special?"

They certainly were—"Um, I'm sorry. What?"

"The sign. It says to try Gus's special of the day. I'm interested."

So was she.

Bella shook her head and tried to scoop up her composure that was melting all over the floor. "It's, um, spinach donuts."

The dimples disappeared. "On second thought…"

Bella laughed. "I know. It takes a certain amount of daring to try them."

"And an iron stomach."

She couldn't help glancing at his. His golf shirt molded nicely to a very iron-like stomach. Probably a six-pack.

Bella tucked some of her stray hair into her ponytail. "Um, so you're saying that your stomach isn't up to the challenge?"

His dark eyes widened. "You're kidding, right? Spinach donuts are *really* his specialty?"

She led him to one of the booths. "We never kid about Gus's specialties. And a few people have tried them." Aside from Harry and Perla, the construction crew came in every Friday to reward the winner of their weekly bet: losers bought the winner Gus's special. Gus, thinking it an honor, was thrilled, and everyone let him think it was. The truth, however, was that the so-called "winner" wasn't the guy who'd done the best job for the week, but the biggest screw-up. "I'll just get you a menu and—"

He—Reese—clamped his fingers around her wrist. "Hang on." He cleared his throat and slid onto the vinyl. "It's not like it's going to kill me, right? I mean, spinach's good for you, and donuts, well, they taste good. So… yeah. I'll give it a try."

Bella blinked. "Are you sure?"

"I am." He didn't look it.

She took pity on him. Some. "If it's any consolation, those who've tried them said they aren't bad." They weren't good either, but at least the donuts stayed down.

"What about you?"

"Me? Haven't tried them." She never did so she wouldn't have to lie to the customers. Or to Gus. "If I sampled everything I wouldn't be able to fit through the door," she said, heading toward the front counter.

"So what's Adonis doing in our humble abode?" Giac asked as she set the hinged countertop back in place.

She'd been wondering that herself. "Having breakfast?" A foreign concept indeed.

"Hmmm, is that what it is?" Giac waggled his eyebrows. "I don't recall you leading Mr. Fazio to his table in a quite so, shall we say, come-hither way."

"Okay, okay." Bella bent down to pick up a napkin she'd brushed to the floor so he wouldn't see her blush. With her composure once more regained, she explained how she'd coerced the poor guy into trying Gus's special.

"Bella." Giac sighed. "You are not doing Gus any favors, truly, by paying or bribing people to eat his 'creations.' " Giac punctuated his statement with air-quotes. "Honey, I know you mean well, but there's nothing to be gained by it. He gets all excited and inventive, and then absolutely crushed when they don't sell. It's getting harder for me to pick up the pieces." Giac shook his head. "I don't think you should encourage him."

"But he wants to be creative and he says the bakery just isn't enough anymore." Bella sighed. "I don't want to lose him."

Giac wiped down the Formica. "Oh honey, don't you worry about that. He'll never leave you. And neither will I. Why, you're like the daughter we never had. We've watched you grow up. There is no way we'd leave you to fend for yourself against that werewolf you live with." He shook his head and scrubbed the countertop a little harder. "If that judge had been more open-minded about Gus and I... Well, that's water under the bigot bridge. But don't you ever again worry that beautiful head of yours about us abandoning you."

Bella smiled and covered his hand. "You two are so good to me and Sophia. I just want you both to be happy. And if eggplant quiche and spinach donuts do that for Gus—"

"Ugh. Don't mention those words to me. I shudder when I even *think* of those concoctions. Now—" Giac turned her around, took the dishtowel from her hand and swept his fingers through her ponytail. "You swish your way over to that very interesting hottie and see what it is he really wants because it sure as heck isn't Gus's special." He gave her a little push, flipped his hands in the air, then strutted back into the kitchen. "And I'll see if I can get Gus to work on something productive, like a death-by-chocolate triple layer cake with whipped cream icing."

Great. Another argument.

She momentarily considered taking Giac's advice to go chat with Reese, but what, really, would be the point? Nothing would come of it.

Madeleine was violently opposed to Bella having anything resembling a personal life that would take from the time she could be devoting to waiting on the woman hand and foot. It only took one threat to Sophia for Bella's relationships to disappear—and not in a *poof!* of fairy dust.

She grabbed the dishtowel off the counter and headed to an empty table—and refused to consider it a reflection of her life.

Besides, Reese had enough people talking to him. Every time Bella glanced over—not that she did so a lot (well, okay, maybe more than she normally would if he were, say, Mr. Fazio)—someone else would be standing by his table. She couldn't blame them; the guy did seem to have a magnetic personality. She should be relieved that she wasn't the only one affected by him so she could put the whole attraction behind her.

Could, but didn't…

"Number seven's up." Giac clanked a dish onto the counter.

Bella took a breath, rolled her shoulders back, and retrieved Reese's meal.

"Go talk to him." Giac smiled through clenched teeth.

"I will." She raised her eyebrows as she held up the plate she was about to deliver to said *him*.

"No, I mean *really* talk to him." Giac added a curly-cue orange rind to the edge of the plate with a heart-shaped strawberry beside it. Bella rolled her eyes. Subtlety was not Giac's forte. "Honestly, Bella, you have to move forward with your life. You don't want to spend your old age with Gus and I, do you?"

That wasn't why she headed to Reese's table with a smile on her face. Or so she tried to tell herself. But just to prove it, she smiled at him, set the plate down, and then left.

Or she would have if he hadn't grabbed her wrist again, sending a bolt of lightning shooting up her arm. Her breath caught and Bella could swear she felt his touch with all seven layers of skin.

Reese cleared his throat and released her arm. "I was, ah…" He motioned to his booth. "Sit for a moment?"

Uh oh. This was not good. That spark between them—okay, bonfire—could *not* lead anywhere. But it didn't stop her from sliding onto the seat opposite him.

Reese stretched his long legs out of the booth, crossed them at the ankles, and looked at her. Just looked.

"What did you want to talk about?" Bella thrummed her fingertips on the table.

*She'd probably be shocked at what he wanted to talk about.*

Reese shifted on the seat, his pants tighter than when he'd walked in, which, if she knew, would probably have her tossing the donuts into his lap and storming off, and that would be the last he ever saw of her. A tragedy he didn't want to think about.

*Business, Charmant.*

Right. He told his hormones to take a chill and glanced around, trying to will some control back into his body.

The place was packed and they were still coming in the door, testament to the restaurant's reputation he'd gathered with a dozen reference calls after his conversation with Jake. Then there was Bella herself. Aside from the fact that she was gorgeous, he'd watched her before he'd come in. She'd had a smile for everyone who's stopped her—and *every*one had stopped her. Bella was obviously very well liked.

He completely understood why.

So, despite the sugar-coated, Popeye version of haggis on his plate, and a libido that was crying with the restrictions he was about to place on it, Reese took a deep breath and a leap of faith. "I'm interested in hiring you."

"I beg your pardon?" flew out of her mouth. Obviously, of all the words in the English language, those five were not the ones she'd expected to hear.

They weren't actually the ones he'd wanted to say to her, but the auction was fast approaching and he was low on options.

"Let me rephrase that." He leaned forward and used his fork to cut a piece of the donut so he wouldn't be tempted to touch her. She even smelled good. Sugary sweet and a hint of spice. Which he so should not care about. All he *should* care about was if she could pull off the job.

Reese straightened, leaning farther from her—but her scent merely followed him.

*Business, Charmant.*

He pulled his legs beneath the table and damn if his foot didn't graze hers, which sparked another layer of awareness he didn't need. "I know you bid on the hospital charity dinner and I want to offer you the job."

"You…" Now it was her turn to sit back. "Why? I thought that contract had already been awarded?"

"There's been a problem with it."

She nodded then nibbled on her lip.

She had great lips.

*Business, Charmant…*

"We've got some top names to donate prizes and services for the hospital, and there are a lot of big hitters on the invitee list. We're looking for upscale fare and white glove service, and I need a local caterer to handle both the cocktail hour and the sit-down dinner." Fastest pitch he'd ever made, including the Hail Mary pass in the final game.

Yeah, that was it; think of football. He'd always been able to think clearly on his feet in a game, and it'd keep him from noticing how a tendril of blonde hair curled down her neck to rest in the hollow of her collar bone.

Or not.

"Any chance you're interested in me—uh, helping me?" Jeez. Talk about a fumble of epic proportions. "Doing the catering it, I mean."

He shoved the donut into his mouth—to prevent anything else escaping.

The taste registered. And not in a good way. He was about to grab a napkin, but Bella blinked those South Pacific blues and he couldn't look away to find one.

"So I'm second best?"

Not in his book and if he'd seen her, there was no way he would have given the contract to Marisa.

Okay, maybe he would have, if only so he could ask Bella out. But it was just as well he hadn't. Because he needed her, and *not* in a way his libido was crying out for.

"No. It's just that we've worked with Conlon's before and your bids were similar. So I went with what I knew." But what he knew right now was that he wanted to lick the crumb of something from the corner of her mouth. "I've called around and you have a great reputation. Any chance you're interested? I'd be willing to bump up your bid by two percent." Hell, he'd go with ten; he needed a caterer.

She tapped her lip with a finger and that crumb fell away. Pity. "Make it three and you've got a deal."

"Done." Reese exhaled. She was in.

And so was he—in a whole lotta trouble.

"I quit!" The cook stormed from the kitchen, crumpling his hat and tossing it to the counter.

"Giuseppe Sorcio! You get back here right now!" The thin guy came running after him, but Giuseppe shrugged away from his touch.

"You think you can do it better? Fine. Do it!" Guisepee's tail wind whisked a stack of paper napkins to the floor as he stormed past, and the bells jangled angrily when he wrenched open the door to head out to the sidewalk.

"Bella, I'm sorry." The thin guy held shrugged as he followed Giuseppe. "I have to go after him. I shouldn't have said—" He shook his head miserably.

Once the bells settled down the silence was deafening.

"Well." Bella exhaled and pushed herself upright out of the booth. "I guess I'm on kitchen duty."

"Need some help?" Reese was as surprised as she was at his offer. He didn't have time to help out. Not that that was going to stop him.

"Oh, you don't have to—"

"Hey, I offered. Might as well take me up on it." He looked out the front window. The men were nowhere to be seen. "Doesn't look like they're going to be back any time soon."

Bella looked at him, nibbling her lip. She was sexy as hell when she did that.

"No, really, that's okay. I can handle it."

"But why should you?" He stood up and swept his hand toward the kitchen. "If we're going to be working together, there's no time like the present to start, so lead on, MacDuff."

Allowing her to lead the way had a lot to recommend it; the view was spectacular.

The kitchen however… wasn't.

"Oh lord." Bella grabbed the toppled stainless steel mixing bowls on the prep table and righted them. The green goo beneath them had congealed into a lump. Just like it was doing in his gut. He'd never eat spinach again.

He grabbed a trash can and slid the mess into it. "Guess it was a limited-time special."

"Thanks," she said.

"No problem. What's on the lunch menu? Please tell me it has nothing to do with spinach."

"No, thank goodness. Gus was planning on lasagna."

"Sadly, not one of my fortes."

"But it is one of mine." She picked up a carton of eggs. "How are you at mixing?"

He flexed his biceps and waggled his eyebrows. "I think I can manage."

She rolled her eyes, then smacked his left arm with a wooden spatula. "Great. First, start with the eggs. Think you can crack them without any shells?"

"You know, I do have some skills in the kitchen." And ones in other rooms he wouldn't mind showing her.

She pointed at the industrial-sized mixer. "Then here you go, Rachel Ray."

*Rachel*? She wasn't thinking along the same lines he was. Which was a good thing. He just had to keep reminding himself of that.

While he was trying to figure out how to turn the machine on, Bella wrestled a large container from the refrigerator. When it landed on the table hard enough to slosh some of its contents over the rim, Reese gave up on the mixer and grabbed the next container from her. "I didn't get these muscles from cracking eggs, you know. Let me do the heavy lifting."

"I can handle it."

"I know, but, again, why should you have to?" He set that container down. "What else?"

She pointed to a measuring cup on top of the cabinet. "I could use that."

He followed her orders as she pointed out other items they needed, then volunteered to grate the mozzarella. After five minutes, he was sorry he'd mentioned his muscles. Grating cheese was definitely not on his Bucket List and there was still the Parmesan to deal with.

"Are you planning for Armageddon?" he asked as he picked up one of five remaining mozzarella balls left to be mixed in with the vat of ricotta cheese.

"Our lasagna sells. I'm just glad Gus cooked the ground beef and made the pasta before he stormed out." She set several trays of the pasta beside each industrial-sized baking dish. "Now we get to put it all together."

They layered the cheese mixture with the pasta and ground beef in each dish, then slathered each with homemade sauce and more mozzarella and parmesan, their assembly line flowing smoothly as they worked together.

He could think of a few other ways they could work together smoothly…

By the time the last dish went into the ovens, Reese felt as if *he* was being cooked. Working so closely with her, their hands and arms accidentally touching as he slowed down or she sped up the process, the close confines of the space between the table and the cabinets ensuring they'd brush up against each other, the way she managed to open the wall ovens and fit beneath his arms… Reese wasn't sure that hiring her had been the best idea. Not when business was the last thing on his mind. No, he was all for saying "screw the lasagna," and just lick the ricotta off several interesting body parts.

Reason enough to move away from her. He did, leaning against the sink and swiping his arm across his forehead. "I can't believe you were going to do all of that yourself. And there's still the clean up to do."

She shrugged and cleaned the spilled ricotta off the prep table. "There's no one else to do it and I'm not afraid of hard work."

"Good thing because the auction is going to require a lot of it." Reese picked up a jar of odd looking yellow-ish beans he'd removed from the fridge when he'd gotten that last tub of ricotta. "Lupini beans? Never heard of them."

She took the jar. "Oh, they're good. And great for target practice, too."

"Target practice?"

Bella got a funny look on her face. "Uh, never mind. I shouldn't have said anything."

A blushing Bella was even more gorgeous. And call him an idiot, but he was enjoying it. "Oh no. What did you mean by that?"

She rolled her eyes. Her beautiful blue eyes that he could spend way too much time looking into if he weren't careful.

"Fine. Here." She popped one of the beans into her mouth and motioned to the giant pot drying on the counter behind him. "Watch."

She did an odd twist-thing with her mouth—which made him focus on her lips, something he needed no help doing—then puckered up, and launched the bean.

She missed the pot.

She didn't, however, miss him. He took the shot on the chin, then the bean bounced down his shirt.

"Oh no." Bella covered her lips with her hands. *That* was the real tragedy. "I'm so sorry."

He wasn't. It was just a shirt and just the thing he needed to get his mind off her lips.

He grabbed an open can of black olives. "Sorry? Not yet you're not." He turned his back to her.

"Don't worry. I'll pay to have your clothes cleaned."

He stuck olives on the ends of his fingers like he'd done when he was a kid. "Oh, you're definitely going to pay." He turned around and lost the battle with his smile as he flicked five "bombs" at her.

They hit her squarely in the chest.

For the space of a heartbeat she looked shocked, then a sly smile slid across those lips. "That was just so wrong." She grabbed an oblong loaf of Italian bread and a hunk of pepperoni that she tossed like a baseball, catching it and tossing it again. "I only got you with one."

"You have to think offensively." He scooped the last spoonful of ricotta cheese from one of the tubs and aimed it at her.

"You wouldn't." Her loaf of bread wavered.

"You willing to risk it?" He pulled the spoon back a little more.

She nibbled on her bottom lip as she looked from the ricotta to his eyes. Reese tried to look stern, but the lip-nibbling was distracting him.

He gave up both battles when she grabbed the turkey baster full of spaghetti sauce and aimed it at him. "Offensive enough?"

"You win." He set the ricotta spoon on the steel table between them and laughed as he raised his hands in surrender.

"Back up." Bella waved the sauce launcher in circles.

"You don't trust me?"

"I don't really know you well enough to know if I can or not."

True, but Reese prided himself on his word being golden. She needed to know that he was a stand-up guy.

So he walked around the table, took the baster from her, and set it down so it wouldn't accidentally go off. "One thing you need to know about me, Bella: you can always trust me."

But then she nibbled her lip and he suddenly didn't want to be trustworthy. No, he wanted to lay her down on that table and start some *real* cookin' in the kitchen, his business and the auction, be dammed.

And, somehow, she was suddenly closer.

It could have something to do with his hands gripping her arms, but one taste; that's all he wanted. One quick, chaste taste of her lips and he'd leave her alone and go about his business and everything would be fine. Then he'd never again have to wonder what it would be like.

It was a pathetic argument that turned into a complete lie the moment their lips touched, and he had to fight with himself to stop from sweeping her up in his arms and doing everything he wanted to with her on that table. She tasted so damn good and her lips... ah, God. Her lips were the softest, plumpest, most delectable set of lips he'd ever tasted, and her body fit against him as if she'd been made just for him, and his blood turned to fire as every ounce of it headed south—

What the *hell* was he doing?

Reese wrenched his lips from hers, his grip tightening on her arms—to keep her or himself upright he wasn't sure. Didn't matter because he shouldn't have done this. Shouldn't have even *thought* about doing this and now what the hell was he supposed to do? He'd come here to *hire* her for God's sake, not *maul* her. How was he supposed to work with her now? Hell, his business was going down the tubes right in front of him and those beautiful blue eyes.

"I am *so* sorry." For so many things, not the least of which was that he needed her for the auction. Damn Luke for scaring off Marisa. "That was inappropriate of me. Here I was saying you could trust me and I go and do something like that." He had to let go of her; touching that soft silky skin was making him think crazy thoughts, like how he could make a relationship between them work.

He couldn't. Been there, done that, screwed everything up.

"I promise it won't happen again, Bella. Please say you'll still consider doing the auction."

"I, uh..." She exhaled and ran a hand through her hair. It helped that he wasn't the only one rattled by their kiss. "Yes. I will. Definitely. I want the job."

"Good. Great." He finally pulled his hands away and shoved them into his pockets. "So, ah... what was that about?"

When her gaze flew to his lips, Reese realized what he'd just said. "I mean, *that*." He nodded toward the dining room. "Out there. Earlier. I take it he does that often?"

"More than I'd like." Bella braced her palms on the counter behind her then leaned against it.

*Away* from him. A smart move he ought to imitate.

He didn't. "So why not fire him?"

"Fire Gus? I can't do that. He's like family to me."

"But when it affects your business, that's a problem. What would you do if I weren't here to help?"

Her pointed look reminded just how much he'd *helped*. "I can handle it. I've done it before."

"But, again, you shouldn't have to."

She crossed her arms and her eyes narrowed, any trace of what they'd just shared gone. "You run your business your way and I'll run mine my way."

She looked just as sexy standing up for herself as she did when she nibbled her lip.

*Not appropriate, Charmant.*

Right.

"Except that your business, Bella, is now going to be my business. I can't have him quitting at the last minute and throwing the entire auction into an uproar." He was one to talk about throwing things into an uproar.

"Don't worry. He won't. He's a professional."

Was that a dig? *He* hadn't been professional and he ought to just leave this entire thing alone and be thankful she wasn't shoving him and his offer out the door. "If you're sure…"

"I am." She grabbed the baster and ran it under a stream of water from the faucet. "Don't worry, Reese. You won't regret hiring me."

He already did. But not for the reason she thought.

# Chapter Six

As Reese left the restaurant, he sent a quick *Thank you* heavenward that he hadn't screwed up and that Bella was still on board.

Then he turned the corner and saw his car. *Someone* wanted to get screwed.

There was a woman draped over his car.

Trouble. With capital double Ds.

"Can I help you?"

The woman, her body melting onto the sleek contours, blood-red manicured hands caressing the hood as if it were a mink coat, gave him the once-over. *Twice.* A sex-kitten smile followed as she pushed herself off the car, her impressive—and cosmetically enhanced, he was sure—chest leading. She licked the slight pout of her lips, their color matching her nails, and tossed a curl over her shoulder as she sashayed toward him.

"I think you certainly can *definitely* help me," she purred, stopping just shy of a chest-on collision.

As if he hadn't seen this before. Women were always throwing themselves at pro players.

Brassy hair color, heavy makeup, size two clothing on a size eight body… Was she working this corner or had a friend of his mistakenly thought it was his birthday?

She looked up, batting fake eyelashes. Why did women think guys liked *fake* anything on a woman?

"I was told that a handsome stud drove that car." Again with the once-over. "My information was correct." She traced a long claw down the front of his shirt. "I'm Staci Fontaine and I just *had* to meet the man who could, um… *tame* that engine."

Someone needed to tame her and he wasn't volunteering for the job.

Reese stepped back, almost choking from the perfume she must have bathed in. "I'd be happy to oblige, but I have an appointment." He got into the car, but wasn't quick enough to prevent her from slithering her way between his seat and the door.

She leaned against the door and rubbed her leg along his thigh. "Do you eat at this restaurant often?"

Christ. As a pick-up line, it was lame at best. As a legitimate question, no way was he going to give her the chance to stalk him. He might have to stay away from Bella, but he wasn't desperate for female company. "I had a meeting with the caterer."

"Bella?"

Great. Dolly Parton-gone-downtown knew Bella. He nodded, and tugged on the door.

The chick could *not* take a hint.

Then, to make matters worse, he heard a nasally, off-key, "Oh, Prince Charming!" from across the street.

Creepy Stalker Chick from the other day was back. Reese groaned. This kept getting worse.

But it quickly got better when the tacky bombshell jumped to her feet and turned toward Creepy Stalker Chick, giving Reese the sliver of space he needed to slam the door. Then he turned on the ignition and threw the stick shift into first in one movement. A quick salute and he pulled into traffic before the women knew what he was up to.

It was just as well they'd showed up; he didn't need to spend any more time mooning over something—some*one*—he couldn't have.

***

Jonathan Griff nearly fell off his chair. Whether that was in glee over their kiss, horror because Staci was acting like a strumpet, or pride because he'd *finally* mastered subliminal messaging, Jonathan didn't know. He was just thankful that Reese had acted on his suggestion to head to the restaurant this morning instead of calling Bella to ask her. He hadn't foreseen just how well it would work out, but he was quite pleased with the results.

Well, until Staci had shown up. He needed to have a talk with that girl's Guardian. Something must be done so she'd act like a rational human being instead of a cat on the prowl.

Jonathan snorted. He believed in miracles—had seen quite a few—but he wasn't sure Staci toning it down was possible even for a Guardian. The Boss knew, Madeleine's Guardian hadn't had any better luck with *her* either.

But Madeleine and Staci were other Guardians' problems and Jonathan had enough issues with his two—most of which could only be helped by that wonderful kiss and their soon-to-happen convergence of agendas.

He sat back in his chair and took a sip of lemonade. Cool and sweet, the perfect thing for a perfect springtime.

And oh, was it going to be perfect.

***

"Now look what you did, Drew!" Staci yelled. "You scared him off!"

"I did not." Drew stomped her foot.

Typical. Staci would have thought that, at some point, her sister would have grown up. It was so embarrassing being related to someone who was still stuck in high school mode.

"You did that all by yourself, Stace."

"How do you know him?"

Drew wobbled her head like the airheaded bobble-head she was. Smug little witch. "I met him yesterday."

Staci didn't like that one bit. "So..." She twisted a lock of her two-hundred-dollar-freshly-colored hair. "What's his name?"

That knocked the air of superiority out of Drew. Good. Her sister should never try to out-think her. It was never going to happen.

"Well, I didn't actually *meet* him." Drew shrugged. "He was helping Bella get up. You know what a klutz she can be."

Staci nodded as if this was an accepted fact, but she'd never known her stepsister to be anything but disgustingly graceful. And competent. And cheerful. On everybody's BFF list. As goody-goody as the real Cinderella, and completely annoying to be related to. Talk about a perfectly cliché-d nickname.

"Anyhow," Drew continued, "I caught sight of that car. I mean, who wouldn't? Then Mr. Gorgeous there was having a chat with good ol' Cindabella. Naturally, I had to save the poor man from a cooking lesson."

"He did say he'd met with the caterer." Staci tapped her lips. Tacky she might be, even cheap in the eyes of a few, but dumb she wasn't. The jury was still out on Drew.

"Let's go find out why," said Drew. "That's twice in two days he's seen her. What's she got that we don't?"

It was on the tip of Staci's tongue to say, "Brains," but Drew would think she meant both of them and that so wasn't true. Instead, she shoved open the door to Casteleoni's, bracing herself as she always had ever since Mother had told them she was going to marry Sal.

The fact that Mother hadn't met the man before her declaration had been beside the point. Mother had known about the accident, his wife's death, and, most importantly, his lucrative business. It hadn't been hard to then make events go the way she'd wanted. Mother never had any trouble making things go the way she wanted, which, at times, was majorly annoying. Just once, Staci would love to be able to beat her at something.

Though, actually… Mother had managed to snag a guy who owned merely a *diner*. Had it been a nightclub or a four- or even three-star restaurant, that'd be something different. But, nope. Diner.

Staci was setting her sights much higher—like six-foot something with a broad set of shoulders, a face worth looking at every day, and a great car. Mr. Gorgeous *had* to be made of money.

She'd find out for sure from *Cindabella*. The cook. Staci always got a giggle over that one. If she were Bella, she would have sold her shares in this place eons ago and be off living the high life somewhere. She'd never understand why someone would elect to bury herself in this hole of a town or greasy snack joint for the rest of her life, subjugating herself for the good of a sister.

And for what? Staci looked around and grimaced. To keep this place operational so some screaming brats could smash cookies on the floor? Or for Mr. Comb-Over over there to meticulously count out his tip to the last penny for a stupid egg sandwich?

Oh no, *this* was not for her. *She* was going somewhere. And with someone. Preferably Mr. Tall and Gorgeous with the car.

Drew waved to Nicky Napoli and ditched her. As if that was such a loss. The *last* thing Staci cared about was being abandoned for some pumped-up, undershirt-wearing, beer-swilling, 'roided-out deadbeat.

Seeing her stepsister's ponytail disappear into the kitchen, Staci headed that way, trying desperately not to touch any of the locals. She shrank against a booth as wayward hands dripping with syrup attached to a three-year-old danced past her. She skirted around a mountain of a man overflowing one of the tiny chairs, his lips smacking as he licked each of his fingers. Staci covered her mouth to keep her own breakfast down. Once past that obstacle, she saw Mrs. Angelelli step back to allow her to pass, a tiny smirk on the woman's face.

*As if* Staci cared that the distaste was a two-way street. As soon as she found out what Bella knew, she was out of here.

***

Bella popped out from the kitchen and caught sight of Staci. She sucked in her breath. Both stepsisters seeking her out in two days? Something was up in the heavens—*not* that she hadn't figured that out about two seconds into that kiss with Reese—

She would *not* think about that. Especially not around Staci. If the girl got even a whiff of Bella's interest in a guy, it'd be all over. Staci's mission in life seemed to be to make her life miserable and she'd stolen more than one boyfriend. True, it'd been in high school when what Staci had been willing to do went a lot farther with boys than hand-holding on the front porch, but Bella wasn't about to test the theory when it came to Reese.

Of course, the fact that she shouldn't be interested in Reese should play a part, too. She still wasn't sure how she felt about being second best.

But a contract was a contract. She could worry about her injured ego once Sophia was safely away from Madeleine. "What are you doing here, Staci?"

"Some guy outside said he had a meeting with the caterer."

*Some* guy? Staci must have passed Reese and now she wanted info. Bella slid past her to deliver another plate of food and plastered a smile on her face. Staci would never know that she gritted her teeth behind it. "Yes, well, we're discussing Casteleoni's doing a charity event." The word "charity" was sure to derail Staci's interest. Her stepsister didn't have an unselfish bone in her body.

But Reese's attraction must have been too great (as Bella could confirm) because Staci wasn't giving up. "Oh, what event is that?

Maybe Mother has tickets for it." The question rolled off her tongue, sugar-sweet, like molasses in July.

Bella gave in; Staci was like a dog with a bone when she wanted something. "It's an auction for Community General. His name is Reese and he's—"

"Reese? Ohmygod. It's *him*!" Staci lost her smug look on the first gasp. "I *knew* he looked familiar." She actually laid a hand on Bella's arm. That was a first. "You *do* know who he is, right? Reese Charmant?" Her eyes widened, the heavy mascara giving her a heroin-chic look that was anything but chic.

Yes, Bella knew who he was—or rather, she knew who the owner of Promotional Sports was and his connections to the industry. It was one of the reasons she'd wanted to win the catering job; if she could hook up with him, she'd get enough business to fund the custody battle.

But she also knew from experience that Staci was going to tell her whether she wanted to know or not. Her stepsister loved lording anything she could over her—and wouldn't *she* just *love* to spill her own knowledge of Reese? How he tasted, how he smelled, how he could overwhelm her with a sigh, and make her tremble with a kiss.

Probably not a good idea. Staci would only use it to her advantage and Bella's *dis*advantage somewhere along the line, and feeling those things about him was disadvantage enough.

"He's the quarterback who won us the Super Bowl." Staci spun around, drama flailing from every fingertip, almost smacking poor little Michael Spaccone in the face. "He's a hero in this town. A very good-looking hero." Staci slid into an empty booth. "And now you're working for him? Hmmm..." Staci strummed her nails on the table, the *clickety-click* of acrylic punctuating her thoughts. "It's going to be a big event, isn't it?" *Clickety-click.* "With lots of people. Wealthy people always to go to those things." *Clickety-click.* "You're going to need lots of help." *Clickety-click.*

An idea was forming and Bella would bet she wasn't going to like it.

She would have won that bet when Staci grinned the same Cheshire-cat smile Madeleine and Drew both had, and her nails stopped mid-*clickety-click*. Even with the noise of the restaurant behind her, Bella heard the ominous silence of the nails.

"I'll help you."

Oh no she would not. Staci was incompetent. With anything. Well, anything but shopping and spending.

*Shopping and spending…* Hmm. Bella knew Staci as well as she knew Drew. If she said no to the demand, Staci would threaten Sophia. Same old pattern. *But* if she gave her something innocuous to do, well, maybe it wouldn't be a disaster after all.

She considered a bit longer and tried one last shot. "I doubt Madeleine will be thrilled to have you working. I thought the Board members' families were above all that."

"Yeah, well, turns out Mother didn't get the nod just yet. Seems there's someone else in the running. She'll actually be thrilled if I volunteer. After all, it'll reflect well on her."

Unless Staci screwed it up. In which case, Madeleine wouldn't get the position and the threat to sell would become much more real. Madeleine wouldn't dare stay around to be publicly humiliated by her defeat. And what that would do to Casteleoni's reputation…

It didn't bear thinking about. Which meant she was stuck with an assistant she didn't want.

"I can do the stuff on the front end, Bella. You know, meet with the client and uh..." Her river of ideas ran dry after that.

*Exactly*. Staci always did have a one-track mind—

Which might actually work to Bella's advantage.

"Fine. Once we decide on the menu, you can help me shop, buy, and spend money." Staci's holy trinity.

"That'll work." Staci jumped out of the booth. "So when do we meet with Reese?"

"*We* don't. *He* has the proposal; it's up to him to make the next move."

"That's your problem, Bella. You should never wait for any guy to make a move. If you want something, you need to go for it."

Words to live by. Too bad they could have nothing to do with Reese.

# Chapter Seven

Bella met with Mrs. DeLeo the next morning to discuss the party Drew had talked her into and was even more hopeful for the upcoming battle with Madeleine. Connie DeLeo and her husband had contacts with almost every business in this part of the state, so not only would the Sophia Custody Fund get a much needed infusion of cash, but her name would get out as a can-do caterer.

The sun was shining through the large maple trees lining the center avenue of town as Bella headed back to the restaurant. The neighborhood teemed with people enjoying the weather. Bicyclists dodged parked cars and rode alongside the light afternoon traffic between the Main-Street- USA style storefronts on each side of—what else?—Main Street.

Bella sidestepped two men in faded t-shirts and jeans who were leaning over a sidewalk newspaper vending machine, loudly flapping the open pages and arguing about an umpire making a bad call last evening. Two boys almost ran her over with their skateboards, and she had to do a quick hopscotch out of little Loretta Pastorius's mad dash of a coach ride with her baby doll.

Up ahead, Maria DeRosa was valiantly trying to grab two of her toddlers' hands while maintaining control of a stroller with her yet-again pregnant belly. Louie Sandone had blocked off an area around Mr. Filipone's hardware store to repair some brickwork. Rosa Angelelli was watering her window boxes on the second floor and calling out to her nephew, Joey, below not to forget the prosciutto at Arena's or there wouldn't be any supper for him that evening. In the midst of the comfortable chaos, Bella offered a quick hello—or in Maria's case, an extra hand—to everyone she met.

This was the town she loved. Home. How could Madeleine think of sending Sophia away?

Bella mustered a smile amid that depressing thought as Maria blew her a kiss before she headed across the street with her boys. "You're a sweetheart, Bell. I don't know why some man hasn't snatched you up. We could be walking our babies together."

Bella just waved to her high school friend and watched her waddle off. She knew, all right, why she hadn't been "snatched up" yet: *Sophia.* To be "snatched," one had to be out there to be "snatched." She hadn't been and didn't see that changing anytime soon. Securing Sophia's future was more of an immediate concern than romance.

Across the street, Maria's husband ran up to his wife, caught her around the waist, and planted a big kiss on her lips, then led his family into Panella's Ice Cream Parlor.

Though romance did have a lot to recommend it…

Bella touched her lips, remembering Reese's too-brief kiss. She sighed. As far as arguments went, hers wasn't the greatest, but it was the only one she had. She just couldn't abandon her baby sister to that woman. Lord only knew where Sophia would end up if Bella didn't win the custody battle. Unless she kidnapped her, won the lottery, or, like Giac suggested, found a Prince Charming who wouldn't mind using his kingdom's unending fortune to pay Madeleine off. Or, better yet, Madeleine could eat a poisoned apple.

Yeah, and unicorns could fly.

Taking a deep breath, Bella opened the door to Casteleoni's, willing the familiar atmosphere to work its magic on her frazzled emotions. The cheers of "Bella!" from everyone in the place went a long way to doing so.

She grabbed her apron from behind the counter and tossed her purse into its hiding spot all in the same movement she'd done for years. She pulled her long hair back into its usual workday ponytail, then gathered a few used dishes and cups, and deposited them in the rinse bin, calling a quick, "Thanks, Aunt Theresa!" into the kitchen where her mother's oldest friend balanced three plates.

"Not a problem, sweetie." Her pseudo-aunt blew her an air kiss. "Glad I could help out." She walked into the dining room and nodded to booth nine. "I'll just get this on over to Tony and Rose and that cute little grandson Petey of theirs, and then I'll be on my way. Did everything work out with Mrs. DeLeo?"

"Yes, it did. Although I'm going to be pretty busy for the next few nights." Bella wiped down Mr. Campanale's place and collected his tip. She had to smile. Every day for the five years since Mrs. Campanale had passed away he would come in, order the same meal, and leave a fifty-cent tip. And Bella would throw the quarters in the big mason jar under the sink. There must be close to nine hundred dollars in there. She'd tried to return it to him many times, but he wouldn't hear of it—told her to use it for something special. She hoped he'd consider Sophia's Custody Fund special enough.

Aunt Theresa returned from delivering the meal and removed her apron. She folded it and placed it on the counter. "Anytime you need us to watch Sophia, just call, honey." She patted Bella's cheek, giving it a little pinch. "Such a good girl you are. Your mama and papa must be smiling down from Heaven, so proud of you."

"Thanks, Aunt Theresa. I may take you up on that offer."

Lunch rush was upon her and Bella found herself wishing Aunt Theresa had stayed. With the warmer weather, people were leaving their offices and taking walks along the shop-lined avenue. Thankfully, Gus was back in the kitchen and Bruno, her busboy, walked through the door at just the right moment.

"Afternoon, Ms. C." he said, tipping a non-existent hat her way.

"Hey, Bruno." She tossed him an apron.

When he raised his arm to catch it, Bella saw a small elf of a man behind him. Barely five feet tall with a bald head speckled with age spots amid a sea of wrinkles, he wore wire-rimmed glasses that magnified startlingly brilliant emerald eyes. Laugh lines ringed his mouth and a deep dimple winked in his left cheek. He looked like a leprechaun, an unusual sight in their Little-Italy neighborhood.

"Good morning, sir." Bella always liked to welcome new guests personally. "Welcome to Casteleoni's. What can I get for you today?"

His smile grew wider, although Bella wasn't sure how.

"Well, hello, lass." No brogue, but the *lass* only added to his leprechaun-ness. "This is a fine place you have here."

"Thank you. We're glad you could join us." She cleaned a spot for him at the counter. "Are you new to the area or just passing through today?"

"Well, you might say a little of both. I've set up my shoe store down the street a ways. We'll see how it goes."

"In the old Colantonio shop?"

"That's the place. Heavenly Shoes, I call it." He thrust his hand over the counter. "Jonathan Griff, at your service."

Bella shook it. "Bella Casteleoni. Welcome."

He studied her. "What a perfect name for you. It means beautiful."

A much better association than the one Staci and Drew had come up with. "Actually, my name is Lucinda Isabella, but it's such a mouthful that everyone calls me Bella."

The man nodded. "Like I said, a perfect name." He took a seat at the counter bar. "So, I heard the place is known for its specials. What is it today?"

Bella was grateful for the change of topic. The nickname was a sore subject. Her mother had declared her daughter to be her princess, so she'd been named after one. Why *that* one, Bella had no clue. Why not Grace or Caroline or Elizabeth? Nope, she got the fictional symbol of perfection. And all the accompanying fairy tale mumbo jumbo.

She offered Mr. Griff some menu suggestions, purposely omitting the now-back-to-work Gus's creation *du jour*. No need to scare the new guy off on his first day. She served him his tea with the splash of vanilla he requested and scones with a generous helping of whipped cream, then settled back into her routine of refilling coffee mugs and wiping down booths, smiling when she heard a pair of familiar voices enter.

"Bella!" they said in unison.

"Hey, Perla. Hi, Harry." Her partners in gastronomic crime headed for their favorite booth. Bella had commissioned a plaque proclaiming it theirs last week and couldn't wait to surprise them with it. It was the least she could do to show her appreciation for their loyalty to Casteleoni's.

She leaned toward them with a conspiratorial grin. "Gus has a new treat for you today."

Perla beamed at Harry's less than enthusiastic moan.

"Aw, come on, Har." Perla flicked a lock of hair off her husband's forehead. "It can't hurt and it does make him happy."

"And gives you your mad money, to boot," he muttered.

"Oh, hush." She tapped his arm as he lifted his coffee. It sloshed over the edge of the mug so she took the rag from Bella's apron pocket and mopped up the spill. "It's our good deed for the day, just like Father DiGennaro says." She slapped his arm lightly with the rag, then handed it back to Bella, who was valiantly trying not to laugh. These two sounded just like Giac and Gus. "It smells wonderful in here. Like apples. No, wait. Cranberries. No. Hmm, I can't place it. What is it today, love?"

"Um..." Bella bit her tongue to prevent herself from laughing long enough to get the answer out. "Carrot waffles."

Harry had no such compunction and groaned, long and loud, before dropping his head onto his crossed forearms on the table.

Perla's mouth twisted as if she'd sucked on a lemon. "You know, maybe we shouldn't encourage him quite so much."

"Or you could direct him to other, less dangerous, pursuits," said her husband.

"Hmmm." Perla tapped a bright red manicured nail against her equally bright red lips. "That's not a bad idea."

Before Perla could continue that thought, Bella headed off to get them Gus's special and enough coffee to chase it down with. Perla and Harry couldn't back out of their arrangement now; Gus would be devastated if no one tried his special and, so far, carrot waffles hadn't gone over as well as the spinach donuts. And those hadn't gone over well at all.

"Hold on, angel." Perla tugged Bella's wrist before she could leave. "Have a seat."

Bella took a quick look around. Everything was, for the moment, under control, so she sat down. "What's up?"

"I have a thought about Gus." Perla flicked one manicured fingernail with another. "I may be talking myself out of my mad money, but our Gus needs to feel appreciated for his creative endeavors. He needs people to enjoy them, but the problem is, no one sees these concoctions of his as creative. Maybe—" She wagged her finger at Bella. "Maybe you should suggest he paint or do interior design. Or fashion." She clapped her hands. "That's it! He sews the aprons for the restaurant, right? He should create a line of clothing. There's always a demand for it." Perla smoothed a hand over her figure.

"Yes, Gus can bake regular food by day and let his imagination run wild on yards of fabric in the evening." Perla stood and patted Bella's shoulders. "Don't you worry, angel, I'll set that man straight." She snorted. "Well, maybe not straight, but I'll tell him my idea. I doubt Giac *or* Harry would be happy if I made Gus straight. Then we'd have a whole other problem on our hands." She flipped her hands and scurried away. "Wish me luck!"

Bella shared a commiserating shrug with Harry. Perla meant well. Just like Gus with his creations.

She returned to the counter, wiped down one departing patron's spot, then was about to refill Mr. Griff's cup of tea when he put some money on the counter.

Bella covered his hand with hers. "Oh, no, Mr. Griff. This one is on the house. A welcome-to-the-neighborhood gift."

He smiled from ear to ear. "Thank you, lass. I always knew you were—that is, er, you look like a generous soul." He put his other hand atop hers. "You must come to my shop someday and I'll find you the prettiest pair of shoes you ever saw—on the house, of course." He winked then hurried out the door so quickly it was as if he had wings on his feet, leaving behind three coins as a tip. Three *gold* coins. Hmmm, maybe he really was a leprechaun.

Bella shook her head. Leprechauns, fairy tales, unicorns… She needed to get a grip on reality.

*Or on a really hunky guy.*

Been there, done that. And, oh, had it been nice.

But then he'd pulled away and apologized. Probably for the best, but still…

She plunked her chin in her hand and toyed with the coins. *If only…*

***

"Kelly, get me a sub's contract, will you?" Reese asked his assistant as he passed her desk on his way to his office.

"Okay, but—" Kelly didn't get the rest of her sentence out before it became obsolete. "Luke Jamison is here to see you."

Through his office door, Reese could see that. And he was not happy about it.

Especially with the guy making himself comfortable behind *his* desk, rifling through *his* papers.

"Something you needed, Luke?" Reese refrained from throwing his fist into Luke's face. Barely. "Or are you trying to see where the benefit was that you missed?"

Once upon a time they'd been friends. Teammates. Business associates.

Once upon a time was over.

"Hey, buddy." Luke extricated himself from the chair—Reese's chair—with the grin that had always saved his ass in the past. He'd been a media bad boy in their football years, but had always managed to come out smelling like a rose with that smile. Pure charm and charisma. But Reese was immune. "Look, Reese, I'm really sorry, but Tanya—"

"Cut the crap, Luke." Reese stormed past him, hands fisted. One more word and he'd put them through Luke's pretty-boy face. "Last time it was your mother, this time your ex-wife. Now I've got a pissed off client *and* an MIA caterer. Not to mention the meeting with *me* you skipped yesterday." He walked behind *his* desk. "It's over. Promotional Sports is finished with you."

He tore a file from the top drawer and slammed it open on the desktop. "This paragraph says no fee is to be paid, and any advance is to be returned, in the event the contractee—you—fails to appear at the contracted event." He slammed it shut, then leaned onto his palms, his face inches from Luc's. "You owe me ten grand."

"Look, Reese," Luke said in a voice Reese knew all too well. The come-on-honey-I-won't-bite voice that had gotten him more gullible women than Reese had thought were on the planet. "The money's gone and without your gigs, well, there's not much left to pay you back with." He sat in the chair facing Reese and grinned. "Come on, man, give me another chance. I'll be there. Promise."

Reese closed his eyes and hung his head. The unmitigated gall. He glared at his old teammate. "You don't get it, Luke. This isn't a game. It's my business, my reputation. While you have no regard for your own, I have a *lot* for mine. I gave you your second chance. Sunday night. And you blew it."

"Yeah, but *you* were there. I knew they'd be more thrilled having the winning quarterback than the tight end there. You could handle it."

"The point being—*you* were contracted. They wanted the guy who caught that Hail Mary pass. Not the one who threw it." Reese shoved his hands into his pockets because they wanted to make contact with Luke's jaw way too much. "We're through, Luke. You've got a month to get me the ten grand or I call my lawyer for breach of contract."

Reese was serious. Even as Luke pursed his lips, Reese hoped the man realized he knew him too well to think about trying to schmooze his way out of this.

"How about I work it off?" Luke lost the grin and, with it, the cocky attitude. "I can't afford another court battle. Tanya's last one used up all my cash as fast as I could earn it."

Reese had heard too many of Luke's "deals" to want to touch this one with a ten thousand foot pole.

"Seriously, Reese. You must have some event coming up where you could use me? I'll do it for the ten grand I owe you and we'll call it even." Luke shifted in his seat. "I promise I'll be there. Tell me where and when. I'll even call you the day before to let you know I haven't forgotten. *Please.*"

Shit. That last word got to him. Luke's motto had always been, "Never beg for what you can win with charm." He'd never needed to beg. Until now. Shit.

Reese shouldn't give in to him. He knew that. Luke had always been unreliable. Well, except in a game. There he'd proven himself, time and again. But he *was* going through a rough patch. His ex-wife— one of the gold-digging groupies who'd followed their team and had managed to catch the uncatchable Luke in the oldest way possible— was demanding almost everything he owned in return for joint custody of their son, Jared.

That "please" had been all about his son, and Reese couldn't punish the boy for his father's misdeeds. Nor risk Tanya getting full custody. Luke might not be a prince, but, in Reese's opinion, he was an infinitely better choice to raise the boy than Tanya. Which said a whole *little* about Tanya.

"Not one word, Luke, to any of the staff I hire. Not a look, a breath, or even a thought in their direction, got it? One fiasco is enough. If you pull off the next event without any drama, we're square. If not..." Reese pulled out the direst threat he could come up with. "I'll testify for your ex-wife."

There was some measure of satisfaction in the color draining from Luke's face. It was no idle threat; he knew more about his old teammate's past exploits than anyone else. Including Tanya.

Luke stood and thrust out his hand. "I'll be there. On Jared's future, I'll be there."

Reese nodded, then filled him in about the auction. "And remember, stay away from the new caterer. She's off limits."

Words he, himself, needed to live by.

"Uh, Reese?" Kelly poked her head into his office after Luke left. "Your caterer is here to see you."

*That was quick.* Reese couldn't deny the surge of pleasure her words and that thought brought. Talk about a hypocrite… "Send her in."

When he saw the woman who walked through the door, he realized he'd gotten what he deserved for considering not following his own non-fraternization rule.

Staci Whatshername, Dolly-Parton-wannabe. Reese grimaced. He shouldn't call her that. The real Dolly was a very nice lady; she didn't deserve the comparison. And he didn't deserve this. Fans had tried all sorts of ways to get close to him before, but posing as a caterer was a first.

This woman, and he used that term loosely, thrust out her hand (and her chest), her artificial talons coming at him like daggers.

Reese chose to ignore both.

"Hello, Reese," she purred as she stood before him, a hair's breadth too close.

A football field would be too close.

"Bella and I were discussing some ideas for your party and I thought I should come talk to you about what, *specifically*—" the word rolled off her tongue as her tongue rolled around her lips—"you want."

He chose to ignore that, too.

The silence grew strained. Sort of like the neckline of that dress, a look that was more tacky than sexy on her.

Finally, her gaze shifted from his to dart around the room. "So… what, um, did you have in mind?"

Not what she did.

Luckily, he was saved from answering by Luke walking back into his office. "And, hey, Reese—" Luke stopped as he caught sight of Staci who gave him a little finger wave. "Well, hellooo."

Mr. Suave had entered the building.

"And who do we have here?"

Reese wanted to deck Luke all over again as the guy sauntered in. Barely restraining himself, he made the introduction, all the while glaring at Luke to back the fuck off. "Luke Jamison, meet Staci Fontaine."

"Hi there," Staci purred as she cocked her hip toward Luke.

Oh, hell. These two were two of a kind.

Luke kissed the back of her hand. "Hello, Staci Fontaine. What brings you here?" He purred every bit as revoltingly as she did, and Staci, like so many before her, fell for it.

"I'm working with Bella on the hospital thing. I came to talk to Reese about it."

"What a wonderful coincidence." Luke tucked her hand in the crook of his arm and led her over to Reese's sofa. "I'm also working on the hospital... thing. We can work on it together."

Not if Reese could help it. Ten grand wasn't cheap even if Staci was. "Uh, Luke?"

Luke looked like was about to argue, but when Reese's cell rang, Luke just smiled instead and steered Staci from the office. "Don't let us disturb you."

If Connie DeLeo weren't the caller, he would explain to Luke just how much—ten thousand dollars' worth—the two of them *did* disturb him. Instead, he scowled at Luke as they left. The guy just did not learn.

Reese blew out a breath before answering. "Hey, Connie. What's up?"

"Hi, Reese. I'm calling to find out if you're bringing a date to the dinner Saturday night. I'm doing my guest list and realized I didn't know if there was someone special in your life."

Subtle Connie was not. He'd met her when he'd been drafted by the team, and she'd tried to get him to settle down ever since. But he'd been too busy proving himself to get serious about anyone.

If only he'd shared that info with Devin.

"You are coming, aren't you? It's a big event."

Which was a big problem. Connie's annual dinner for everyone involved with the stadium meant that Coach would be there. They hadn't spoken since Reese had gone on the disabled list, and a public place wasn't the best idea for a first conversation.

"I don't know yet, Con."

"Oh, please, Reese. It'll be good for you. And Coach, too. Just the thing you need to break the ice. Start over. A new beginning. Please say you'll come."

Actually, bringing a date could be a good thing. A buffer.

Right. Buffer. He knew who he wanted to bring, but it wasn't so she'd be a buffer.

"I won't take no for an answer, Reese."

He knew that, too. Well, he could always tell Bella it was a site visit so she could see what he had in mind for the auction.

That was lame. Even for Luke.

Reese sighed. "I'll be there. Not sure about a date yet, though. I'll have to check her schedule." And his own sanity. But if he and Bella were going to work together he had to get over this attraction.

Connie was right; the party could be the perfect beginning for a lot of things.

# Chapter Eight

 ophia tugged Bella's hand on the sidewalk two blocks from the park. "Come on, Bella! Let's race! I want to see the hot air balloons."

"All right, but be careful." Bella rumpled Sophia's hair.

"I will! Ready, set, go!" Sophia took off down the sidewalk toward the park where the annual regatta was set up.

Slowing her stride to meet Sophia's furious one, Bella pretended to struggle. Couldn't let Sophia win too easily or she'd catch on.

Suddenly though, Bella no longer had to act as she landed hard on the concrete. "Ouch!"

Sophia spun around and hurried back. "Bella! Are you okay?"

Bella examined her ankle. Then her hip. Both seemed intact, but sore. The same could not be said of her running shoe. The seam was ripped, the rubber sole hanging by threads.

She got to her feet, wincing at the twinge in her hip. "I'm having the darnedest luck with shoes these days."

"We could buy you a new pair in that store over there." Sophia pointed across the street.

*Heavenly Shoes.* Talk about luck…

The store's door chimes sounded a lot like the bells of St. Gabriel's Church as Bella followed Sophia inside, and Mr. Griff's smile was almost angelic as he hurried from the back room.

"Bella, it's so good to see you. And you must be Sophia." Mr. Griff dropped to one knee and took Sophia's hand in his. "I'm so glad to meet you."

Sophia giggled while she shook her hand. "It's nice to meet you, too, um…"

"Jonathan Griff, lass." He stood up. "Welcome to Heavenly Shoes' opening day. I can't think of a better opening than to have two such beautiful ladies stop by." He winked at Sophia which sent her into another round of giggles. "Now, what brings you here?"

"Bella needs a new pair of running shoes." Sophia held up the damaged one. "See?"

"Tsk tsk. I'll say she does." Mr. Griff took it from her. "It's seen better days, I'm sure. But not to worry, ladies. Running shoes are my specialty." He led them to a bank of chairs. "Have a seat and I'll be right back with a selection for you to choose from."

Bella sat, but Sophia rushed over to the shoe displays in the glass case beneath the counter.

"Look Bella! Here's a pair like Dorothy wore in *The Wizard of Oz*." Shiny ruby pumps glittered in the twinkling lights lining the case. "And this pair looks just like the ones Mary Poppins had on the carousel ride." Sophia walked along the case. "These look like the Sugar Plum Fairy's ballet shoes. And these look like a genie's slippers. And—oh, Bella! Come see! These look like Cinderella's!"

The transparent shoes did look as if they were made of glass with the way the lights sparkled in them. The velvet purple cushion they were displayed on didn't hurt the image, either. It was a great marketing tool. Little girls would be dragging their mothers in by the mini-van-full once word got out. And with Sophia doing the talking, that wouldn't take very long.

Mr. Griff returned then with a tower of boxes teetering over his head. "You should find something suitable in these, but if not, I'll bring out more."

"I'm sure I'll find something. Thank you, Mr. Griff." Bella sat down and his gold coins clinked in her pocket. She took them out. I believe you forgot something earlier."

Mr. Griff shook his head and wouldn't take them. "You keep them. They're a gift."

"But that meal was the gift, and these are worth more than the food."

"I'll not hear of it, lass. They were a gift to you for being so generous. Now try those shoes on while I see to our Miss Sophia." He walked over to the case Sophia had her nose pressed against. "Do you see something you like?"

"Oh, yes!" Sophia squealed. "Cinderella's glass slippers. They're beautiful!"

"Would you like to try them on?"

"Oh, yes, please!" Sophia squealed, hopping out of her running shoes quicker than Bella's mishap had gotten her out of hers.

Mr. Griff winked at Bella. "Lucite, but it gets their attention every time. I do so love to fire up people's imaginations."

"I bet you get a big run on them during wedding season."

He shook his head. "I probably would, but I only have the one pair and they're not for sale, though I do lend them out on occasion."

"Can I borrow them for my wedding day, Mr. Griff?" Sophia asked as she paraded around the store with a very-practiced royal wave. "They make me feel like a princess."

Bella laughed along with Mr. Griff. Sophia would have enough time to learn that fairy tales didn't exist, but childhood was the time for dreams and wishes and believing in magic.

She flicked Sophia's ponytail as she paid for the running shoes. "Sure you can, Soph. Every girl deserves to feel like a princess at least once in her life."

***

"Bella's not here," said Giac when Reese called Casteleoni's. "She's probably with Sophia at the park."

A crash in the background was followed by another round of angry Italian so Reese didn't have a chance to ask who Sophia was or where in the park they'd be. But since he was within walking distance, he figured he'd find out for himself, using the exercise to burn off his anger at Luke.

Yeah, that was lame, too.

Still, Reese headed down the tree-lined path to the river, where, apparently, half the town had congregated, dodging rollerblading teens, stroller-pushing mothers, and dog-walking grannies. He was going to need some major luck to find Bella in this crowd.

When a little old man barreled into him and almost knocked him over, Reese realized he should have specified which kind of luck he wanted.

Instinct, however, took over and a few pattern drills he used to do in practice kept him from going down. Unfortunately, the old guy wasn't as successful. Reese caught him by the arms just before he landed.

"You okay, sir?" he asked, easing the guy back to his feet. Short little guy. Bald, wrinkled, with the brightest green eyes Reese had ever seen.

Reese blinked. When had he ever noticed another man's eyes?

The man brushed off his suit jacket. "I am now. Thank you, my boy." He patted Reese's arm. "Nice catch, though you're usually the one doing the passing, are you?"

Ah. A fan. "Not anymore." The words caused his breath to catch. He'd really hated leaving the game.

"Now, now, my boy. When one door closes, another opens." The man removed some items from his pocket and handed them to Reese. "And here's something to help that along."

Reese looked in his palm. Gold coins. "I can't take these."

"You'll insult me if you don't, and besides, there's a wishing fountain at the end of this path. Surely you can use a few wishes?"

Insulting a fan was never a good thing. And, hell, yeah, he could use a few wishes. "Well, okay. Thanks. I appreciate it."

"Not yet you don't," said the old guy, patting his arm once more before he headed off in the opposite direction, adding, "But you will."

Reese jostled the coins as he watched the guy walk away and tried to figure out that cryptic message. When he couldn't, he put it down to old age and headed toward the fountain.

A loin-clothed marble statue of a man with a massive set of wings on his back stood in the center holding a jug that spouted water into the pool. Dozens of children ringed the marble edge, tossing pennies in with squeals of laughter and shouts of "A new puppy!" "My own room!" "A pony!" One little girl scrunched her face so tightly it looked painful. Another toddler leaned in too far and was rescued at the last moment by his mother.

Reese fingered the coins. This was silly; wishes were for children.

"Make a wish, mister," said a little boy who'd jumped onto the edge of the fountain beside him. "They really do come true." Then he tossed his own coin in and scurried away just as the color of his eyes registered. Green. Bright, sparkling green.

Reese shook his head. He was being ridiculous.

So he went with that theme, made the wish, and skimmed a coin into the fountain. It skipped five times, then sank at the statue's feet.

"Looks like you spent hours skipping stones when you were a kid," said a voice behind him.

He looked at the statue. No, it didn't have sparkling green eyes, but he almost wouldn't have been surprised if it did. He turned around. "Hi, Bella."

"Hello, Reese."

"Hi," said a high-pitched voice beside her.

Reese looked down. A younger version of Bella stood beside her—

She had a daughter?

"Uh, hi." He'd always prided himself on being able to adjust to any situation in a game, but this blew him away. Bella must have been a teenager when she'd had her—

His gaze shot to Bella's left hand. No ring. *Phew.*

Although… she *did* work with food all day; she could have removed it.

The thought ripped into his gut worse than the spinach donut had.

Grasping at the shred of hope that he hadn't kissed another man's wife, Reese prayed that Sophia was her niece. Sister, maybe.

"Hi. I'm Sophia Casteleoni." The little girl smiled with the same enthusiasm—and dimple—as Bella.

"I'm Reese Charmant. Pleased to meet you, Sophia." He was also pleased that he managed to sound composed. But this was definitely *not* what he'd been expecting when he'd come here today.

"What brings you to the park?" Bella asked.

"I, uh, was actually looking for you."

"Is there a problem?"

In a word, yes. She had a daughter.

Did she also have a husband?

"Reese?"

Problem. Right. "Staci Fontaine came by my office."

"My stepsister?"

"What'd Aunt Staci do now?" asked Sophia with more maturity than someone her age should have. Poor kid sounded like she was used to Aunt Staci doing things she shouldn't.

"Honey, you don't have to call her 'Aunt Staci.' She's not really your aunt," said Bella.

"I know, but Mama—"

"Let's not go into it now." Bella brushed her hand over Sophia's hair and the image of a glowingly pregnant Bella flashed before him.

*Mama.* Hell, Sophia *was* her daughter.

Reese took a deep breath and pulled his head out of his ass. What difference did it make if Bella had a daughter? Or a husband? He needed her for her cooking abilities, not her procreation ones.

He was *not* going to think about procreating with Bella—"Uh, yeah. Your Aunt Staci. She came to my office to discuss the auction. I didn't know she would be working with you."

"Staci will *not* be working with me. She doesn't know the meaning of the word."

Sophia giggled. "Yeah, she tried working at my daddy's restaurant once and she sprayed water all over the place and made a big mess."

"It will be yours, too, someday, Soph."

*Daddy.* Shit. He had a hell of a lot of apologizing to do for that kiss. But not in front of the kid. Any idea of asking Bella to Connie's party was definitely out of the question. Reese clinked the coins in his palm again. He'd made the wrong damn wish.

Sophia, her eyes sparkling just like her mother's, touched the coins. "Are you going to make a wish with those?"

Yes he would: that the ground would open up and swallow him. He just couldn't get over that he'd kissed her. Thank God he'd ended it when he had. And that his idiotic action hadn't cost him her services the way Luke's had cost them Marissa's.

*Yet...*

Reese shook his head. *Never.* "No, I've already made my wish." He held out the coins to the little girl. "Here, you take the rest."

Bella put her hand on his arm and it was all Reese could do not to jerk away. "Reese, you don't have to—"

"I want her to have them." Not that they in any way made up for his huge breach of manners or common sense, but it was the least he could do. The very least. "Go ahead, Sophia. Make a wish."

He dropped them into her palm, then shoved his hands into his pockets, Bella's touch still lingering on his skin. "And, Bella, I'll have my assistant Kelly set up a time we can discuss your proposal as soon as I get back to my office." He turned around and started to do just that. "Have a nice afternoon."

***

Jonathan smacked his forehead. *Married*. He thought she was married.

Honestly, it was no wonder these two needed help. Too noble for their own good.

Jonathan scratched *Fountain Wishes* off his list. He needed to come up with something else fast before Reese blew it.

# Chapter Nine

*W*hat just happened?

Bella stared after Reese as he walked away, and, while it was a nice view, she couldn't figure out how they'd been discussing the auction on minute, and the next, he'd clammed up, hands in pockets, all stiff-necked and polite, then left. The conversation about Staci could have been handled with a phone call, so she had no idea why he'd come to the park in search of her.

And her traitorous hormones had been gearing up for round two.

"He's cute," said a too-sophisticated ten-year-old.

"I don't know that I'd say cute." No, she'd use words like *sexy, delicious, hot*. Words a ten-year-old didn't need to know at this age.

"He is, too." Sophia crossed her arms. "You should marry him."

*Yes she should—*

Bella sighed. Hormones and Subconscious were staging a coup over Common Sense and Familial Duty. "Soph, you don't marry someone because he's cute."

"Well, duh. But it doesn't hurt."

Bella did a double-take. She didn't want to know how Sophia had formed this opinion. "But Soph, if I married him, who'd tuck you in at night? Meet you off the bus?"

"You, silly. I could live with you guys."

"That would be nice, wouldn't it?" Bella's heart twisted. It *would* be. Everything she wanted under one roof. But it'd never happen. Madeleine would never let it happen. Not when it meant losing her majority hold over Dad's estate.

It always came down to money, and how sucky was that? Bella sighed and, once more, relegated another *what-if* to the Someday corner of her brain.

It was nice in that corner. Wishes and hopes and dreams danced around like fairies amid a meadow full of flowers and unicorns—

"Oh, no!" Sophia's cry yanked her back to reality.

She'd barely made the transition when Sophia took off, racing across the grass toward…

Reese.

Reese?

Bella ran after her—and realized she'd had no reason to slow her pace earlier on the sidewalk because Sophia had quite the sprint on her.

"Reese!" Sophia shouted. "Help!"

Bella couldn't for the life of her imagine what had happened. Reese looked just as confused when he spun around, but he jumped into action with a move she was sure came right off the playing field, dodging a kid on a tricycle and a little old lady walking her Maltese.

"What's wrong?" Reese got to Sophia a few steps ahead of Bella.

"Please, you have to help." Hopping from foot to foot, Sophia grabbed his hand. "Please."

"What happened, Soph?" Bella hunkered down in front of her sister, visually checking her to make sure she was okay.

Sophia pointed to the branches above them. "There. Can you see it?"

Bella looked up.

"A cat." Reese saw it first. The animal's soft gray fur blended in with the bark and its green eyes could pass for leaves.

"It's a kitten," said Sophia. "And he's scared. You have to get him down, Reese."

"How on earth did you see that, Soph?" Bella walked closer and held up her hand. The kitten shrank from her.

"He was chasing something and ran up the tree."

"Sophia, he'll come down when he's ready," said Reese. "Cats like to climb."

"They like to climb *up*. He can't get down. Please, will you help him?"

"Soph, I'm sure Reese has better things to do—"

"It's no problem. I'll get him." Reese rubbed his hands together, then leapt to grab the lowest branch.

The kitten backed away.

"Are your shots up to date?" Bella asked.

"It's not mine I'm worried about." Reese swung his legs onto a branch, giving Bella the perfect view of his backside. A sight she would never forget, God help her.

The kitten sneezed.

"Oh, please, Kitty!" Sophia wrung her hands. "Stay where you are. Reese will rescue you."

Reese grunted as he hoisted himself onto his feet on the branch. He grabbed the trunk with one hand and leaned toward the kitten with the other. "Come on, cat."

The kitten scrambled backwards.

"He's a kitty, Reese, not a cat." Sophia walked around the trunk so she was facing Reese. Bella was quite content to stay where she was because the view was pretty spectacular. "You have to make kissy noises for him to come to you."

Bella snorted. Kissy noises. She'd pay to see that.

"Keep laughing, Bella. I will eventually get down, you know."

"Me? Laughing? Sorry, Reese. I was clearing my throat."

"Uh huh." He tested his weight on another branch. "Come on, cat, er, kitty."

"Like this, Reese." Sophia held out her hand and rubbed her fingers together. "Here, kitty, kitty."

The kitten looked at her, giving Reese the chance he needed to grab it.

"Oh!" he yelled when the little thing clawed on for dear life.

"Yay, you saved him!" Sophia bounced around the base of the tree until Bella took the kitten from Reese and handed it to her. "Can I keep him?"

Oh, yeah. *That* would go over real well with Madeleine. "How about we keep him at the restaurant, Soph? We can always use a good mouser. Not—" she looked at Reese—"that we have mice."

He swung out of the tree. "Of course you don't. And the Health Department won't have an issue with him living there either." He brushed off his hands, then patted the kitten's head. "What are you going to name him?"

Sophia looked up with all the hero-worship a ten-year-old could muster. "Reese, of course."

Bella choked back a laugh. "That'll be interesting when we take him to the vet for the, ah, procedure."

Reese got a sick look on his face. "I'm flattered, Sophia, but why not something a little more cuddly, like Fluffy or Sweetie or something like that."

Oh, Bella didn't know… she had a feeling Reese could be quite cuddly.

"I guess you're right." Sophia scratched the kitten's head. "I think I'll name him Pussy-willow. Cause he's a kitty and he's gray and furry. What do you think?"

Bella thought it was a mouthful, but definitely better than calling him Reese. "And how about Willow for short?"

Sophia hugged the kitten closer and Bella made a note to pick up a bed, some litter, and food on the way home. Unfortunately, she wasn't sure exactly where "home" would be for the little guy. Madeleine was not about to let a cat into the house and Bella wasn't up for defying her on this small item.

"What do you say to Reese, Soph?"

Sophia beamed that megawatt smile at him and crooked her little finger. Reese knelt down and Sophia kissed his cheek. "Thanks, Reese. You're my hero."

"You're welcome, Sophia. Take care of the little guy, okay?" Reese brushed a hand over Sophia's hair and Bella's heart clutched at the sweet gesture.

Her heart clutched even more when he looked at her and smiled. "I'll talk to you. Have a nice day, ladies."

She watched him walk away until he disappeared down the path, her conscience battling with her heart. Why'd he have to be such a prince of a guy?

***

Jonathan curled in Sophia's arms to enjoy head-scratching with a contented purr. His "rescue" was just a baby-step in getting them together, but finally something had gone right.

# Chapter Ten

The party was in full swing as Reese mounted the brick steps to the DeLeo's Georgian estate in the Mirror Lake Development Saturday night. Two softly lit topiaries flanked the double mahogany front doors that opened when Reese raised his hand to the bell.

"Good evening, sir," said the uniformed doorman. "Mr. and Mrs. DeLeo are with guests on the back terrace."

Reese crossed the travertine marble foyer with its curving staircase. A balcony above it overlooked both the entranceway and the great room. He turned sideways through the group of people congregated in the archway to the dining area, snagged a beer from a guy heading to restock the bar, and grabbed a few hor d'oeuvres from a pretty brunette. Some of his old teammates nodded as he passed them, but he didn't stop. He wanted to see Coach and put the past to rest.

He caught a glimpse of blonde hair as he passed the kitchen. Did everyone have *her* color hair these days?

Drink in hand, he walked through the open French doors to the flagstone terrace beyond. Twinkling white lights shimmered in the trees flanking the patio, and the low drum of crickets provided a subtle musical backdrop. If he didn't know of Connie's incessant penchant for gardening, he'd swear the heavy scent of hyacinths was from some industrial-grade candles instead of the flower beds beyond the lights, in front of which a small crowd gathered around Coach. Devin was beside him.

Reese took a deep breath. At least he'd get the whole awkward thing over with in one shot.

Connie extricated herself from the group. "I'm so glad you came." She gave him a quick peck on the cheek. "We've been wondering where you were."

He wasn't sure who the *we* referred to, but it didn't matter; he was here and it was time to deal with the situation. Reese slid his arm around Connie's waist and led her back toward the group. "Sorry, I'm late. Some loose ends to tie up took longer than I expected. You know how it is when it's your name on the line."

She patted his arm. "Always working. Don't forget to have some fun tonight. And be sure you don't miss out on the food. It's fabulous. The poor caterer, she had to throw it together at the last minute since the woman I had originally booked had a family emergency come up. Thankfully, my son's girlfriend knew someone, and, well, you know I wouldn't have been able to pull it off."

They shared a laugh. Anthony DeLeo hadn't married Connie for her cooking, which was a good thing because she would have put their concession business under within the first year of marriage.

"I'll get some later," he assured her, then met Coach Randy Meade's gaze. "Coach." He held out his hand as the conversation around them trickled off to an uncomfortable silence. Luckily, the rest of the group drifted away quickly.

He took a quick breath. "It's good to see you." He held out a hand. "Congratulations on your new granddaughter. You, too, Devin, on the baby. You're looking well."

"Thanks, Reese. You, too," said Devin, nudging her father.

Coach glanced at Reese's hand. Considered it for a few seconds that stretched into what seemed like hours. Then he took a healthy gulp of his drink.

And turned his back.

"Oh, but Randy—" Connie reached for Coach's shoulder, but Reese stopped her.

"It's all right, Connie." He nodded at Devin who looked as stricken as he felt. "Devin. All the best." Nothing like getting shot down in public.

Reese took another deep breath and left them standing there. He'd made the first move; the ball was now in Coach's court. Unfortunately, they'd stopped playing ball altogether.

He took another swig of his beer, the taste souring on him. He set it down and decided he might as well get something to eat since good manners and his ego prevented him leaving so soon after arriving.

And then he saw her. Only in profile, but there was no mistake.

Even in the typical caterer's uniform of black pants, white shirt, and bowtie, with her hair pulled back in a ponytail, he should have recognized her earlier. No one else had that shade of blonde, that curve of a smile, that grace as she arranged the dishes on the table.

Bella, simply put, was stunning.

She looked up. "Hello, Reese."

And she was married.

"Hi, Bella. I didn't know you were catering Connie's party."

Bella stirred the pasta dish, giving him the perfect view of that hollow beneath her ear. The one he hadn't had the opportunity to taste—

Hell. He should have stayed home tonight.

"I picked up this party at the last minute," she said without a clue of what was going on in his mind, thank God. "But I'm working on updating the proposal. Your assistant sent the VIP list yesterday, so I'm looking into any possible allergies, likes and dislikes, that sort of thing. I should be able to have it to you by Tuesday."

Tuesday was too far away.

Jesus, he really needed to get his head in the game here; Bella was *married*. The mess with Devin would be nothing compared to the issue Bella's husband could have with him.

"So, are you having a good time?" she asked.

*Only because you're here* would be an inappropriate answer, and *No* would be wrong, at least at this minute. "It's nice to see my old teammates."

"But you still see them through your company, right?"

"Yeah, but it's not the same. Nothing can take the place of the game. Best time of my life." And Coach had just flung all of it back in his face. What did that say about him? Given that he was now lusting after someone else's wife, not a whole hell of a lot. Some prince he was. "So, er, how's the cat? Settled in?"

Bella laughed. "He's going to weigh twenty pounds in no time."

"Sophia a little too generous with the table scraps?"

"No. Gus. Seems he has a new audience for his creations. I'm hoping the little 'present' Willow left on his apron will deter him." She picked up a plate. "Here. Would you like to try this? It's one of Casteleoni's signature dishes. I was thinking of serving it at the auction, but if some of tonight's attendees will be there, maybe I shouldn't. What do you think?"

He was thinking that her husband was one lucky SOB. She was gorgeous, personable, sexy as hell, could kiss like nobody's business—especially not his—and she could cook. Every man's fantasy.

"Reese?"

*Head in the game, Charmant. Not your pants.*

He would've shoved his *hands* into his pants… pockets, but he couldn't refuse the food, though he doubted he'd taste it. The whole episode with Coach had left a bad taste in his mouth. Still, that wasn't Bella's fault, and she was looking at him as if her world were hanging on his opinion.

Or that could be wishful thinking.

"I'm sure whatever you serve will be fine. Connie has been singing your praises, and the hor d'oeuvres are fantastic."

"Oh. Good." She waited for him to take a taste of the shrimp and asparagus pasta dish.

He'd never been more self-conscious in his life of someone staring at his mouth. Which, of course, made him stare at hers.

Was she remembering the kiss? He really should apologize.

"Bella, about the other—"

"Reese." Devin strode up to him and put her hand on his arm. "Do you have a minute?"

Not for this. Not now. "Actually—"

"That's okay, Reese. I should get back to work." Bella took a step back and smiled at Devin.

*Smiled* at his ex-lover. Because she wasn't thinking about him the same way he was thinking about her. Because She Was Married.

Right. "This is good, by the way." He held up the plate.

"I'm glad you like it." She took another step back, her smile unchanging, and she even nodded at Devin.

He cleared his throat. "What do you need, Dev?"

"I wanted to apologize for my father. I told him to let it go. That it wasn't your fault. It was mine."

"Not rea—"

"It doesn't matter anymore, Reese. You'll always hold a special place in my heart, but you never promised me anything. That was all me. I've tried to explain it to Dad, but he's just so stubborn about this. He can't see past the fact that I'm—"

"His little girl. I get it, Devin. And I understand his point of view.

I do. If I ever have a daughter—" No he wouldn't think about Bella's daughter. "Well, I'm sure I'll be just as overprotective, too."

"He'll come around. Eventually." Devin smiled. It was a nice smile, but it didn't do to his insides what Bella's did.

God, he was screwed. He needed to get out of here. He'd put in an appearance; Connie had gotten what she'd wanted.

At least someone had.

"Dev, it's been great seeing you. If your dad comes around, hey, my door's always open. If not…" He brushed a kiss on her cheek. "I wish you well. Truly."

"You, too, Reese. I'm sorry things worked out the way they did."

He held up her left hand where her wedding ring sparkled. "No, you're not."

"True." Devin laughed. "I wouldn't have Troy or Maggie, and I couldn't imagine my life without them."

Is that how Bella felt about her husband?

Reese gritted his teeth. He was keenly aware of her standing behind them. Keenly aware that he was thinking of her in a way he had no business thinking. And that he couldn't stop himself.

He set the plate down. "I'm really happy for you, Dev. If you'll excuse me…" He looked at Bella. "Bella, we'll talk."

And that's *all* they'd do.

***

Jonathan almost fell off the lintel over the door to Connie's dining room when he clapped his hands. He quickly steadied himself, praying that his lack of focus hadn't removed the Ethereal charm. It and Animal Transformation were some of the few he could do without help, though he did have to concentrate more than most. Story of his Afterlife.

But how could he concentrate when sparks were practically flying between those two? Celestial ones actually were; it was how members of the Realm knew when soul mates had found each other. Sometimes the sparks were so vibrant and explosive that they managed to manifest themselves in reality, the proverbial fireworks or lightning strike some mortals have claimed to have experienced. Bella and Reese were so perfect for each other that Jonathan wouldn't be surprised if they were among those who did.

Actually, they could be… *if* he could get them to look beyond the obstacles they mistakenly thought were bigger than the path of True Love and see each other for who they were inside.

Jonathan sighed. Easier said than done, but if anyone could do it, there wouldn't be such beings as Guardians.

He looked at the plate of food Reese had left behind, limbered up his fingers, and materialized another lucky charm in Reese's pocket. For added insurance, he sent another one into Bella's purse because, obviously neither one of them had read The Manual. Food truly was the way to a man's heart and Bella had just handed it to him, literally, on a platter.

Now to get her to do it again.

***

Bella returned the smile Reese's ex-girlfriend gave her before she headed back to the patio, but it wasn't easy. Petite, blonde, and pretty, with a body that did *not* look like it had carried a child… but those weren't the reasons Bella was jealous of Devin Meade-Taylor.

The relationship she'd had with Reese on the other hand… Bella would bet he'd never apologized to *Devin* for kissing her. She still couldn't get over that. One minute he'd been all caught up in the moment and the next… Apologizing.

She picked up the plate he'd left behind and told her ego to chill out. They were going to be working together; anything else would be a bad idea. It was *good* that he'd apologized. *Good* that he'd stopped. Lord knew, *she* hadn't wanted to.

And that had been the biggest problem of all.

# Chapter Eleven

H ey, Reese."

Luke. Great. Just the person he didn't want to see.

Then he saw Staci clinging to Luke's arm like a sucker fish on a shark, the analogy all too real. "Luke. Staci." He nodded, and thankfully saw an out in Connie and Anthony's eldest son walking up behind them. "Hey, Jimmy. Great party, as usual."

"Yeah, Mom sure knows how to throw them." He ushered another girl forward and Reese had to stifle a groan. So much for the escape. Stalker Chick. "This is Drew. The third sister."

"Stepsister," said the two women at once.

"Whoa. Okay, ladies. My bad." Jimmy held up his hands and backed up.

Right into Bella.

Reese grabbed her as she stumbled. It was a becoming a habit. "You okay, Bella?"

Bella smiled, but it wasn't one he was used to seeing from her. Unless she'd tried the spinach donuts. "Um, yes. I am. Here, Reese. You forgot your plate."

"*Bella*?" Luke's eyes, shoulders, and probably a certain part of his anatomy perked up. "*This* is the Bella I've been hearing about?" He took the plate from her, shoved it at Reese, then raised her hand to his lips. "So very nice to meet you, Bella."

Reese gritted his teeth and had to restrain himself from punching Luke out. He had no right to feel so protective of her. It was The Husband's fault for letting her out of the house.

*Let her out?* Now he had to restrain himself from punching *him*self. Since when had he gone caveman? He'd never felt like this before in his life. God, he needed to get a grip—and release the one he had on Bella.

Hell, he also needed to get laid, too. Just to take the edge off. Maybe then he wouldn't see Bella every time he closed his eyes. And considering that he blinked probably twenty-five times a minute—and saw her each and every damn time—that'd be a good thing. Except the thought of touching anyone else right now was enough to turn him off. Of everything and everyone except Bella—which took him right back to the dilemma at hand as Luke leered at her chest under the guise of bending over to kiss the hand he held. He'd seen Luke pull that trick too many times to count.

Staci, thank God, saw through it, too. If Reese wasn't mistaken, she pinched Luke's ass. And not in a good way.

Luke shot up and glared at Staci before turning his charming smile on Bella. "I'm Luke Jamison. I understand we'll be working together on the hospital auction."

"We're *all* doing the charity thing. Together." Staci sidled close enough that her breasts rested on Luke's arm. For once, Reese and the bimbo were on the same side. "We were just thinking that we should all, you know, go take a look at the place this Friday night." Staci included him and Bella in the *we all*. "Go over how the auction is going to be laid out and that sort of thing. You guys busy?"

Bella's smile disappeared altogether as she slid her hand from Luc's. "Stace, I don't think that's necessary—"

"I think it's a great idea," Luke chimed in. "It'll give us the lay of the land, so to speak. Right, Reese? Don't want to leave anything to chance, you know?"

It wasn't *land* Luke wanted to lay. And *The Midnight Maiden* would play right to that. The top deck, with its twinkling lights that reflected off the water beneath a starry, moonlit sky, was one of the most romantic dining experiences in the city. *That* wasn't something Reese wanted to chance.

"We don't need to go together," he said. He'd been there half a dozen times in the last week alone.

"Sure we do," said Staci. "Otherwise, how will Bella and I know what you and Luke want?"

He had a feeling Staci knew *exactly* what Luke wanted.

"Yeah, come on, Reese," said Luke. "I want to make sure I know exactly where it is and what's expected of me. Don't want to blow it again."

Which meant if Reese didn't go and Luke decided not to show up, Luke would blame him.

"Fine. Let's say seven. But Bella, if you can't make it…" Or if her husband wanted to have a romantic dinner or something… He should probably invite the husband. That'd be the polite thing to do. And would show him once and for all that Bella was Off Limits.

But he wasn't going to.

"Great. It's a date." Staci wiggled against Luke. "We'll have so much fun. Right, Bella?"

Bella blinked and that spinach-donut smile reappeared. "Uh, sure. I'm going to have to get a babysitter for Sophia."

"Oh Drew can do that."

"Hey!" Stalker Chick spoke up. "What if I have something to do?"

"Do you?"

"Well, no, but you don't know that."

"I do now, so you're on babysitting duty."

Jimmy whispered something in Drew's ear. Her blush was nowhere near as attractive as Bella's.

"Okay, then. That's settled," said Bella. "But now I have to get back to work."

A loud silence followed her departure until Luke's, "*That's* the serving girl I've been hearing about? She doesn't look all that homely to me" broke it.

Reese wanted to break *him*.

Instead, he grabbed him by the other arm and extricated him from Staci's cleavage, then steered him away from the others. "Knock it off, Luke. What the hell was that all about?"

"What was what about? You don't want to go? I thought this shindig was a big deal."

"Don't fuck with me, Luke."

"Trust me, Reese. It's isn't *you* I want to fuck."

Reese got that. "What happened to staying away from the caterer?"

Luke arched an eyebrow. "I am. We both know Staci isn't doing a thing for this auction. You never said anything about steering clear of family members. Besides, I figure the event will run much smoother if I keep her busy."

His logic actually made sense. "Fine. But another stunt like that hand-kissing move and we're done."

"Fine. No hand-kissing. I hear you."

Problem was, he thought Luke saw right through him, too.

***

Luke massaged his wrist as Reese stalked away. So *that's* the way it was, huh? Reese was all hot and bothered by one pretty little caterer.

Luke almost laughed. He hadn't ever seen Reese this tied up over anyone. And it had only taken one comment to set him off. That could make things really interesting.

He tucked that morsel away as he rejoined Staci, Drew, and Jimmy. "So what's the deal with your stepsister?" he asked the girls. "Is she seeing anyone?"

Jimmy's mouth fell open and Drew giggled.

Staci, however, turned to stone. Ah, good. He liked his women a little jealous and a lot unsure of his intentions. Though, seriously, the way her tits were all over him, she couldn't be *that* unsure of what he intended tonight.

"Bella? Seeing someone?" Drew snorted. "Depends if you count a ten-year-old as someone. Bella never dates. She's always at the restaurant or taking care of her little sister, Sophia."

"Oh, yeah, she's a *whole* lot of fun." Staci straightened which *just so happened* to make her tits the center of the conversation again.

God, he loved cheap and tacky. And easy. Easy was good.

"Any guy Bella ever dated dropped her after about a week. She's too boring." Staci leaned back into him, tits and all. "But let's not talk about her. I'd much rather hear all about that Super Bowl catch you made."

And then she got that calculating look in her eye just like Tanya had had when they'd first met. He'd thought it'd been genuine interest. Instead, it was the sign of dollar signs calculating in her head. He'd learned from that mistake big time.

Still, a man did have needs and the way Staci curled his arm around her and leaned her head against his shoulder might as well be a written invitation. Looked like someone was going to get lucky tonight and it definitely wasn't poor Reese.

He grabbed Jimmy's newly-opened beer and allowed himself to be sidetracked by football. Hell, he'd told this story so often he could do it in his sleep.

But all the time he was reciting the thirty-yard reception and three tackles he'd avoided for the winning touchdown, Luke was thinking about Reese. And Bella.

The guy needed to loosen up and live a little. Too much stress wasn't good for anyone. Luke knew that first hand.

In the old days, it would have been fun to see if he could win her out from under Reese, but he really didn't want to trash the repairs he was making to his business relationship with his old friend. Especially over some chick.

Maybe he could help Reese and Bella along. That could cement things with Reese once again. He'd fucked up big time on the business end, and with Tanya pulling her shit, he couldn't afford to be out of a job. He needed Reese's gigs.

He also needed Reese to keep his mouth shut around Tanya's lawyer and the best way to do that was keep it busy with something—*someone*—else.

Yeah, he could be as calculating as Tanya and Staci, but Luke had to look out for Number One.

His son.

***

Reese checked his watch and was surprised to find it was so late. He'd stayed. He hadn't been planning to, but when Metzner had pulled him into a conversation about the playoffs, well, hell. He missed the game. The camaraderie. His injury had stolen it; he wasn't about to let Coach's stubbornness and the ill-advised attraction to Bella to take it from him, too.

So he, Metzner, and Baldwin had hung out on the patio until everyone else had gone. Bella, too. She'd broken the set up down almost an hour ago. It was safe to head out.

And how ridiculous was it that he was avoiding her? He was a grown man, for chrissake.

Connie had walked the other guys out while he and Anthony closed down the outside. Anthony was off to the pool house to kill the lights while Reese headed into the kitchen to dispose of the trash.

Bella stood at the sink washing dishes. Her back was to him, her black outfit a bold contrast to the blonde ponytail resting between her shoulder blades. It swished as she turned and he had a momentary image of those strands swishing over him.

Good God, what was wrong with him? She was just another pretty woman.

Yeah, and his hotrod was just a car.

"Need some help?" he found himself saying instead of doing the smart thing by leaving.

Those gorgeous eyes of hers widened. "That's not necessary. I'm almost done."

"Well, then, let me help you get out of here quicker." He took a breath; he didn't want to say it. Really he didn't. Why punish himself more? But he said it anyway, if only to remind himself that someone else had already staked a claim on her. "I'm sure you're anxious to get home." There—he'd been magnanimous. Even if it killed him. Somewhere on the big tally sheet in the sky he should get very high marks for this offer.

"Oh. Thanks. I *am* tired after being at the restaurant so early." She handed him a dishtowel and they worked in a silence that, if it wasn't comfortable, at least it wasn't strained.

"Bella."

"Reese."

They spoke at the same time, then laughed.

"You first," again in unison.

He spoke first. His conscience had been gnawing at him. Plus, if she was going to quit on him, he wanted to do a pre-emptive strike. As he'd said to her in her kitchen, it was better to be on the offense. "I wanted to apologize again for that kiss. I had no right and it won't happen again. I don't want it to affect our working relationship. I was really impressed with what you put together for tonight so quickly. If this is how you do business, the auction is going to be a big hit."

The look on her face told him nothing. Was she mad? Offended? Disgusted? He had no clue—and that didn't sit well with him either. "Your turn." He finished the last dish, then rested his hip on the granite countertop.

Instantly Bella shoved him off the counter, her hand searing into his skin like a branding iron, knocking the breath from his lungs as if a dozen linebackers had just tackled him.

"Sorry." She yanked her hand away as if she'd been burned—he sure as hell had—then pointed to the water pooling next to where his hip had just been. "Your pants... they were going to get wet."

He wouldn't have cared. But if it meant he'd have her hands on him, even for the briefest of moments, he'd willingly sacrifice his pants.

But there was still the matter of The Husband.

"Thanks." Reese took a step away, knowing he had to. It was the right thing to do.

And so was leaving. "I guess I'll see you Friday, then. By the river. For the site visit. It's a good idea." God help him, he was babbling.

Reese Charmant did *not* babble. Ever.

"So, um, have a good night." He shoved his hands into his pockets, his fingers fiddling with a coin, and wished he could just get out of here with his sanity, his dignity, and his honor intact.

He thought he had until he realized that her scent had followed him all the way home.

***

She'd touched his hip. What had she been thinking?

Bella snorted as she sank onto a chair at the DeLeo's kitchen island, her knees wobbly from the searing awareness of that contact. Thinking? She hadn't been thinking. She'd been reacting. To him. To his apology. To that stupid water that was going to ruin pants she really shouldn't care about ruining. *Especially* if he was apologizing for kissing her. He must have really regretted it.

Which made her feel about as attractive as her namesake in the rags-to-riches rags days.

Okay, enough of the negativity. It'd been a long day and she was wiped out. Add the added sexual awareness she'd been dodging all evening and she was ready to call it a night.

She grabbed her purse and reached inside for her car keys. A gold coin rolled out. Hmmm. She thought Sophia had tossed them all in the fountain.

Oh well. With as distracted as she'd been lately, anything was possible. She just hoped Reese had no idea that *he* was the cause of her distraction.

***

Back on Front Street in his half-furnished apartment, Jonathan groaned and shook his head as he sat back in his chair, the television before him turned off, but still filled with images.

Did *anyone* know what to do with lucky charms these days? Wishing for the opposite of what they wanted was *not* the purpose the coins had been manifested for.

He dropped his head into his hands as the split images of Bella in the DeLeo's kitchen and Reese zooming off in his car faded from the screen.

This was going to be harder than he'd thought.

# Chapter Twelve

"Lucinda Isabella!"

Bella counted to ten. Twice. Madeleine calling her in that tone of voice was never a good thing; using her full name was even worse.

Saying a swift prayer to keep her cool, Bella backed through the French doors to the patio, the breakfast tray balanced precariously in one hand, a pot of steaming coffee in the other.

"Your breakfast just came out of the oven." She set the tray on the glass-topped wicker table in front of her wicked stepmother. Some days she really wouldn't mind the fairy tale coming true.

"It's not the breakfast." Madeleine snapped the front page of the Society page in her face. "You failed to mention the party you catered last night was at the DeLeo home."

Because she knew the woman would have finagled a way to attend. Connie DeLeo was who her stepmother aspired to be.

"Constance DeLeo is the on the Arts Center Board." Madeleine rattled the paper again. "How did it go? Did you make any beneficial comments about me, any kind words or recommendations for me to be on the Board?" Her stepmother arched a perfectly-plucked, wickedly-black eyebrow.

"Actually, Madeleine." Bella set the coffee pot on the table, just out of arm's reach away, her own little rebellion. "I was there to work for the woman, not do your PR. My main goal was to see that her party ran smoothly." Before Madeleine could interrupt—because she would; she always did—Bella took the newspaper, folded it in half (just below a line mentioning the catering, she was happy to see), and set it beside the coffee pot—also beyond arm's reach. "Working so diligently speaks well of Casteleoni's, and since you *are* a Casteleoni, I'd think you be glad that I care about our name."

"Yes, well it is fortunate that the staff seems to be up to the task." Madeleine helped herself to a portion of the breakfast casserole, then reached for the coffee, only to glare at Bella as she had to stand to reach the pot. "I'd be unhappy if there were poor reviews from one of your events. If that happens, I'll have to get involved with the day to day running of the company."

Over her dead body. Madeleine's, not Bella's.

"As I said, everything went well. And will continue to do so despite your threat. I will handle it as I see fit—just as I did with Mr. Tildwell and his son after my father's funeral." She couldn't resist the barb. That situation had been a defining moment in their relationship.

"That is one of the reasons I am *not* on the Board today." Madeleine sat back down and poured the coffee.

Bella had the urge to dump the entire pot on Madeleine's head. "For God's sake, Madeleine. The man caught his son cornering me in the back hall of the funeral home and had the gall to say *I* was trying to trap him into marrying me since my parents had both died, and you really expected me to *apologize*?"

"You could have used it to our advantage."

"You mean *your* advantage, but I'm not going to compromise my principles for your ambitions."

"Oh, I think there's something you'll compromise for, my dear." Madeleine's mouth stretched into that thin, teeth-bared grin she was so bloody good at. "Or should I say *someone*?"

Sophia.

It was always Sophia. When Madeleine had wanted to be head of the PTA, Bella had had to show up at a meeting and tell all the members—in tears, no less—how wonderful Madeleine had been to her and her sister, and how special it would be to share Madeleine's generosity with the school community by electing her president. That Madeleine had never run after her term was over was quickly forgotten by the woman herself—the position hadn't been prestigious enough for her.

Since then, Bella had tried to keep away from those predicaments. But the stakes were higher now. And Madeleine, damn her, knew it.

"I thought you aren't on the Board because there's someone else in the running?"

"Where did you hear that?"

"Staci."

Madeleine's eyes narrowed. "Anastasia needs to learn to keep her mouth shut."

*Good luck with that* was what Bella wanted to say, but wisely, kept her own mouth shut.

"I trust you to keep this information to yourself. I don't need rumor and innuendo running rampant while the Board is making its decision. Of course, they can't possibly pick anyone other than me. Casteleoni's has been around for years. We're a fixture in this town."

"No worries, Madeleine. My lips are sealed," Bella replied as she headed back into the kitchen. She talked about her stepmother only when necessary and hated being lumped in with that collective *we*. She hated that Madeleine *was* a Casteleoni, and she especially hated that the woman was using her family's reputation to make her own name. But if it kept Sophia where she should be, Bella would make the sacrifice.

If only she didn't have to sacrifice everything…

Reese had looked so good last night, relaxed and joking with his buddies. She'd had to escape to the kitchen to stop from staring at him. But that hadn't stopped the replay of their kiss from cycling on an endless loop during the monotony of dishwashing.

Then he'd come into the kitchen and, well, it'd made for both a sleepless night and some pretty nice dreams when she'd finally drifted off.

She could only hope Casteleoni's would become so inundated with business that she'd amass the money for the custody battle quickly because once it was over, she might try making her own wish come true.

***

"What's up with washer-woman?" Staci asked her mother as Bella walked past her without so much as a hello. And after all she'd done to set her up on a date with Reese. Honestly, the girl just didn't have a clue how to do anything when it came to guys.

"Oh." Mother waved her spoon dismissively. "We were simply having a meeting of the minds." She took a sip of her coffee. "Hers was meeting the directives of mine."

Staci "hmmmed" and slid into the cushioned wicker chair across to the table. Mother could be very *persuasive*. All three Fontaine women could. All they had to do was dangle the threat of sending Sophia away and Bella would do whatever they asked. Just like a puppet.

Sometimes—rarely, but sometimes—Staci felt bad about that. Sophia wasn't really a problem. She was actually a neat, well-behaved child. But it was the only way they could keep control of Bella and, well, if Bella didn't do things around the house, she and Drew would have to because there was *no* way Mother would ever dirty her hands. And that was *so* not happening.

Shrugging, Staci picked up the newspaper. "Hmph," she grumbled as she read the Society page. "Not a word about me in this article, but there's good ol' Bella's name."

"What?" Her mother set down her spoon. "Why should there be a mention of you?"

Staci didn't bother hiding her smile. It wasn't often she could one-up her mother with gossip. "Because I was there, too."

"Bella actually let you work with her?"

"No, Mother!" Staci slammed down the article. "You know, I do have some worth as a person. I went with one of the football players. The one who caught the winning touchdown in the Super Bowl if you must know. As his date."

"Which player? That Reese Charming person?"

"Not him." It figured *he'd* be the one whose name Mother knew instead of Luke's. Even unintentionally, Mother had that knack of always making Staci feel second best. "And it's Charmant, Mother, not Charming. You'd better learn it because he's a big-wig in this town with a successful business and," *la-la-la* was what she wanted to add, but opted for, "he's hired our little Bella to cater the annual charity auction for the hospital next month."

"Bella?" Mother's coffee cup rattled on the saucer, spilling it onto the hand-embroidered placemat she'd had made for her wedding to Sal. The fact that she made no move to blot up the mess spoke to her level of upset at this news.

Staci had never seen her mother so flustered and had to admit there was a certain satisfaction in having been the one to do that to her.

"Yep. Bella's going to be working with him." Staci sat back. If she were a cat, she'd be puffing feathers from her mouth.

"You mean Bella is in contact with that man?"

"Yes. She spoke to him last night at the DeLeo's and he's been to the restaurant at least twice."

"She could ruin me." Mother absently mopped up the coffee. "Why, he's—" Mother shook her head, as close to sputtering as Staci had ever seen her. "She could ruin everything."

"Relax, Mother," Staci took the napkin and cleaned up the rest of the coffee as much as possible. That placemat was a goner. "It's just some big dinner. She does those all the time. Plus, I'll see to it that she doesn't mess it up."

"You?" Mother's eyebrow arched in the derision Staci had come to expect over the years.

Someday, Staci was going to master that movement because it conveyed so much more than just the acidity in her mother's tone—acidity that, once again, was directed at her. God, she was so sick of never measuring up to Mother's expectations.

"Yes, me, Mother. *I'm* working with Bella on the auction so I'll be around to make sure nothing happens."

"Honestly, Anastasia. It's a nice thought, but drama follows you around like a puppy. If only you'd learn to keep your mouth shut. Why would you tell Lucinda about the other candidate for the Board position? If she says anything about that, it'll all be over. Why, I'd be better off if—"

All of a sudden Mother's eyes narrowed and Staci swore she felt daggers being thrown at her from those little slits.

"Wait." Madeleine snapped her fingers. "I have a better idea. You—" She pointed at Staci—"are to drop this catcher guy—"

"He's a tight end, Mother."

"I really don't care to hear of his physical attributes, Anastasia." Madeleine took her time slicking her pinky finger over that damned eyebrow. As *if* Staci could miss it or what it meant. "You need to drop him and start dating that Charming guy."

"Charmant, Mother. Reese Charmant. The quarterback."

"Yes, whatever." She waved her hand. "You'll need to keep tabs on him, spend time with him, enthrall him as you've done with so many other men."

This was new. Mother was usually berating her for her choice in guys. "I don't know that that's possible. He seems to have a thing for her."

"I don't care if he wants to marry her, Anastasia. Well, actually I *would* care about that; it'd be disastrous. I want you in his face," said her mother and Staci wasn't enjoying being on the receiving end of Mother's *directives*.

"But, I'm dating Luke, Mother. He's perfect for me."

Madeleine slammed her fork onto the table top. "And that's precisely the problem with you and your sister. You have no idea who or what is perfect for you. You're always willing to settle for good enough. I did, and look what happened. We end up here, stuck on the fringes of society. I thought Sal was good enough, rich enough, *pliable* enough, to mold for our entree into society. But then he had to grieve himself to death over that *woman*."

Madeleine never could say Ana's name. She could barely stomach the thought of her, which was why she'd removed every trace of their stepfather's first wife from this house after she'd married him.

Every trace except for Ana's look-alike daughters.

"You are not going to settle for some hind end, Anastasia."

Staci couldn't help snorting at that. Luke would go ballistic if he ever heard his position called a "hind end."

"You are going to make sure Reese Charmant knows who you are. And wants you, not Bella." Mother took another sip of her coffee. "We'll go shopping today."

"Shopping?"

"You don't think you'll hold his attention looking like that, do you?" The look Mother gave her would have done a construction worker proud. "Tacky, but the genes are there. No, you're only good for a weekend fling looking like that. And much as I hate to admit it, Lucinda does have a certain style. Obviously, you'll have to be more like her to catch his attention." She gathered the paper and, wonder of wonders, picked up her own plate. "I'll take care of it. We'll start with a cut and color, and then move on to your wardrobe."

"But, Mother—"

"There will be no more on the subject, Anastasia. Your stepsister *cannot* have anything to do with that man."

Staci followed her. She had no idea why Mother was so set on this, but the woman's will was formidable. She just wondered who was going to tell that to Reese.

# Chapter Thirteen

Cheers greeted Bella as she entered Casteleoni's for her shift Monday morning, the Society page on every table.

All the regulars were there: Mr. Campanale raised his cup, Tony and Rose stopped talking to smile and wave, Mrs. Angelelli—and even Joey, her nephew, was there early to take his aunt to her morning bridge club.

Giac flew from the kitchen and threw his arms around her neck. "Congratulations! We saw the write-up in the paper." He steered her toward the counter and pulled out one of the vinyl-covered stools.

As Bella allowed herself to be settled on the seat, Giac pulled another one up for himself and slid onto it, his elbow coming to rest on the counter, his palm cradling his chin. "Tell me all about it." He tapped her arm. "What was Constance wearing? Was it a little black number or did she do belle-of-the-ball? Sleek and sexy or uppercrust?" He sighed. "That woman has looked gorgeous since grade school."

Bella chuckled. "She had a very pretty dress on. But what's with the interest in fashion?"

"Oh." Giac actually blushed—and that was odd because he *never* blushed. "I can't tell you right now, but we've had some success. Gus has found a new creative outlet, and, *phew*! the man has been on fire."

"You are not telling my secrets?" Gus boomed from the back.

"No, but hurry up or I might!" Giac shouted back.

At least they weren't arguing, so that was something.

Hopefully this new *creative outlet* didn't involve cooking. Since Gus had started experimenting with their menu, he'd put on considerable weight. And so had poor Willow.

Speaking of which, she wondered where the kitten was. She'd brought him back to the restaurant and he'd made a beeline for the trashcans out back. Not that she could blame him, and thankfully, he always showed up whenever Sophia came around. It wasn't optimal, but at least it kept the Health Department off her case and Sophia happy.

"Fine, fine. I'm coming." Gus shoved himself through the door, and flourished a gift-wrapped box from behind him and set it on the counter. "For your success."

Everyone in the restaurant stopped talking as Bella opened the box. Inside was the most beautiful soft pink satin fabric.

She lifted it out. It was a blouse. But not just any blouse; there was nothing ordinary about this. The delicate fabric was cut into a tuxedo style with three-quarter sleeves with flared, angled cuffs. The neckline Vee-ed to an opening fastened with three oversize opalescent buttons and a tapered waist, and her name was embroidered in silver on the left side.

"It's beautiful, Gus. Thank you so much." She squeezed his hand, squeezing her eyes at the same time so she wouldn't cry. He'd made this just for her and it touched her more than any expensive gift ever could.

"Black, she is no good for you," Gus said, gruffly—because he was a softie when it came to her and Sophia. "Now, when you work the big parties, you must look beautiful. As good as the food we make." He puffed out his chest, tapping it with one meaty fist. "I make the gift for you so people ask, 'Who is this girl? I meet her and learn her name.' " He brought his thumb to his first two fingers and shook them backward in a familiar gesture from the old country. "They see, they talk, they like, and they buy." He kissed the grouping of his fingers with a loud smack. "You make much money and we say 'Ciao, Madeleine!' Good idea, eh?"

Bella laughed. It was good to see him happy and excited about something. Even though his logic was faulty—it'd take more than a piece of clothing to best Madeleine—she couldn't fault his attitude. Or his effort. The blouse was truly spectacular.

Bella leaned across the counter and kissed his cheek. "Thank you, Gus. This is perfect."

Gus beamed and tapped Giac on the chest with the backs of his fingers. "My first Giuseppe Sorcio original. But not my last, eh?"

"No, Giuseppe." Giac kissed those fingers, then folded them against his heart. "Definitely not your last."

The bells jingled then and Perla's "Dollface!" curtailed the rest of what Bella wanted to say to her two friends while everyone else went back to their normal routine.

She hurried over as Perla tottered in on spike-heeled sandals. Nice weather signaled the advent of pedicure season and Perla was the leading dignitary at Nina's Nails. She even bought her shoes to display them accordingly. Shoes that Casteleoni's had helped finance.

"Quick, doll," Perla stage-whispered to her, "what's Gus's special today? I want to prepare myself before Harry hears it." She tapped her manicured fingers on the Formica.

"Actually, Perla, it looks like Gus is taking your suggestion to heart. I got a beautiful new blouse today and there is no special."

Perla clapped her hands together, bangle bracelets clanging, with a small hop in her heels. "Oh, wonderful! When do I get my new outfits?" She pushed off from the counter. "I'll go talk to the dear man right this instant. Harry and I are going to the beach with the family this summer and I need a whole new wardrobe." She scurried off. "Won't Francesca just *die* when I show up with designer originals," she said to no one and everyone; that was Perla. "Of course, I'll need shoes too. I should probably try that new shoe store, too—oh, doll. I almost forgot. There's a cute guy asking for you over there." The word *subtle* was lost on Perla as her voice carried throughout the restaurant. The cute guy—*Reese*—was sure to hear.

Bella's stomach flip-flopped as she turned—

But the flips flopped as she saw, not Reese, but someone else. Tall, dark, and definitely good-looking, he wore a business suit and carried a briefcase. Gray eyes and hair the color of steel completed the whole package, but Bella had no idea who he was. Referral business from the DeLeos' party, perhaps?

Bella pasted her most professional smile on her face and walked over, arm extended. "Hi, I'm Bella Casteleoni. What can I do for you?"

"Hello. I'm Jake Adams. Reese's business partner." He lifted his briefcase. "He asked me to stop by and give you our subcontractor contract. Do you have a few minutes?"

"Sure. Let's have a seat here." She led him to the booth in the back corner and tried to squelch the disappointment that Reese hadn't been the one to bring it by. Of course, it was probably better that he hadn't. Allowed her to concentrate on business rather than the hot guy sitting across from her.

"Is Reese out of town or something?" She asked oh-so-nonchalantly as she signed the paperwork.

"No, just tied up with meetings and since I was on my way to see another client, it made sense for me to bring them."

The explanation, however logical, didn't make her feel any better. Her illogical reaction to it didn't either.

And Madeleine entering the restaurant at that moment *really* didn't make her feel good at all because the last time her stepmother had set foot in the restaurant had been when she'd wheeled her father in right before she'd wheeled him down the Justice of the Peace's courtroom aisle.

This time, as then, Madeleine coasted into the suddenly-silent restaurant like the lady of the manor, a nod here, royal wave there. To whom, Bella couldn't imagine.

And she didn't want to waste time trying to. She excused herself from Jake to intercept her stepmother before she could make it to the kitchen. God only knew what havoc the woman was planning to wreak now.

Madeleine's eyes flashed, but she quickly reigned in her temper. Madeleine was always calm, cool, and collected in public. Always image-conscious. Too bad she didn't pay that much attention to her soul.

She smoothed a hand over the French twist she'd probably spent a week's worth of receipts on, then rested it on the top of a booth. Carlo Marinelli shrank back. Took a lot to make Carlo back off; the guy was tough.

"Why Lucinda, dear, is that any way to greet a member of your family?" Politeness dripped from every syllable as Madeleine's obsidian eyes skirted the interior of the restaurant.

"Don't remind me," Bella gritted through her teeth. "What could possibly bring you here?"

"I thought it might be a good idea to see how the restaurant operates, meet the clients, that sort of thing."

The whole speech was said through the phoniest smile Bella had ever seen. Who was the act for?

"What's going on, Madeleine?"

"Whatever do you mean, dear girl?"

*Dear girl?* Madeleine had never entertained the idea of Bella being dear to her in even the most remote sense. Bella tried to figure the woman's angle, but no answers came.

"Why shouldn't I watch over Sophia's interests? I am, after all, her *legal* guardian."

She smiled at someone. Bella fought the urge to see who had betrayed her by greeting this witch. Though, in all fairness, that person probably only returned Madeleine's smile to keep from getting struck with her metaphorical fangs.

"Are there any of your catering clients here today?" said witch asked, a tad too interestedly.

Ah. She'd heard about the auction. And since Staci came through the door just then, it was no surprise where that info had come from—

Actually she *thought* that was Staci, but the resemblance stopped somewhere at the eyes.

"Staci? What did you do to yourself?" The tasteful outfit her stepsister wore bore no resemblance to any article of clothing the tacky girl had ever worn. If it didn't show cleavage, Staci wasn't interested.

Staci gave her sleek new cut a pat. "Do you like it? I thought it was time for a change and since I'm going into business with you, I thought perhaps I should hide my... um... charms a little more. Keep the customer focused on the little hor d'oeuvre-y things instead of the help." Her smile was a glittery, gloss-wrapped nightmare.

"Going into business with me?" Bella almost shouted. "Going into business? I don't think so." She slammed her hands on her hips and glared at Madeleine. "If you're so anxious for Casteleoni's reputation to get you on that Board, I suggest you think twice before making me take her on. She may have cleaned up nicely on the outside, but the minute she opens her mouth, the whole façade crumbles."

"But you already hired me for a job," said Staci with a pout she'd perfected years ago. Bella knew; she'd caught her practicing it in the mirror when they were younger. "This is just the next step and since it's Casteleoni's and I'm—"

"You are *not* a Casteleoni, Staci Fontaine. And even if you were, that doesn't entitle you to just declare yourself my partner. I only gave you a job because you insisted."

Madeleine's fire engine red lips formed her famed feral grin as she patted Staci's arm. "And *I'm* insisting that you take her on as your partner. I know she's a bit rough around the edges, but we'll work on her. After all, she does have a degree in public relations."

"That's because she'd thought she could get a TV anchor position with it." Bella was so angry she wanted to storm off, but Jake was sitting there, watching. It wouldn't look very professional of her to pitch the fit she wanted to. "She just wants the glitz and glamour. There's no substance to her. She doesn't know the first thing about catering, and the last thing I'd do is let her talk to a client."

"Now, Lucinda." Madeleine turned on what she apparently thought was charm, but in reality was completely fake and saccharine-sweet. "Just think how busy you're going to be with all these catering clients. You couldn't possibly care for Sophia as well, now, could you? We'd just have to send her off to that boarding school where there are people to take care of her and help her with schoolwork." Madeleine wiped a non-existent crumb from the corner of her mouth, letting the threat sink in. "Of course, if Anastasia were to help you…"

Bella looked between the two mistresses of evil. What could Madeleine possibly want with Reese? And, Staci? She already had Luke under her spell; surely she wasn't after Reese as well?

"Is there a problem?" Jake walked toward them.

He and Reese ought to re-think the name of their business. She'd vote for Prince Charming, Inc., Rescuers of Damsels-in-Disgust.

Madeline turned around, her viper eyes taking him in quickly. "Hello." She held out her hand with such *noblesse oblige* Bella almost laughed.

Almost.

"Bella?" Jake ignored Madeleine's hand. "Is everything all right?"

She nodded, both to clear it and to answer him. "Everything's fine. This is my stepmother, Madeleine Fon—er, Casteleoni—"yeah, that name still stuck in Bella's craw—"and this is her daughter, Staci Fontaine."

"Hello," Staci purred.

See? The inside hadn't changed.

"Are you hiring Bella for something?" Madeleine let go of the booth and sidled up next to Jake.

Carlo Marinelli exhaled and mopped his forehead with a napkin.

"Yes, I am. Well, *we* are. I'm Jake Adams. Of Promotional Sports."

"Oh, you're Reese's partner." Staci perked up at that. "Is Luke here?"

*Staci* didn't want Reese; *Madeleine* did. The question was, why? Surely she didn't think she had a shot with him?

That time Bella did snort a little.

Madeleine's eyes narrowed.

"No, Luke's not here." Jake disengaged himself from Madeleine's clutches—a very impressive move—and handed Bella the papers she'd signed before Hurricane Madeleine had blown in. "Thanks for this, Bella. I'll be in touch."

Madeleine clenched Bella's arm as Jake left. "Why did you let him leave?"

Bella held up the papers. "Because our business is done. Now I have to get back to work. We'll discuss this later."

"There will be no discussion, Lucinda." Madeleine's hissed whisper could have frosted an entire day's worth of fountain sodas. "Staci will be partnering with you. I want her to learn everything about running this business. Or Sophia will be going on a very long trip."

Bella kept quiet. This was odd, even for Madeleine. To put Staci on the job... She wanted something. Badly.

Bella was going to figure out what Madeleine wanted, why she wanted it, and how to beat her at her own game.

***

"She signed, then?" Reese asked Jake when he picked him up around the corner from Casteleoni's. Yeah, it was a cop-out having Jake deliver the paperwork, but he had to make the break and the only way was to keep his distance.

"What asinine thing did you do to think she wouldn't?"

"Nothing." He certainly couldn't tell Jake that he was lusting after their new caterer. His partner already wanted to take Luke to court for the ten grand and was skeptical that Luke would actually work it off.

"Yeah, right. I've known you since we were kids, Reese. You can't pull one over on me. What'd you do? Why'd you have me do this? Oh, and by the way? That family of hers is whacked. The stepmother is unbelievable and the sister—"

"Stepsister."

"Yeah, an important distinction. But you still haven't answered my question." Jake quarter turned and stared him down with his "lawyer glare." "What'd you do?"

Reese checked the rearview mirror, then crossed to the left lane.

He'd drop Jake off at the office before heading to the other side of town. "Nothing. Really. You were the logical person since you're the lawyer. You handle the paperwork; I handle the staff. That's why we work so well, remember?"

"I remember that you could bullshit yourself out of pretty much any situation. But not with me." Jake drummed his fingers on the dash. "Is there something I need to know?"

"If there is, you'll be the first to know it."

Jake exhaled and turned back in his seat. "Just promise me we're not going to run into another Luke situation."

"I can definitely promise you that."

"Good. Then it's your problem, man. Just make sure it doesn't interfere in our business."

"You got it."

Now if only he could make his libido remember that.

# Chapter Fourteen

My prince has come."

The singing voice greeted Reese as he entered the house. Wincing, he looked up as a cloud of diaphanous female floated down the stairs and flung herself at him, slender arms slipping around his waist.

He expelled an amused breath at the theatrical entrance. "Hello, Mom."

Carolyn Charmant looked up, all five feet nothing of her, with a smile bright enough to light up an entire block for a month. "My darling son, I am so glad to see you." She disengaged herself from the hug, grabbed his hand, and tugged him into the living room, half prancing in her haste to get there.

She patted the seat next to her, tucked her legs to the side, ankles crossed, and folded her arms gracefully in her lap, her back ramrod straight. The perfect lady.

He couldn't help but smile. Five children, six grandkids, and she still looked like the movie star she'd been. No wonder his father had talked her into early retirement.

"You look beautiful, Mom."

She waved her hand dismissively, but she still blushed. "You must want something to try to flatter me."

"Geez. Can't a guy compliment his mother without a reason?"

"Some can, my darling, but you've always had an ulterior motive with your flattery." She brushed his cheek. "Usually it was to get yourself out of trouble. Or if you had girl trouble. Not that you had much of that, unless you call being able to take your pick trouble." She folded her hands in her lap again. "So which is it?"

His mother had always been able to read him. It'd been pretty annoying in high school; he'd barely been able to get away with anything. "Not trouble, exactly. Just an unhealthy interest in someone else's wife."

"That's not trouble?"

"Only if I act on it. Which I'd never do." Well, *again.* He pinched the bridge of his nose. "I just can't get her out of my head."

"Oh, Reese, honey." His mother might embrace her movie star image, but when it came to life's ups and downs, there was no one more practical. "I don't think I can fix this one for you. But you know you can't act on it, so you'll have to stay away from her. Find someone else. Bury yourself in work." She winced. "Clichés, I know, but I don't know what else to tell you that you don't already know. I'm sorry."

He scrubbed his face, then stood up and walked to the fireplace. "They're clichés for a reason, Mom, but they're easier said than done. She's working for me as a subcontractor. I hired her for a function next month."

"Before or after checking her references?"

"Before I knew she was married." He faced the fireplace and grasped the mantle. "And she has a daughter."

He met Mom's gaze in the picture above the fireplace.

"You really care for her." It wasn't a question.

He spun around. "How can I? How can I feel like this for another guy's wife? Mother of his child?" He sank into a side chair and dropped his head into his hands. "I know I should stay away from her. I know I should forget her." He raised his head, hands flung between his knees. "Hell, I've only known her a few days and I can't stop thinking about her. Can't get her out of my head."

His mom walked over and hugged him. "I'm sorry, honey." She wore the perfume he'd been buying her ever since he'd been old enough to shop for Christmas gifts. She stroked his hair just like she'd done when he was a child. God, it was nice to come home. "Do you want to tell me about her?"

He shook his head and removed her arms. "No, I've got to let it—her—go, but thanks for listening. I'll be all right." He kissed her cheek, then smiled the smile he'd inherited from her. "But I didn't come to talk about Bella. I came to take you to lunch if you're free."

"You must really want something badly if you drove all the way here to take me to lunch."

He feigned offense. "I can't take my mom to lunch?"

"In the middle of the week with an hour drive from one side of our fair metropolis to the other?" Her slate eyes sparkled beneath her raised eyebrows. "Try another one."

"You got me." Yeah, he'd never been able to pull one over on her. "But it was only forty-five minutes."

"Reese, just because your car has that stallion logo, doesn't mean you have to treat it like a racehorse. You're lucky you didn't get pulled over. Or worse."

"Mom. I'm thirty-four years old. I don't need driving lessons." He grinned again. "But you're right. I do want something."

"I knew it."

"I want you to come with me to lunch."

She shrugged and took his arm. "Well, then, I guess I'll have to go. After all, who can resist Prince Charming?"

"Mom, please." He exhaled. "Don't you think we're a little old to believe in fairy tales and happily-ever-afters?"

She pretended to look put out, but Reese knew better. His mother was an Academy award-winning actress for a reason.

"You're never too old for dreams, my darling."

***

Bella felt as if she were in the middle of a nightmare.

Madeleine had insisted that Staci begin her education that very minute. The problem was that if it didn't come from a national restaurant chain, Staci couldn't grasp the subtleties of the food. To her, pigs-in-a-blanket were gourmet.

Bella winced. Not that she had anything against pigs-in-a-blanket, but she wanted upscale for the auction.

Madeleine couldn't really believe this was a good idea. Why sic Staci on her? It made no sense. *Unless* Madeleine was trying to sabotage the event. Which also made no sense. If Casteleoni's failed, Madeleine's bid for the Board could as well. Not to mention her bank balance. And Bella didn't even want to consider the effect on Reese's business.

The thoughts whirled around in her head, mingling with that damn threat. Just once she should call Madeleine on it. She'd thought about doing so many times, but she couldn't risk it. Sophia would suffer.

Then a call had come from Reese's assistant that he'd had a cancellation tomorrow and could she make a two o'clock appointment? She'd have to finalize all of the plans, cover her shift at the restaurant, and find a friend for Sophia to get off the bus with, but it was business; she'd make it.

Staci had taken off the moment Giac had hung up the phone, declaring a "shopping emergency" for a new outfit. Bella wasn't sure what was wrong with the one she was wearing, but she was fine with Staci leaving. She'd had more than enough of the Fontaine family.

And then Uncle Vinny arrived, which was always cause for celebration. He traveled a lot with his job and was rarely in town. She loved him as if he were her father and missed him terribly when he was gone, but his arrival now only added to the day's upheaval.

"Mi Bellisima!" Her father's second cousin's booming voice echoed through the restaurant as he enveloped her in a hug.

Uncle Vinny had been there for her when the accident had shattered her existence, and he'd tried to help her put the pieces together ever since.

"Ah, Bella. It's so good to see you again." Uncle Vinny kissed her on both cheeks, then held her away from him with a smile on his face and a twinkle in his Mediterranean-blue eyes—just the way she always pictured him. Vinny might be a top-echelon golf course designer and shrewd businessman to the rest of the world, but to her, he was an old softie. "I heard Connie DeLeo's party was a success."

"In more ways than one. We've gotten two referrals so far from it."

"I told you, Bella, I'm willing to give you a loan—"

"And we both know the message it'd send to the judge: that I can't take care of Sophia on my own, and that would negatively affect my case. Why would a judge alter the current custody arrangements if I can't provide for my sister from the outset? No, we've been over this, Uncle Vinny and your lawyer confirmed it. I have to show the court that I can take care of her myself, or it'll be tossing money away. And if I lose, God knows where Madeleine will send Sophia. I can't take the risk; I have to go into this with a clear shot at winning." And until then, she had to play by Madeleine's rules.

Uncle Vinny bit back the words she knew he wanted to say. He had the same opinion of Madeleine that she did, but there was nothing he could do about it. With all his traveling, there'd been no hope of him getting custody after Dad had died. His lawyer had said that Madeleine's lack of a career actually *helped* her cause.

Bella bit back the bitterness. Madeleine didn't have a job because of Dad's money and this business. The very thing Bella was counting on to help her out of the mess was the thing that kept her in it.

Luckily, Gus barreling through the swinging door from the kitchen got her mind off the endless loop of helplessness.

"Vincenzo! About time you visit!" Gus grabbed Uncle Vinny by the arms and pulled him into a double-cheek kiss. "Is good to have you back. You stay a while, eh? See Bella's big night? She is a good business woman." He tapped Vinny's chest with the back of his fingertips. "Our little angel, she flies high these days. And with an American football player, no less!"

"What?" Uncle Vinny raised an eyebrow.

Bella rolled her eyes. Leave it to Gus to make more of the situation with Reese than it merited.

She tugged Uncle Vinny into one of the booths. "Don't listen to Gus. I'm doing a job for Reese Charmant. The annual hospital auction. Gus's food sealed the deal."

"She lies. It is because of our Bella that we do this." Gus wagged a plump sausage of a finger at her while pushing his way into the booth beside her. "The man, he saw her—" he held her chin in his hand—"and this beautiful face. He was *incantato*. The man, he knows beauty when he sees it."

"Enchanted?" Bella tugged her chin away. *If only*. "Really, Gus. Even if I were Miss America, Reese wouldn't hire me if the food wasn't good. You sealed the deal for us."

Gus and Uncle Vinny looked at each other with such a look that Bella knew when to throw in the towel. "All right, I can tell when I won't win against you two." She untied her apron and scooched across the booth, making Gus stand up. "And I'm not even going to try. You two stay here and chat all you want about something completely incorrect while I get Sophia off the bus." She kissed both men on their cheeks. "Behave. Both of you."

She didn't believe their angelic expressions for one minute.

***

92

"He's interested in her, isn't he?" Vinny asked Giuseppe the minute Bella left.

"*Sì*. But Giacomo and I, we don't know in what way. Well, of course, we know in *that* way—the man, he is not dead—but we will watch to be sure he treats her as a princess, *capisce?*"

"Yeah, I understand." Vinny scratched his jaw. He and the guys had been looking out for Bella ever since Sal took sick after the accident. Vinny was all for Bella having someone in her life, but he was around pro athletes all the time, and while most were decent, there were those who had an ego bigger than the venues they played in, and behaved—or *mis*behaved—accordingly.

He ought to tag along with Bella on this appointment. Check the guy out. He knew *of* him, of course, and what he knew he liked. But the real guy? That took firsthand knowledge. And since his own celebrity status gave him some common ground with Reese, no one would think anything of him tagging along. One sports guy to another.

Vinny chuckled. Okay, maybe *he* had one of those egos he was talking about, but that only made his radar hum for Bella's sake.

So, yeah, he was definitely going to pay Mr. Reese Charmant a visit. Bella needed someone to watch out for her; it's what her father would have wanted. Since Sal couldn't, it was up to him.

After all, he *was* her godfather.

***

Madeleine paced in the master suite and, for the first time since she'd married Sal, she didn't care what her heels were doing to the plush carpet.

Bella could ruin everything.

That Board position had been *right* in her hands. Talia had suggested it would happen at the flower show last week and, as the Recording Secretary, she would know. They'd been waiting for the tea to tell her.

Then there'd been the frantic whisperings when Talia had arrived. Of course she'd been late so Madeleine had had to deal with her devastating disappointment while surrounded by the rest of the Board. *She* ought to get an Academy Award for her performance, not that *actress* they were now considering.

She sat on the settee at the foot of the bed. How dare they take this from her. That woman had done nothing for this town but leave it to make a name for herself. Then she comes sashaying back as if she were royalty, expecting all doors to be opened to her, all accolades bestowed upon her.

*Madeleine* deserved this. *She'd* worked her fingers to the bone taking care of Salvatore Casteleoni. *She'd* hurt her back helping him to and from that godforsaken chair. And then she'd had to play the grieving wife, always at his hospital bed when the man hadn't had a prayer of recovering. She'd known that from the day they'd admitted him. Yet she'd done her duty. Acted the concerned and caring wife, always mindful of the respect the townspeople held for him. Her. She'd been the face of Casteleoni's and how did they pay her? By making her second best?

No. It could not happen. Some Hollywood chippy was *not* going to take what was rightfully hers.

# Chapter Fifteen

ella and a Mr. Casteleoni to see you, Reese."

Reese was halfway out of his chair when Kelly's announcement registered.

The Husband.

*Now* he was meeting her Husband? Father of her child, the man legally and morally entitled to do things to and with her that Reese had no business imagining. *That* Husband?

He wasn't ready.

"Oh, yes." Kelly's barely contained amusement interrupted his dread. "And a Miss Staci Fontaine, as well."

Reese could hear Staci "humph" in annoyance as Kelly cut her off.

Never had he imagined he'd be glad to see Staci, but today she'd be a buffer between the happy couple and his wayward thoughts.

Okay, he could do this. "Send them in."

Bella, looking beautiful in a light pink frilly feminine blouse and cream pants that brought to mind a vanilla ice cream cone he'd love to lick, walked into the office with a presentation portfolio clutched in front of her and a mountain of a man walking behind her.

Reese immediately started summing the guy up—as the guy did to him—and the air suddenly came alive with testosterone zinging around the room like wayward bolts of lightning. Bella seemed oblivious. How, Reese couldn't begin to guess. He sure as hell wasn't.

And he'd thought puberty had been a trial? It was nothing compared to having The Husband stare him down like a man staking his claim. Which was exactly what the guy was doing. Alpha male to alpha male, they squared off.

"Hello, Reese." Staci pushed past the Casteleonies to greet him with more warmth than was professional, but just the right amount to provide cover for him. At least, he hoped so.

"Staci. Bella." He greeted the women before turning to The Husband. "You must be—"

"Vincent Casteleoni," the mountain answered, a large hand extended.

Reese shook it, his mind reeling as he made the connection he should have guessed. Vincent Casteleoni? *The* Vincent Casteleoni? The famous golf course designer? Married to Bella? Why, she was young enough to be the man's daughter, for God's sake.

What had possessed either one of them? No *wonder* he hadn't met The Husband—the guy had probably been jetting around the country half the time.

And where did that leave Sophia? Without a father for most of her life?

Reese's manner turned cooler than he knew it had a right to. But he was appalled. Indignant. Angry. Pissed.

Jealous as hell.

"My Bella tells me you're having her cater the auction."

Vincent Casteleoni skewered him with his gaze. He *knew* Reese was having thoughts he shouldn't. And he was letting him know that he knew.

The cavemen vibes sailed over the women's heads. Bella seemed absorbed in her own thoughts and Staci was being Staci: sidling up to him and coiling an arm around his as if he were a meal for a pet snake. The woman was an open book.

"And me, too." Staci pouted. "Bella and I are doing it together. Right, Reese?"

She dug her nails into his arm, literally getting her hooks into him. And yet, he wasn't discouraging her.

That would be because he didn't have a death wish.

He put on his game face and answered her Husband's question. "I *have* hired Bella. Your business came highly recommended."

"Oh, it's not my business. It's all Bella's, start to finish." The lucky SOB wrapped his arm possessively around Bella's shoulders and squeezed.

Reese couldn't even think of him as Vincent Casteleoni, who, in any other situation would be a potential celebrity to book for jobs. Now, he was just The *Husband*. With that damn capital H.

Staci, showing more smarts than Reese had given her credit for, ping-ponged her gaze between them. "Reese." She tugged on his arm. "We brought updated menus to go over with you."

He ushered them to the conference room adjacent to his office. Filled with floor-to-ceiling windows that framed the river beyond like a painting, with plush gray carpeting and maroon wainscoting, the room normally had a calming effect on him. It didn't now.

"Please have a seat." He indicated the head of the table closest for The Husband, then took the one at the far end for himself. He had to put as much distance between them as possible.

Not that it mattered. The entire time Bella was speaking, Reese had to struggle to focus on the content and not the way her lips moved when she said things like *asparagus spears*.

God, he had it bad.

And The Husband knew it. Reese could feel it rolling off the guy in waves.

"And for dessert—"Bella shuffled more papers and brought out another list that Reese barely saw because he was thinking exactly *what* he'd like for dessert—"I wasn't sure if Baked Alaska would be too predictable or too over the top, but it always makes a great impact when the wait staff parades it in in flames. It'll be a spectacular ending, especially under a starry sky."

Reese forced some words past the pasted-on smile that was purely for The Husband's benefit. "I think it's a great idea. We're going to have fireworks over the river and that will tie in nicely."

*Nicely*? What was he, a choir boy? Thinking of licking that Baked Alaska meringue off her body, one stroke at a time, was so much more than *nice* that he was amazed *he* didn't suddenly go up in flames.

He should be shot. Right here. Right now.

"So that's it." Bella closed the portfolio. She ran her hands over it, smoothing out the surface.

Reese all but groaned at the thought of those hands doing the same to him.

Staci ran her fingertips across the back of his hand, the look on her face saying she'd like to run them elsewhere. He wasn't willing to go that far, but he let her hand stay where it was when he saw The Husband's shoulders relax.

His own did, too. Finally. This nightmare was almost over.

"We're still on for Friday night, right, Reese?"

Until Staci asked her not-so-innocent question.

The Husband leaned forward. "Friday night?"

Staci leaned sideways, the cleavage she rubbed against his arm doing nothing for him. "Reese is taking us to the Riverfront Landing Friday night to see how it's all going to play out."

Except, what he'd planned sounded nothing like her innuendo-laced statement.

He really didn't need Staci to help him hang himself—the thoughts he knew Vincent could read were doing that for him.

Reese cleared his throat. "Luke Jamison is one of the celebrities participating in the event and he wants to go over the layout. We agreed on Friday for the site visit. You're more than welcome to come along." There. He'd earned a few more hash marks in the *Good* column of his permanent record for when he arrived at the Pearly Gates.

"That's a good idea, but, unfortunately, I can't make it." Vincent Casteleoni sat back, hopefully with zero idea of Reese's relief at that news. "I have a dinner engagement that evening." He squeezed Bella's hand. "I was going to invite you along, but I see you've already made plans."

A knock on the door interrupted the domestic conversation and Reese was insanely grateful to whoever had caused the problem that would now demand his attention.

Jake poked his head and a manila file into the room. "Sorry to interrupt, Reese, but there's a glitch with the bank opening tomorrow that you need to deal with as soon as you're free."

Reese gripped the edge of his chair to keep himself from jumping out of it. Instead, he stood slowly. "We're about done here." Thank God.

He looked Vincent in the eye, the first time since meeting him that he could. "If you'd like us to reschedule the site visit for a time when you're available, please make arrangements with Kelly. She's got my calendar." He shook his hand, if only to prove to himself—and Vincent—that he could, then handled the usual *We'll talk*s and *I'll send it over*s, before finally escaping into the sanctuary that was his office.

Unfortunately, though, the tension from the meeting followed him in. He couldn't stop seeing the image of them. Bella and Vincent. Together. Nor the fact that they'd created Sophia. The two of them. When Bella must have been a teenager.

Reese flopped into his chair. Their relationship was none of his business.

Then why couldn't he let it go?

Jake did his perfunctory knock as he opened the door. "You okay, Reese?"

No. "Yeah. What's up with the bank tomorrow?" If someone had robbed it, it'd take his mind off Bella.

Maybe.

Jake bypassed the chair in front of the desk and walked to the window. "Nothing."

Reese spun around in his chair. "What?"

"Nothing's up. I saw you in there and the look on your face suggested you could use a break." Jake leaned against the window, crossed one foot over the other, and tapped the file folder against his palm. "Was I wrong?"

Reese exhaled, his eyes closing long enough that when he opened them again, they were focused. *He* was focused. On the future of his company.

Not a future with Bella.

"No, Jake. You were absolutely right. I owe you one."

Jake grinned. "Oh, you owe me more than one, buddy. I'll just add it to the list." He walked toward the desk and tossed the empty file folder onto the blotter. "You're sure there's nothing to talk about?"

No. But he would. Because they'd known each other their entire lives and Jake was the brother he didn't have. *And* because Jake wouldn't let it go until he got the whole story. It was the lawyer in him.

"Yeah. I'm sure." He scratched his head wishing he could remove Bella from it that easily. "She's married."

"You're not referring to the one practically sitting in your lap, I hope."

That got Reese to smile. Finally something to laugh about. "Staci? Hell no. That'd be too easy. No, I'm talking about Bella. And her husband."

"No wonder you wanted me to take the contract in to her." Jake sat and swiped a hand along his jaw. "He can't know you have a thing for his wife."

"He might have guessed. I can't seem to stop staring at her."

"Reese, if you thought Luke's actions caused problems—"

"I know, I know." Reese pushed himself up from his chair and circled the desk, shoving his hands into his pockets. He slumped back against the edge of the desk. "I'd already talked myself out of asking her out before the auction because I didn't want history to repeat itself." He held up a hand as Jake started to speak. "I know. We talked about this. And I said it wouldn't interfere with our business. It won't. Never mind Luke's stupidity with Marisa, I have firsthand knowledge of the nightmare that comes from mixing business with pleasure. Like I said; I get it. And I'm not about to risk another career or our investment."

"Glad to hear it." Jake had invested his nest egg into Promotional Sports; Reese wasn't going to lose it for him.

"The thing is, Jake, consciously I understand that pursuing something with her is a stupid move on so many levels. Besides the fact that she's married. But subconsciously?" Reese tried to shrug but couldn't be so nonchalant about this situation no matter how much he wanted to. "There's just something…"

"Well, you better make up your mind what's more important to you: this company or the lawsuit we're going to be hit with for trying to break up a client's marriage."

Reese shot off the desk. "Fuck you, Adams. You know I'd never do that."

"Exactly." Jake stood up, toe-to-toe. The sonofabitch never backed down. It'd made him a good lawyer, but a pain in the ass as a friend. "Which makes this conversation pointless. She's got a husband and we've got a caterer to replace Marisa. Win-win situation in my book."

"For everyone but me." Shit. Had he said that out loud? Reese sighed and leaned back onto the edge of his desk.

"Come on, man." Jake ran a hand through his hair. "I'm as human as the next guy, regardless of what they say about lawyers. She's hot, I get that. But maybe you're so fixated on her because you haven't been out in a while."

"You get your shrink's license when I wasn't paying attention?"

Jake arched an eyebrow. Reese hated when he did that. Had pummeled him more than a few times over the years for it. Mainly because Jake had been right most of the time.

"Go out." Jake ignored the dig. "Find someone else. Trust me, nothing gets your mind off one woman like another. You've always had your pick; go pick one."

Right. As if he were buying a car. "Look, Jake, this is pointless. Let's just leave my love life—"

"Or lack thereof."

"Whatever." Reese crossed his arms. "Let's just leave it out of this and let me focus on making a name for myself off the field."

"As long as you remember that, Reese." Jake headed toward the door. "Because, unlike that playoff game, now's *not* the time to go for a Hail Mary pass."

Reese glared at Jake's back as he walked out the door. Monday morning quarterbacking never stopped.

# Chapter Sixteen

ella was quiet on the ride back in Uncle Vinny's car. She'd let Staci sit up front, expecting inane chatter to fill the silence, and her twitty stepsister didn't disappoint. But though Vinny appeared to fully participate in Staci's conversation, he kept glancing at her in the rear-view mirror.

Bella didn't—couldn't—meet his eyes. He might have questions for her, but she was angry at him.

That was the *last* time she let him come on a sales call. She'd thought having him along wouldn't be a problem. After all, two sports figures who knew a lot of the same people… how bad could it be? Plus, she'd hoped he'd be a buffer to Staci's and Madeleine's machinations.

She should have known. Uncle Vinny with his "My Bella" and stern handshake… She'd recognized the tension coiling between the men and had wanted to drag her uncle out of there by his ear at the first whiff of testosterone. He'd acted like such a he-man/caveman type that she would've laughed if it hadn't been so pathetic.

Pathetic because Reese hadn't exactly been fighting Staci off.

And, yes, that bothered her, but not for any reason other than her stepsister's behavior had been utterly unprofessional. Truly. This was *her* chance to get her name out beyond her normal clientele and she didn't want Staci to blow it. How Madeleine thought having her stepsister go after Reese in a personal manner would benefit the business was beyond Bella. And then, with Uncle Vinny and his posturing… She'd be lucky to still have this gig the next time she talked to Reese.

Uncle Vinny dropped Staci off at the mall—no surprise—then motioned for Bella to join him up front.

Bella got in, weighing her words. "What was that?"

Uncle Vinny raised an eyebrow as he steered the car back into traffic and pulled up to a traffic light. "What?"

"That. Back in Reese's office."

"I believe they call it a business meeting." He had yet to look at her.

"Not that. That… that he-man thing you were doing."

Now he had the audacity to laugh. But he still didn't look at her. "He-man? Honey, I think you're overreacting."

"No I'm not and don't try to placate me. I'm trying to run a business and you went and got all protective just because he's a good-looking guy. I don't—"

"So you think he's good-looking?"

*Now* he looked at her.

Bella exhaled. "Look, Uncle Vinny, whether I find him attractive or not is beside the point. He's a client and—"

"So you do find him attractive?"

He narrowed his Casteleoni-blue eyes and Bella couldn't speak. This third degree was so unlike him that she almost wouldn't be surprised if he turned into a pumpkin at midnight. "Uncle Vinny—"

A car behind them honked so Vinny pulled onto the shoulder of the road. He flicked on his flashers, then faced her. "What I don't understand, Bella, is why you were allowing Staci to stake a claim to him. If you want him, you're going to have to let him know—"

"Uncle Vinny, there's nothing for him to know. I want his business. That's it. And I plan to have a talk with Staci about her behavior. Just like I'm trying to have a talk with you. You can't get all protective around every client I meet with."

"Reese and I we were just coming to an understanding. That's all." He ran a hand over his mouth. "He *is* a successful, good-looking guy, you know. About your age, too. I wouldn't be so quick to dismiss him if I were you. He's not interested in Staci. The girl's too obvious. She saw fame, looks, and dollar signs, and signed on for the project. Reese is a smart guy; he'll figure it out if he hasn't already. You won't have anything to worry about on that front, but you *do* to have to let him know you're interested."

"I'm *not* interested." *Liar*. "I can't be. I already have Madeleine breathing down my neck. Getting involved with Reese is a bad idea A) because of our business relationship and B) because Madeleine will never permit it to play out. Everything I do is for Sophia. I can't forget it and neither can you. I'll think about guys and settling down and all the rest once she's out from Madeleine's clutches."

"I don't like it."

"I don't like a lot of things, but I've learned to live with them. I just have to keep my eye on the prize."

As far as Vinny was concerned, *Reese* was the prize for her. Not this on-going tug-of-war with Madeleine.

Vinny ground his molars. The woman had been a pain in the ass ever since he'd met her. He should have confronted Sal about her, but Sal had been through so much and Vinny had been on a big commission. Then the fall had happened and it'd become moot.

God, he'd love to tell that woman a thing or two. Not that it'd work. He'd actually tried to buy her off years ago, something Bella knew nothing about. He'd been surprised when Madeleine had turned him down. A gold digger like her, he'd thought for sure the two mil would be a reasonable price tag.

But she hadn't even bargained. Just gotten a smirk on her face, raised her nose a little higher, and turned her back on him. It'd been the last time he'd spoken to her.

He could see now that he'd been wrong to walk away. Oh, he'd always been ready to listen to Bella. Ready to help out financially, but he should have been here, keeping an eye on things. On Madeleine.

He'd underestimated her. The woman from the wrong side of the tracks had a huge chip on her shoulder—and was taking it out on the two people who didn't deserve it.

And there wasn't a damn thing he could do about it. He'd made inquiries into getting custody, but his lawyer had told him the same thing he'd told Bella. Madeleine had more support in the court's eyes than a single waitress who only owned a third of a business. Madeleine's two thirds percent control gave her everything.

But if Bella weren't single...

Reese would look good in the court's eyes. Young, successful and the two of them married: together, they had a shot.

And the guy was interested. He'd seen it in Reese's gaze. The one that had rested anywhere but on Bella. Well, most of the time. But there'd been those few lingering glances...

He'd laugh if it weren't such a touchy situation. Bella was right; Madeleine liked controlling her own little kingdom and would never allow Reese to enter.

# Chapter Seventeen

By eleven o'clock Thursday morning Bella had a headache that wouldn't quit.

The only reason she hadn't had one earlier was because Staci hadn't decided to come in until ten fifty-eight. And after three days of working with her, two minutes was all it took for a headache to show up.

"So, what do you think?' Staci twirled around in yet another new "non-Staci" outfit, doing a little "ta-da" dance at the end, almost clipping little Michael Spaccone again with her designer bag. Poor kid would probably have flashbacks for the rest of his life any time Casteleoni's was mentioned. "Is it me, or what?"

Depended on which Staci she was talking about.

Her black skirt didn't hug her curves like a mummy's wrappings, the frilly beige top camouflaged the silicone torpedoes into a silhouette fit for polite company, and her hair was tamed to a manageable mane.

"You can't wait tables in that, Staci."

Staci's sank back on her heels and Bella inexplicably felt as if she'd hurt a puppy. "I know that, Bella. I wasn't planning to. This is what I'm wearing Friday night."

"Oh. Well, it's nice." It also meant that Staci wasn't here to work. Which was also nice.

Though Madeleine had said she wanted Staci to learn all aspects of the business and Bella was actually looking forward to seeing Staci try to wait tables. That'd be a kind of karmic retribution.

"What are you going to wear?"

"Probably my blue suit."

"A suit?" Staci's mouth fell open. "You can't wear a suit to dinner on a Friday night. We're going on a boat, not some museum. Where's your sense of fun? Of adventure?" She put her hands on her hips. "Of *dating?*"

Bella wiped off another table, her ponytail slipping over her shoulder. Impatiently, she flicked it behind her. "Staci, this isn't a date. It's a business meeting. We're going over the set-up and checking out the site, remember? That's all it is."

"And after all that boring stuff?" Staci leaned against the edge of the booth and then apparently remembered what exactly it was she was leaning against. She stood up, checked her sleeve for sticky finger residue, and crossed her arms in front of her instead.

Bella tucked the dish towel into her apron pocket and brushed her hair off her forehead. "*Afterwards*, I intend to come home, make some notes, and get a good night's rest. I'm taking Sophia to the zoo on Saturday and I'll need to get up early."

"Please tell me you're kidding." Staci's mouth dropped again. "After a night out with two of the hottest guys in this godforsaken town, you're going to call it quits and go out with your baby sister?" Her hands jammed back down on her hips. "Are you out of your mind? No wonder you're still single."

The headache went nuclear. Bella had had enough. Ten years of insults, threats, snide remarks, and slurs ruptured through her carefully composed shell. She threw the dish towel onto the just-cleaned table. "For your information, *one* of the reasons I'm still single is because of *your* mother. She always seems to come up with some event or other after I make plans to go out, and ends up threatening to send Sophia away if I don't stay home to take care of her. Enough of that and guys decide dating me isn't worth the trouble, especially if they could end up with a stepmother-in-law like her."

Staci opened her mouth to say something, but Bella was having none of it. She shoved her finger into Staci's brand new shirt. "And you and Drew have been no help. Any time you don't get your way, off you go, running to your mother."

She poked the shirt again. "None of you seem to realize that there is a blameless little girl at the bottom of your self-centered plots. And not one of you seems to care. Sophia has lost both parents. She doesn't even remember them." *Poke.* "And the closest thing she's got to compare to a loving parent is a manipulative woman bent on furthering her own ends at the expense of a child. What a wonderful role model. What a wonderful way to grow up." Another jab. "So if I focus all my free time on Sophia, that's my business, Staci, not yours." Bella poked

Staci's shirt one last time, slowly becoming aware that every voice in the restaurant had gone silent, every mouth had dropped open. Mrs. Angelelli didn't even seem to notice that her dentures had gone askew.

Giac and Gus, however, were smiling. Giac raised his arms and began clapping. Gus quickly joined in. Within two seconds, not one pair of hands remained still in the place.

Her finger still in its position, Bella looked around. Staci did, too. They glanced back at each other, then looked down at Bella's finger.

Bella yanked it—and herself—away. Oh, God. What had she done?

She closed her eyes. Bad enough she'd told Staci off, but in public? No matter that it was long overdue; Sophia was going to be the one who paid for her lack of control.

"Well." Staci's voice was a little higher pitched once the applause died down, but it was a far cry from shrill. Definitely not threatening. Which was utterly surprising.

As was the fact that Staci didn't storm out.

Instead, she brushed off the spot where Bella had poked her, then looked at Bella.

A dropped pin would make more noise than there was in the restaurant at that moment and Bella cringed inwardly. She should probably start packing Sophia's bags—to be followed by her own.

"I guess that's been building up a while." Staci said into the silence with a tentative… *smile*?

Okay, who'd taken Anastasia Fontaine and replaced her with this new model?

Half afraid the attitude was a trick, Bella nodded slowly.

Staci flipped her hair back, straightened her blouse, smiled a weak little smile, raised her chin, and walked toward the door. No eye contact with anyone, no running, no slinking, no storming. She just walked out the door with her back straight, her shoulders squared, and zero ounce of her normal wiggle.

And Bella had no idea what she was planning to do.

Everyone erupted once the door closed, congratulations and "atta-girl"s abounding, but Bella couldn't celebrate with them. She shouldn't have lost her temper and now that the adrenaline rush of telling Staci off was subsiding, all she could think about was, God, what had she done?

***

Jonathan scurried out through the cat door Giac had created in one of the windows and followed Staci. This was unprecedented. None of the charts he'd studied had showed this possibility. He had no idea what to do now. All he knew was that he had to follow Staci and if she tried to cause trouble he had to stop her somehow.

He looked down at his little gray paws. He wasn't quite sure how he would do that in his present form, but it was safer to tail her in this form than in the human one.

His mind raced as he dodged the foot traffic. Boy, stilettos took on a whole new meaning when one was ankle high to them.

He couldn't believe Bella had finally stood up for herself. He *really* couldn't believe it and not because he didn't believe she had it in her—The Boss knew she did, but He also knew that she tempered it with common sense, something Staci had none of.

Yet the girl hadn't gone off on Bella. And that worried Jonathan. When mortals didn't follow prescribed patterns, they became loose cannons.

The light changed and Jonathan had to stop. Dodging stilettos was a whole lot less riskier than dodging automobiles.

Up ahead, Staci turned a corner.

He was going to lose her.

Looking around, he didn't see the proverbial phone booth to make his transformation in. He couldn't just materialize out of thin air with all these people around.

Which meant he'd just have to materialize *into* thin air.

Scooting beneath a mail box on the off chance that someone would notice a cat *poofing* out of existence, Jonathan took a calming breath—a necessity to get this transformation to work properly—and willed himself to become a wisp of his former self.

He had to do something to save his Charge from herself.

***

Staci tried to muster her dignity as she turned onto Pine Street. She couldn't believe Bella had said those things to her like that. In public.

Staci cringed. All those people looking at her as if she were…

Mother.

Her foot slipped out from under her and she landed hard. In a gob of something. Great. All over her new skirt. Mother would kill her.

Staci tried to get up, but one of her new Manolos slipped off and went sliding away on something black and slimy. Ugh. Oil. That would never come out. Mother was really going to be pissed.

Staci couldn't prevent a shiver. Mother had a very determined nasty streak. The woman could flay the skin off your back with her tongue from across the room, and do it so damn quietly that no one would ever know.

But Staci… she'd know.

She stopped trying to get up. Was this what Bella felt all the time around Mother? Like walking on coals, never sure which one would burn her?

And all those people, staring at her as if she were just like her mother…

She dropped her hands into her lap. She'd never really thought about what life was like for Bella. Especially since Sal had gone into the hospital.

Those few months after Mother had married him had been good ones. For the first time, Staci had hoped that they'd found a true home. Sal had treated both her and Drew as if they were his own. But then he'd gone into the hospital and life had gone back to the way it'd been before with Mother, though this time there'd been more money so it'd made Mother's demands less annoying. Plus, Bella had been there to take the brunt of it all.

Something slithered beneath Staci's calf and she scrambled to her feet. The skirt was a goner. Hopefully, Mother wouldn't notice.

Fat chance. Mother noticed *everything*. She'd blame Bella; she always did.

And she and Drew had always gone along with it.

Guilt slithered up Staci's spine like the oil along her leg. Maybe they hadn't treated Bella all that nicely. After all, Bella's life *had* completely changed and not for the better in the space of a year. And as for Sophia… Bella was right. The little girl didn't have a clue what a normal life was like and it wasn't fair of them to threaten the life she *did* have just to keep Bella as their servant. The poor kid had lost enough. *Both* of them had.

"Hey, Stace!"

Drew. Staci tried not to groan. Her sister was cut from such different cloth. Polyester to Staci's silk. Staci fingered her skirt and for the first time felt pity for her sister instead of derision. "What's up, Drew?"

"What happened to you?"

Staci grimaced. "I slipped on some oil." She schlepped over to the missing Manolo.

"You did a lot more than that. Are you sure you didn't smoke something funny?"

Staci stopped mid-schlep. "What are you talking about?"

Drew's head twitched as if she'd stuck her finger in a light socket, waving her hands all over the place. "This. You. Those clothes. The hair. What'd you do?"

"Oh. You like?" Staci did a little twirl. Even with the oil, she was looking fine—though she did wish Mother hadn't forbidden the ruby red lipstick. She'd made her buy coral, a "more subtle color." Staci smacked her lips. Subtle? Try colorless. But Mother said it'd get Reese in her clutches, so it was worth it, right?

"Like it? I guess. But why?" Drew cocked her head, her eyes narrowing. Unlike the brown eyes Mother had, Drew's were green, a recessive gene that explained so much.

"Mother thought I needed a new look."

"And you listened?" Drew snorted. "Since when did you turn into Bella and start jumping through Mother's hoops?"

Staci slammed her hands to her hips. Damn, she missed how her old long nails pinched into her skin when she was mad. These functional, so-called "classy" ones were so bland. "Of course not, Drew. But if I'm going to interest Reese, this is what he likes, apparently."

Drew snorted again. "Yeah, the old you didn't have much of an impact on him. But that Luke guy… I thought you were interested in him?"

"I am. Was. But Mother says that Reese could cause trouble for her, so I have to get him interested in me. She thinks dressing like this will do it. And since I'm going to be helping Bella with the party business any way, I ought to look the part."

Drew's mouth dropped open.

"It's not all that bad, is it? I can get oil out, can't I?"

Drew shook her head, her ginger ponytail bouncing over her shoulder. "Whoa. You're getting a job? A real job? With Bella? Are you *kidding* me?"

Oh, God. She *was* doing exactly what Mother wanted. Drew actually had a point.

Staci bit one of the acrylic nails—and ruined the French manicure. She exhaled and tapped her teeth instead. "It made sense at the time."

"To who?"

Staci winced. "Mother."

"Exactly."

"Well, me, too." She guessed. "I mean, you have to admit I look different." She didn't really want to think she looked better because that would mean she'd been exactly what her mother had called her.

"Yeah, it's definitely different, but you're giving up the guy you want for Mother's plans. Just like Bella."

Staci gripped her hips harder. Hmm, the acrylic did have some pinch to it after all. "Hey, I'm my own person. Perfectly capable of deciding what I want to do with my life and how I want to live it. And if I want to follow Mother's suggestion to restyle my hair and choose more sedate, classy clothing, then I will, and it's none of your damn business." Staci spun around to leave, then turned back. "And if you thought about it, Drew, you'd realize that Bella doesn't really have a choice about listening to Mother. I do. See the difference?"

The words sounded good, but Staci couldn't squelch the niggling little pointy finger hitting her in the middle of her brain just as sharply as the one Bella had jabbed into her shirt. *Did* she have that choice or was she as tied to Mother's apron strings as Bella was?

Staci swiped her hand over the skirt one more time. She *did* have control of her own life. And she was going to prove it. She'd start by keeping Friday night a secret. She did, after all, want to go with Luke. What Mother didn't know wouldn't hurt her. Or, at the very least, it wouldn't hurt Staci.

Still, she couldn't shake the feeling that she was missing something. Something big. And that maybe, just maybe, Drew was right.

***

Jonathan leaned back on the window ledge and wiped the back of his hand across his forehead. Saints alive, (and many of them were, walking the earth among mortals who had no clue), but that had been close.

And not just for Bella. The Archangel had told him to use whatever means possible, but manipulating another Guardian's charge without permission was always a little tricky. Far more advanced than Jonathan's meager skill set, but he'd been desperate to stop Staci from doing something rash like telling Madeleine, so he'd had to improvise.

The oil had been a last second stroke of brilliance. *Not* that Jonathan was laying claim to brilliance, but he was encouraged that he'd come up with it so quickly and had put it into play without a snippet of suspicion on anyone's part.

But, still, his job was far from over.

# Chapter Eighteen

Bella rolled another gold coin through her fingers and stared at the fountain in the park, feeling more than a little foolish that she was even thinking about making a wish. But given the disaster that was sure to be facing her at home, she was willing to try anything to mitigate it.

She should have kept her mouth shut. But once the dam had burst, she'd been as powerless to stop it as stopping the water from rushing out of the statue's jug in the center of the fountain.

She'd be just as powerless facing Madeleine.

Bella looked at the coin. This was ridiculous. She didn't believe in fairy tales or magic amulets or whatever mumbo-jumbo people used to get themselves through the tough spots in life. She'd been in those tough spots before and all her prayers and wishes hadn't made any difference. They wouldn't now either, but she was here and had nothing to lose except a gold dollar.

Well, that and hope.

No. She wouldn't lose hope. Hope was what kept her going. As long as she had the ability to stash cash away for the custody battle, she had a chance of winning.

Bella closed her fist and her eyes. There were so many things to wish for: for her parents to be alive, for Madeleine to never have come into their lives, for Sophia to grow up well-adjusted, for the strength and money necessary to fight for her...

She couldn't decide, so, in the end, she left it up to the universe, closed her eyes, and took a deep breath.

"Whatever will make it all work out right," she whispered as she threw the coin into the water.

She opened her eyes.

Nothing. Just as she'd expected. No Prince Charming, no glass coach, and definitely no fairy godmother waving a magic wand.

So much for her nickname.

Bella made it to the front stoop of her home just as the grandfather clock in the living room chimed the hour. Fifteen minutes left before Sophia's bus arrived.

Fifteen minutes left to undo whatever Madeleine was planning to do. Or, at least come up with countermeasures.

Except there were no countermeasures to be made. Madeleine would make whatever decision she wanted about Sophia's education and there was nothing Bella could do about it.

Fourteen minutes.

Bella straightened her shoulders. She was wasting precious time. Best get this over with before Sophia arrived home to witness it. Bella would keep her little sister in the dark about their living arrangements for as long as she could.

She opened the door. "Hello? Anyone here?" She looked in the living room, but the only thing that moved was the clock's pendulum, softly marking time in its etched glass-fronted case.

The *Jaws* theme would be more appropriate.

No one was in the dining room. Nor the family room. A glance into the kitchen showed someone had poured a drink and left the empty glass on the island. Typical.

Where were they? She knew they were here; the Fontaine vibe was insidious, crawling through the house like the ribbon of dread that wound around her heart at the thought of what was going to happen with the confrontation. She should never have let her temper get the best of her.

She opened the French doors and Staci looked up from a magazine. "Hello, Bella."

What? No screaming? No sarcasm? No fingernails clawing at her eyeballs?

Bella stepped purposefully onto the faded uneven bricks. "About earlier..."

Staci stood and—

Smiled? Again? What in heaven's name was going on?

"Before you say anything," Staci said calmly, "I'd like to say that I'm sorry for the way I've threatened you with Sophia over the years.

You're right. I did forget that your sister was the one really affected by all of this." Surprisingly, she held out her hand. "Can we go forward from here?"

Bella felt as if someone had knocked her into the Twilight Zone. First Staci had wanted a job, then she'd gone for an extreme makeover, and now… this? "What's going on, Staci?"

Staci bristled for a moment.

Aha! A normal reaction. To be followed, Bella was sure, by a tirade.

But Staci surprised her yet again.

Releasing a taught breath, Staci's eyes actually filled with tears.

Bella didn't think her stepsister was that good an actress. "What's happened? Is it Sophia? Is she okay?"

Staci shook her head. "Sophia's fine." She pulled a chair out from the table and motioned for Bella to sit.

Bella slid into it, never once taking her eyes from her stepsister.

Staci looked up, nibbled on her upper lip, and grimaced. "It finally hit home with me today, all you've gone through, and all we've put you through. I mean, I've always known my mother was manipulative, but I never considered the effects of what she did." She clasped her hands together on the tabletop and Bella saw the knuckles go white.

Another deep breath. "Now, my mother is trying to manipulate me, and, well, I've found out it stinks. She's making me go after Reese and I don't want to. I like Luke." She unclasped her hands and smiled a genuine smile this time. Small, but genuine. "Your little tantrum thingy actually opened my eyes to what she's doing and I just want to tell you that I won't use Sophia as a threat anymore. And I've talked to Drew. I don't think she will either. I'm not going to mention this conversation to Mother, so you don't have to worry about that either." And now she actually reached out and grasped Bella's hand—and not to dig her nails into her flesh. "I'll stay away from Reese, too, Bella. Mother never has to know. But I would like to continue working with you. I know I have a lot to learn, but I will. I promise."

Bella felt as if the wind had been knocked out of her. All the anxiety, all the sick feelings, the wish-making, and now this? She glanced skyward and sent a silent "thank you" to whoever was looking out for her Up There.

Jonathan Griff, stacking shoe boxes in the back of his store, did a little jig.

***

Forty-five minutes later, Bella's good mood disappeared.

Madeleine had arrived home.

"I want an invitation to the auction." The witch swept into the kitchen as if she were a debutante at her first ball. Madeleine always made an entrance. Bella could only imagine the kind she'd make at the auction.

Actually, she didn't want to imagine it. She didn't want the woman to even *be* there.

Bella looked up from the dinner preparations and glanced at Sophia who was sitting at the table absorbed in her homework. She considered her next words carefully. Telling Madeleine *no* was always risky, but after Staci's capitulation, Bella was starting to feel empowered.

"Tickets to the event aren't part of the contract, Madeleine."

The woman patted her never-out-of-place ebony hair, brushing some imaginary strands to the back. "Did I mention that I'm meeting with a gentleman next week who has offered to buy the restaurant? It might be in your best interests to ensure accepting his offer would be less favorable than what being the owner of Casteleoni's can do for me."

Bella dropped the asparagus into the steamer, clipping off more than a few tips. So much for being empowered.

*Buy the restaurant*? Sure, Madeleine had threatened it before, but this was the first time she'd mentioned an actual buyer. Bella was *not* going to lose Sophia *and* her family's legacy.

"I'll see what I can do."

"I thought you'd see things my way." Madeleine slid her bony talons to Sophia's shoulders. "Hello, Sophia. Did you have a nice day at school?"

Her sister, oblivious to the undercurrent—for which Bella was profoundly grateful—smiled up at their wicked stepmother and began telling her all about her day as if the woman gave a damn.

But that was Bella's cross to bear, not Sophia's. Which was why she'd ask Reese for those extra tickets Friday night.

# Chapter Nineteen

I wish Reese could have picked us up. This van isn't exactly my idea of a good ride." Staci may have changed her tune, but the whining melody was still the same.

"His car only seats two."

"Well Luke's then. A Beamer isn't something to sneeze at."

"And Madeleine would have seen him. Isn't that what you want to avoid?" They'd staged their departures from the house so Madeleine had no idea what they were doing or that they were doing it together.

"Oh. Yeah. Good point." Staci rearranged her skirt. "But Luke's bringing me home. Or… not."

"Up to you." Staci hadn't changed all *that* much, apparently. But the part she had, Bella was grateful for. Not completely trusting of it, but grateful. She'd take whatever help she could get in beating Madeleine.

Her stomach roiled. Sell the restaurant? No way in hell. Not only was it her livelihood, but also her family legacy. She wanted to be able to pass it down to her children someday.

An image of a little boy with chestnut hair and dark eyes flashed into her head, the same coloring as the guy getting out of the sportscar in the dockside parking lot.

Staci whistled. "Man, that is one sweet car."

"Uh huh." Bella didn't want to start the comparisons to the man.

"I love that rearing stallion logo on the front."

Too late.

"Kind of gets you all jumpy, like anyone driving one would be all rearing and stallion-y."

Bella groaned. Images she did not need. "Stallion-y? Is that even a word?"

"You know what I mean." Staci dragged her gaze from the car and looked at Bella. "Or maybe you don't. Maybe that's the problem. You know, Bella, you really should—"

"Staci." Bella put the van in park. "Let's stick to business. The rearing stallion can run out to pasture, for all I care. Come on, let's go." She breathed a sigh of relief as the conversation ended right before Reese reached her van. That was one conversation she did *not* want him to overhear.

"Ladies."

Good Lord above. One word and she was ready to melt at his feet.

She tugged the neckline of the coral dress up and pulled her wrap tighter around her shoulders. She should have worn the suit. Would have, but Staci hadn't let up, and, well, the dress did look good on her. She'd even left her hair down. Not to impress anyone of course, but it'd be windy aboard *The Midnight Maiden*, so it only made sense to, pardon the pun, go with the flow.

Stacy dashed around the front of the van. "Hey, Reese. Where's Luke?"

That's what Bella had to admire about Staci—her subtlety.

Reese didn't do a very good job of hiding his smile, but he coughed to cover it and pointed to the pavilion. "Over there."

Staci's one track mind—and body—went full steam ahead, leaving Bella alone with Reese, the evening crickets, and the supreme awareness of how delicious he looked in a chest- and shoulder-hugging navy blue crewneck sweater and camel jacket. A pair of dark jeans molded powerful thighs that she could only imagine—and, yes, she did—had been an asset in his football career.

She wouldn't mind getting in a huddle with him.

Reese cleared his throat. "So, Vincent was fine with tonight, then?"

Thank God he'd said something because she wasn't quite sure how to recover from the hormonal bath her nerves were awash in. But Uncle Vinny? After the pissing contest they'd had in Reese's office the other day, she wouldn't have thought he'd want to discuss her uncle.

"Fine? Um, yes. He was. Is there a reason he shouldn't be?" She took her iPad out of her purse and the night breeze lifted her wrap and sent it fluttering to the ground.

Reese bent down to pick it up, taking those few seconds to get his emotions under control. There definitely was a reason Vincent Casteleoni shouldn't be fine tonight. Hell knew, *Reese* wouldn't be, sending her off to a romantic locale for a dinner with some guy who was lusting after her, looking way too good in a peach dress that brought out the blue in her eyes and clung in all the right places.

God, he really should be shot. He'd brought up Vincent—The Husband—as a blatant reminder to himself to keep his hands off. His eyes, too.

Right. Reese stood up and tried to find some way to put this wrap around her shoulders without touching her.

There wasn't one. So he tried to do it with minimal contact and probably ended up looking like a big, uncoordinated oaf. Which was much better than a lascivious wife-poaching bastard. "Uh, no. No reason. Shall we join Luke and Staci?"

"Okay. Thanks for getting my wrap."

"No problem." Reese tried to come up with some small talk on the short walk over, but it eluded him. Kind of like what he'd been trying to do all week when it came to Bella. He'd even forbidden himself from checking her out online. Look for wedding photos, that sort of thing. He'd made it a point to immerse himself in other clients' events and recruiting new celebrities. Business. Where his focus ought to be. He was pretty damn proud of his self-control.

But then she tucked some hair behind her ear and he caught the slight lift of her breast in his peripheral vision, and one part of him had absolutely *no* control. It went to half mast in an instant.

God, he needed to get a grip. And *not* on that part.

"Hey guys," said Luke and Reese had never been so glad to see him in his life, including the Hail Mary play. God, the irony of needing *Luke* to provide a buffer with a beautiful woman around.

Luckily, Staci and Luke ran interference on his thoughts while they discussed the set up for the cocktail party beneath the pavilion. Reese had a few changes to the initial plan, they discussed the timing of the presentations, and generally managed to get the job done.

If only he weren't so damn tuned in to the fragrance of her perfume, the fruity scent of her shampoo, and the alluring essence that was all hers. She'd left her hair loose tonight and the wind tossed it around her shoulder in a flowing curtain his fingers were itching to caress.

He shoved his hands into his pockets since his imagination and libido didn't seem to be on board with tonight's agenda.

"I think that covers all the bases here." Bella made a few more notes on her tablet.

She looked up at him with those beautiful blue eyes and lips he'd tasted and all he could think about was tasting them again. About taming her hair by wrapping it in his fists and kissing her senseless. Pulling her soft, curvy body into the hard planes of his, one hardness in particular, and ripping the thought of Vincent right out of her head.

"Yes, we're done here." He more than the rest. "Let's finish up with the auction itself. We're planning to have the dinner on the deck of *The Midnight Maiden*. I'm concerned about the baked Alaska presentation if the wind keeps up like this. The captain won't be very happy if your fire burns up his ship." Never mind that her fire was burning up his—

Yep, he was going to hell. One way ticket. First class.

"It should be fine unless it's really windy," said Bella preceding him past the line of people with dinner reservations as they made their way up the roped gangplank. "Typically it'll burn out by the time we reach the farthest tables and you'll have the effect. But if it's too much, we can do a controlled flame. I've done it before at weddings with small pitchers of brandy that we'll light at the table. It takes a little longer and you won't have that wow factor, but we'd rather have people safe than sorry."

He was sorry he'd let her precede him up the stairs to the top deck. The wind was doing riotous things to the hem of her dress which did riotous things to his libido. Tanned, smoothed, toned legs in sexy-as-hell heels. He hoped it was ten degrees cooler on deck because he'd need it.

Except then the wind messed up her hair exactly as if she'd spent a night of hot, sweaty sex, and the chill did nothing to cool him down.

He took a deep breath, trying to regain that self control he'd been so proud of minutes ago. "The hospital administrators will sit here." He motioned toward the starboard side of the bow and put a few extra paces between them. "And we'll put the band over there. The dance floor will be cleared of tables after the fireworks."

"How long is the band playing?" Staci asked.

"You won't have to stay until they're finished." Reese said. "Dinner's usually over by eight and the auction rarely goes past ten or so. We've got the band until one, but once dessert is over, you and Bella will be free to enjoy the party. The bartenders will be earning their tips at that point."

And if there was a God, Bella would leave and Vincent would never show up in the first place and he'd never have to have the torture of watching Bella in the guy's arms.

"We're going to have a lot of serving dishes to run up and down that gangplank. Where do you want us to park?" Bella, thankfully, dispelled that image with her question.

"There's a reserved area by the service entrance at the back."

"Okay, then. That all sounds good." She powered off her iPad and stuck it into her purse, then turned to Staci. "I guess that covers everything. Ready to go?"

Staci propped a hand on her hip. Regardless of the clothes, that pose was designed to get attention and Luke's eyes were all over her, the lucky SOB. At least the woman *he* lusted after wasn't married.

"Aren't you forgetting something, Bella? Like, uh, dinner?"

"We hadn't planned on staying for dinner, Stace."

"I had." Staci grabbed Luke's arm and plastered herself to his side. "Right, Reese? We're having dinner?"

It took Reese a few seconds to process that Staci was asking *him.*

Took Luke a few, too. "Stace, I thought—"

"No, no." Staci linked her other arm with Bella's. "We need to have dinner here to get the full experience. And I'm sure one of you guys has enough of a name to bypass all those people down there in line, am I right?"

She definitely knew which button to push for Luke; his ego wouldn't let that challenge go unanswered.

"I'll be right back." He sprinted toward the maitre d'.

Yeah, the guy was a sucker for a pretty face. Or easy lay as the case may be—except Reese couldn't figure Staci's angle. He would've thought she'd want to be alone with Luke. Use the opportunity to get her claws into him.

"I really can't, Staci," said Bella. "Remember, I'm taking Sophia out tomorrow? I should get home to bed."

There was an image he didn't need.

"Oh no you won't." Staci trapped Bella's arm tighter to her side. "You're staying. We're going to have some fun."

Fun wasn't the word Bella would have used. Not when she'd been trying to concentrate on what they'd been talking about and not notice the way the twinkling lights danced across the planes of Reese's face.

Or the way the wind rippled through his hair like her fingers wanted to. Or the flex of his abs beneath that shirt… She'd been way too aware of him for her own good and spending another minute, let alone hour, in his company was really going to be a test.

"It's all set," said Luc, returning. "They have a table for us below deck."

"There. See?" Staci didn't let go as she followed Luke back to the stairs. "No waiting. You'll get home at a reasonable hour."

So Bella found herself sitting across a candlelit table in the darkly intimate belly of *The Midnight Maiden*, with hurricane glass lamps providing soft lighting, and the tables way too small and close together for a supposed business meeting, and all she wanted to do was, just once, forget about her responsibilities and her problems and let herself pretend *what if*.

"So what celebrities are coming?" asked Staci once the waiter had taken their drink orders.

Reese rattled off an impressive list for this part of the country. He'd really put a lot of work into this event. She was proud that the Casteleoni name would be affiliated with it.

"And my mother, of course. *If* I can convince her. She doesn't seem to think anyone remembers who she is."

Staci, was obviously a fan. "*Carolyn Charmant* is coming? Ohmygosh, I *loved* her last movie."

"Don't tell her that," said Reese, setting down his wine glass. "The word *last* in conjunction with *movie* is a sure way to get her to cry. She loved performing."

"Why did she stop?" Staci asked.

"My dad asked her to. He had a heart attack and, you know they say you re-examine your priorities when things like that happen. She didn't mind, actually. They're more in love than the day they got married, I think. They're always doing things together, especially spending time with the grandkids. For all that my mom enjoyed the limelight, give her a baby and she turns into Grandma."

It sounded so perfect. A family. A real, normal family. That's all she wanted out of life. To find someone to spend her life with and create a family.

An image of Reese and his child wound its way through her mind. And lodged in her soul.

She closed her eyes, savoring it if only for a second. She was, after all, playing *what if* tonight.

The conversation eventually turned to football, and Bella actually relaxed and enjoyed herself. The banter between Luke and Reese as they shared stories of games and pranks players had played on each other had them all laughing through dinner.

"Metzner said you roped him into donating a dinner." Luke said when dessert arrived. "Can you see him making small talk with people he doesn't know?"

"Hey, it's for a good cause. The proceeds benefit several children's funds that the hospital administers."

"So Bella," said Staci. "You should ask Vinny to donate something."

"Yeah, that's a great idea," said Luke. "Maybe a three-hole design for someone's backyard. That'd up the resale value. What do you think, Reese?"

"It's not necessary. We have enough."

And just like that, the mood was over. Reese sat up straighter in his chair and fiddled with the edge of the napkin he'd tossed onto the table.

She *knew* Uncle Vinny should have behaved himself. "Oh, but I'm sure he won't mind."

"It's fine, Bella. All taken care of."

"Yeah, but, just think, Reese," said Staci once more oblivious to anything but herself. "Vinny's got a big name in this town. People would bet tons of money."

"Really, not necessary. The auction is big enough." Reese lifted his empty wine glass and rolled the stem between his fingers. "But thanks for the thought. No need to put yourself out on this, Bella."

Message received loud and clear: stick to what she knew and back off his end of the program. Okay then…

"Well, sure. Fine. But if you change your mind, all you have to do is ask." She grabbed her purse and stood up. "I'll be going. Thank you for dinner. Staci do you need a ride?"

Staci looked sideways at Luke. "Do I?"

Luke stroked her arm. "You got one right here, babe."

Bella had to look away. Sure, *Staci* got the guy. Bella got a lonely bed and useless dreams.

She nodded and made sure to look at Reese one last time before she left. This was business and she was a professional. "Thank you again for dinner. Have a nice evening."

"Well, geez. I was only trying to be helpful," said Staci as Bella left. "I wonder what crawled up her butt."

Reese tried not to groan as he pulled his eyes *from* Bella's butt. He was an ass. He'd overreacted and hurt her feelings. God, what was wrong with him?

"I know you were, Stace. There's no need to apologize." Luke put his hand on hers, but drilled Reese with his gaze. "You, on the other hand…"

Reese sighed. Luke was right. He tossed a few bills onto the table. "Have a good night, you two." Then he set off to fix the one he'd ruined.

# Chapter Twenty

ell, now." Luke turned on his charm. Not that he needed to; Staci was ripe for the, er, plucking, but it was good to keep the skill up. "I thought we'd never get rid of them." He ran his hand up Staci's arm. She shivered and he grinned. No matter what Tanya said, he still had it.

"I hope you don't mind that I invited her to stay tonight. She never gets out."

Altruism? In Staci? This was unexpected.

"No. I don't mind." And he hadn't. It'd given him some foreplay time. Running his fingers along her thigh, touching her foot with his… He liked to get that shit out of the way early. Left more time for the main event when they got to it. And they'd get to it, no doubt about it. "Want to dance? I've been dying to get you in my arms all night."

She blushed. Yeah, he still had it.

"Okay. Let's."

She shivered again when he took her hand and pulled her into his arms. Could be the breeze, but he'd take it. Nothing like having a beautiful woman cuddle into him.

She smelled nice. He'd noticed at dinner. Funny, but when he'd met her in Reese's office he could have sworn she had on some overly commercial sharp perfume, but tonight, she'd toned it down. Like with the outfit.

Soft, frilly blouse that covered more than he wanted it to, a skirt that let him know she had curves but not quite how curvy… He'd been expecting something that left nothing to his imagination, and this outfit made his imagination work overtime—as in, getting her out of it. Undoing the buttons with his teeth and licking every centimeter in between.

"I had a good time tonight," he whispered. Women liked that shit.

She smiled against his cheek. "Me, too."

"Good." He moved his hand a little lower.

Staci moved it back.

What the fuck?

He pulled back. "Stace?"

She smiled. Sort of. "I want to take it slow, Luke. Savor the moment."

Aw hell. Frustration razored along his back and lodged in his balls. He wasn't getting any, dammit.

Surprisingly, his interest in her picked up a notch. Not that he hadn't had anyone play hard to get before, but there was something about the way she'd said it… the way she'd behaved this evening.

"Yeah, sure, Stace. That's fine with me. I'm not a Neanderthal, you know."

Now her smile turned genuine. Real. And, shit, it socked him in the gut more than that creep Mackenzie's tackle that'd broken his hip and put him out of commission for good.

He just hoped that analogy wasn't at work here. The last thing he needed was another woman grabbing some real estate in his life.

A couple next to them briefly bumped them. A chorus of "sorry"s followed, but Staci wasn't sorry. She was enjoying this moment. Sure, Luke felt good against her—there was not denying that body—but he'd gone with her moving his hand away. Hadn't gotten all pissy like she'd thought he might. Which just proved that he wasn't some player. Wasn't after only one thing.

Mother was right. Who knew?

Except she wouldn't know that Staci was using her newfound look on Luke. Reese didn't want her, and, frankly, Staci didn't want him and Mother would just have to deal.

She wanted Luke. For a lot longer than a couple of hours. Which meant that she had to play her cards right.

Well, she'd take a page out of Bella's book and try the classy act—*not* that her stepsister had any clue how close Reese was to drooling over her. Poor guy; all through dinner he'd been like a deer in the headlights while Bella had been oblivious. Heh, maybe there was something Staci could teach her when this was all said and done.

But like Bella, she wasn't going home with anyone tonight. She was done being an easy lay. If Luke wanted her—and that bulge pressed against her abdomen said he did—he was going to have to work for her. No matter how much it hurt both of them in the interim.

The band segued to the next slow song and Staci was all for enjoying Luke pressing against her a little longer.

Their thighs brushed as the soft strains of Spandau Ballet's "True" wove around them. *True*. Ha. She'd had a lot of *true*s tossed her way lately, the biggest being that her mother was an overbearing tyrant. Staci was ashamed that she'd fallen in line with Mother's plans so easily.

But no more. Mother wasn't going to run her life or ruin Sophia's; Staci was taking charge of it all as of now.

Luke's hand moved lower.

Okay, so maybe she wasn't going to take charge of anything *right* now. Once this song was over would be soon enough. Luke's arms around her felt good. And she liked allowing him to lead—the guy not only knew his way around women, he knew his way around the dance floor and it'd been a long time—try never—that she'd been with someone who had his flair.

Something flared all right—right in the middle of her stomach when his fingers made little circles on her back, warming her flesh as heat seeped through her shirt and traveled south. It was going to be tough to stick to her decision if he kept doing that.

"Any chance you want to get out of here, Staci?" Luke whispered in her ear, sending shivers all over her body.

Yes.

No.

Hell.

Damn her conscience and re-awakened common sense anyhow…

"Yeah, let's go."

***

Reese followed Bella, needing to apologize for overreacting. It wasn't her fault he was a jealous ass. But there was only so much he could handle, and having Vincent Casteleoni on the agenda was his breaking point. He had to be civil to the guy, he had to keep his hands off his wife, but he did *not* have to do anything more than that.

And what about the kids who would benefit from the auction? Weren't they important enough to set his ego aside and suck it up?

Hell, yes, they were. And not having Vincent on the agenda wouldn't change the fact that the guy still went home to Bella every night.

He caught up with her by her car. "Bella, wait."

She slowed, and looked at him warily. "Yes?"

"I'm sorry if I was a little sharp back there."

"Sharp? Try deadly." Her tone stung and wouldn't let him off the hook. Not that he deserved to be.

"I know. And I really don't have an excuse except that I—" What? Was a jealous ass? A stupid, horny bastard? A lowlife scum lusting after another man's wife? What? What could he say to salvage this?

Hell, he didn't need Luke to screw up the catering part of this business for him; he was doing a damn good job all by himself.

"You're what?"

"I… I'm sorry."

"That's it? Sorry for embarrassing me? Sorry for humiliating me? Sorry for insulting me? Which one, Reese, are you sorry for?"

That he hadn't met her before Vincent.

Yeah, he *was* a horny, lowlife scum bastard to lust after her this way. "All of the above? Forgive me? Please? And you can ask Vincent. We'll make room for him."

He held his breath as she looked at him, hoping he hadn't screwed up everything.

"I guess I have to forgive you since you owned up to all of it."

She gave him that same smile that Sophia had, blinking those big blue windows into her psyche and Reese blew out a breath. At least he was still a good judge of character—if not of marital status.

If he were Vincent Casteleoni, he'd make damn sure she wore thick, horn-rimmed glasses tinted a nice shade of gray to hide the impact of those eyes because they could turn a rational man's thoughts to mush. And another part of his anatomy to stone.

He took a huge breath and willed himself to take a step back. He did not hit on someone else's wife. "So, um, we're okay then? No hard feelings?"

She shook her head, the ends of her hair swishing across the bit of cleavage above her neckline and Reese wanted to follow its path with his tongue.

Jesus.

He grabbed her driver side door handle and yanked it open, being sure to stand behind it as she climbed in, away from any part of her that he could inadvertently touch, or stroke, or… *lick*. He motioned for her to get in.

Of course, she stopped before she did so. And of course she put her fingers on his arm.

"Oh, I wanted to ask you…" She nibbled her lip and Reese was so freaking glad there was a big piece of steel between them. "Is there, that is, do you have an extra pair of tickets to the auction? I'd pay for them of course."

Two tickets. Sophia and Vincent. It only made sense.

"Sure, Bella, no problem. And don't worry about paying for them. They're on the house."

And then he sent her back to *her* house. The one where Vincent waited.

# Chapter Twenty-One

Reese's bad mood carried over to the next morning. Given that he'd left the parking lot in one after Bella had driven away to come home to an empty house, that shouldn't be a surprise.

What had been was that his house which, until that moment, hadn't seemed particularly empty, suddenly had. He'd stared at the four walls that made up his living room, and later those of his bedroom, and acknowledged that he needed more in his life than what he'd been living with. The looks Luke and Staci had been giving each other, not to mention the sexual awareness he'd almost been able to touch, had grabbed him by the throat, and Bella looking stunning in the glow of the candles, her eyes sparkling, the breeze brushing her hair across her skin, her soft laughter wrapping around him like a caress hadn't helped matters.

Sending her home to The Husband had only made things go downhill.

He wanted to punch something just for the sheer frustration of not being able to have her.

Luke strolled up his front walk just then, his usual morning-after swagger making Reese want to punch *him*.

He yanked open the door before Luke had the chance to knock. "What do you want?"

Luke, damn him, smiled. "Sleep well?"

Reese swiped a hand over his chin, then raked it through his hair. "Is there something you need or are you purposely trying to sabotage your chances of getting back in my good graces?"

"Oh, I don't know." Luke looked at his fingernails, the pompous prick. "I thought I was doing you a service last night by trading my signature to a lucky couple for their table so Bella wouldn't leave."

Reese checked the fist he wanted to swing. Luke had one warped sense of humor. "Remind me to thank you sometime."

"I'll take it now, but do we have to have this conversation on your front porch? How 'bout a cup of coffee?"

Sadistic bastard. But Reese let him in anyway. Luke wanted to brag. He always did. Staci was just one more in a long line of notches on a bed post.

"Going somewhere?" Luke's toed the suitcases stacked in the foyer.

"A conference. Is there something you need, Luke?"

"I came by to drop off your change."

"You could have kept it."

"And give you reason to distrust me more than you do now?" Luke dumped the cash on the end table. "No way. I told you I'd be on the job and I plan to prove it." He tapped his shoe. "Uh, any chance of that coffee? From the looks of it, you could use some, too."

"Gee, thanks." Yeah, he had been up half the night—and he didn't mean just being awake.

Shaking off the memory—and the erotic dreams he'd had once he'd finally fallen asleep—Reese headed to the kitchen. He grabbed a bag of coffee beans from the fridge, poured them into the grinder, then turned it on, the harsh whir of the motor combined with the remnants of last night's wine  and lack of sleep giving him one hell of a headache.

Luke sat at the breakfast bar and drummed his fingers on its surface. "So, how'd it go with Bella?"

*Like shit*, but Reese opted not to say it as he poured the grounds and water into the coffee maker and set it to perc. Luke didn't need to know his feelings toward Bella—not that the fact that she was Vincent Casteleoni's wife would matter to him; marriage had never stopped Luke before.

Reese grabbed two mugs from the cabinets above the breakfast bar sink and placed them on the granite countertop. "She accepted my apology. We're good."

"Yeah, what's with *that*? You sure clammed up in a hurry. I mean, hell, snagging Vincent Casteleoni for the event was a brilliant idea."

"That, surprisingly, came from Staci." From another cabinet, he pulled out a sugar bowl and a cardboard cylinder of non-dairy creamer, then handed them to Luke. "I don't know how you can use that stuff."

"Hey, a guy's gotta have a few vices. Mine just happens to be for something sweet in the morning."

Reese could think of something sweet he'd like to have as his vice in the morning.

"So. You and Staci." Anything to take Bella out of the conversation.

"Hey, don't get on my case. She's not really working with Bella. We both know that. I'm just keeping her busy and out of the way."

"Regardless, Luke, the problem is, you always pick the ones who think they can be the exception to your no-involvement rules." He filled Luke's mug.

"Yeah, but Staci's different. I made one move, and, bam, she was out the door of my car like lightning. Shocked the shit out of me." He took the coffee from Reese. "I think there's more to her than she lets on. I mean, did you see what she was wearing last night? Totally unexpected."

Unless she was trying to keep Luke off-kilter enough to intrigue him. Reese wouldn't have thought Staci smart enough for that, but then, looks could be deceiving.

"I mean, yeah, she comes off all brassy and tacky, but once you start her talking, you see she's a real person. Not some ditzy chick with no brains and a great body. We went to a coffee shop after *The Midnight Maiden* and had an interesting conversation. There's actually depth to her."

Surprising words coming from Luke; normally, the guy was as shallow as a puddle two days after a rainstorm. "Depth, huh?"

"Yeah. For instance—" Luke drained his mug and motioned for another. "Did you know she graduated at the top of her class in college?"

"Yet she remains unemployed."

"She admitted that was due to not wanting to look for a job. She took some time off to enjoy life."

"And, who, exactly, is paying for this decadent lifestyle?"

"She said her stepfather left them comfortable, so she doesn't have to work."

"Yet Bella is working her tail off at the restaurant." And had a family with one very lucky SOB. "Now, why do you suppose I find Staci's story hard to believe?" Reese shook his head. "How much longer are you going to be gullible for something in tight pants, Luke? Didn't Tanya teach you anything?"

Luke slammed the mug down on the counter, coffee splashing over the top. The handle cracked off and he tossed it into the sink. "I don't need a lecture from you, Reese. At least I haven't let myself turn into some freak, with nothing else in my life but a bunch of parties I don't get to enjoy." He grabbed a napkin and mopped up the mess.

"You know, you used to be fun. We had some great times in our playing days. Now, you're like the suits we used to make fun off, all tight-assed and number-crunching. Sometimes, Reese, you actually have to take a chance and go outside your safe little world." The napkin followed the mug handle into the sink. "And, yeah, it's not always nice out there. Tanya may have been a mistake, but having Jared never was. So, stay off my case about Staci. What I have, or don't have, going on with her won't affect your precious auction."

He stood up and poured the contents of the mug down the drain. "I can't believe I thought you might be interested in Bella. I can't believe I thought you might bend your ironclad rule about fraternizing with the help to go out with her." He set the mug on the counter. "Do you know I was almost going to volunteer to babysit today so she wouldn't have to take her little sister Sophia out so you two could go do something? That's how nice I was trying to be to you. I'm really glad now that I didn't waste my time." He shot a disgusted look at Reese. "Have a good day, Reese. A good, *lonely* one."

Luke punctuated his departure by slamming the front door hard enough to knock a picture off the wall while Reese's world shifted, turned sideways, and dumped him off the edge with it.

Little sister? Sophia was her *sister*?

Then who the hell was Vincent Casteleoni?

He grabbed his iPad, finally allowing himself to do the search he'd been wanting to do all week—

Her uncle. Vincent Casteleoni was her *uncle*.

Jesus. He was an idiot. A stupid, blind, lovesick moron.

He sat down and read the article about her parents' accident. Saw her father's obituary, listing Sophia as her sister.

His damn nobility had put him in hell for a week.

Well no more.

He grabbed his cell. She was taking Sophia somewhere today. He wanted—no, *needed* to know where.

***

133

Staci hung up Bella's cell phone, a smile on her face, then brushed her hands together. There, that was her good deed for the day.

She turned around and came to an abrupt halt.

Mother stood in the doorway, her eyes narrowed.

Staci knew that look. And had recently learned to fear it.

"Why did Reese Charmant want to speak with Bella?" An icy chill followed Mother's words.

Staci gulped and suppressed a shiver. Now that her eyes had been truly opened to Mother's scheming, she realized she did not want to get on her bad side. "I don't know. I didn't ask."

"That was your second mistake." Mother folded her arms over her chest with military precision, her starched white collared shirt crinkling like cellophane. With the pencil-straight charcoal skirt, her black hair sleeked back into a French twist so severe it looked as if her cheekbones were going to be pulled to the back of her head, and black pointed heels, Mother could be commanding an army. Or terrorizing a town of defenseless Munchkins.

She whipped her hands to her pointed hips so fast Staci thought the air whistled. "Honestly, Anastasia, must I think of everything?" Her mother advanced upon her with all the deadly grace of a big cat stalking its prey. "I suggest you call the man back and ask him what exactly he needs, and tell him you'll get him the answer. There is no need to encourage a meeting between them."

"I don't know Bella's pass code for her phone. And he was calling from his car and I don't have his cell number."

"Then I strongly urge you to march that well-wiggled derriere of yours down to the zoo and catch him before he finds her." Mother's eyes narrowed. "I don't have to explain any further, do I?"

Oh no. She came through loud and clear. But Staci had other plans for the day. Plans that would be futile unless she did what Mother wanted. "Fine. I'll try to find him before he finds her and Sophia."

She was almost past her when Mother's hand shot out and caught her arm. "Don't *try*, Anastasia. *Do.* Remember, Salvatore's money only takes us so far. We cannot buy our way into the country club scene. However, if I become a member of the Board of the Arts Center, our entrée is all but guaranteed." Her grip got tighter. "Unless you want to be second rate all your life."

Staci yanked her arm out of the vise. "I get it, Mother. Say goodbye to Luke and play nice-nice to Reese in exchange for helping you out. Gee, I'm so glad I get something out of it. Do the words 'world's oldest profession' mean anything to you?"

Fury rushed into Mother's face. "Don't you ever speak to me in such a manner again, Anastasia. I'll not have it. I've given up the best years of my life trying to do better by you girls than that slob who sired you ever did! I put up with enough of his garbage to last me a lifetime, and then, when I was finally able to land a good prospect, I had to play second fiddle to a ghost!" She wagged a long, pointed finger in Staci's face. "I've done what's necessary to keep you in the tight clothes you so enjoy and a decent roof over your head, and this is how you repay me?"

Staci took a step back as Mother came closer. She'd never seen her like this. Usually Mother's *words* spoke volumes, not her tone.

"I struggled to claw out of the slum where I was born. Do you have any idea what it's like to be so hungry you'll eat other people's bread crusts?" Mother was beyond stopping. She backed Staci against the foyer wall, jailing her in place by planting her hands on the wall beside Staci's head.

"I swore I'd never do that again, that I'd do whatever it took to get out of that hell and rise to the upper echelons of society."

Mother's face was so close Staci had a hard time focusing. But Mother's tone got through and it frightened her. She'd never seen Mother so out of control.

"And what happened once I worked and saved and struggled just to get beyond Fifth Street? I find a man who promises to be everything I need him to be. Your father. Only his promises turn out to be gin-soaked."

For a brief second, Staci swore she saw the glint of a tear. But only for a second. Mother never cried.

Mother turned away and straightened her shoulders. "A man who saw a young girl and swept her off her feet by pulling the rug out from under her. As he continued to do with any pretty girl he met. Five years and two kids later, I was right back where I started. But at least then I had smarts." She spun back around. "And a plan. No man was ever going to take advantage of me again. And when Sal came along, it was just too perfect to pass up. A financially well-off man who was completely dependent on me. Who was I to pass up the gift that'd been dropped into my lap?"

Probably not the time to remind Mother that she had, in fact, gone after Sal when she'd read about the car accident.

"But, no. Again, I'm thwarted by the lust of a man. This time for a dead woman." She pointed one of her long fingernails at Staci. "But you, Anastasia, you will learn from my mistakes, from my experiences. I don't ever want you to be at the mercy of some fickle man, to be used and cast aside as the mood suits him." She picked up Bella's phone and held it out. "Which is why you are going to end whatever this little fling is with this Luke person. We need to keep an eye on Reese, and, so help me, Staci, I will send *you* away with Sophia if you ruin this. I need you to keep tabs on that man and make sure Bella is never alone with him."

"Why, Mother? What good will that do any of us?"

Mother yanked Staci to her until they were nose-to-nose. "Because his mother is the woman vying for my place on the Board and I'm counting on you to ensure that she doesn't get it."

"And just how do you plan for me to ensure that, Mother? No one on the Board is going to listen to me." Mother was putting a lot of confidence in her. A first. And it made Staci suspicious.

"Please, Anastasia. We both know you are not cut out for this time of work. It's bound to turn into a fiasco. And if by some grace of God it runs smoothly, you'll be on board to turn it around in our favor. His mother won't want her son's name dragged through the mud if she gets appointed."

"You want me to *sabotage* the auction?" Staci didn't know whether to be insulted or appalled. Though the fact that Mother *expected* her to fail, had meant for her to work with Bella so that she *would* fail, was a pretty compelling reason to go with insulted.

"Sabotage is such a harsh word, Anastasia. I want you to make sure that Reese's sterling reputation is tarnished just enough to reflect poorly on his name."

"But that will do the same thing to Casteleoni's."

"Not if you play your cards right. And with me dealing your hand, you will. You just have to do what I say."

So nothing had changed. Mother still thought so little of her that she thought she could insult her with no repercussions.

But she wasn't the brainless idiot Mother obviously thought she was. She had her own plan for her life and just because Mother hadn't found a man to stand by her didn't mean Staci couldn't. And, yes, Luke was a long shot, but he'd come around. He would. If she stood her ground and didn't give in to him until he realized that she wasn't like anyone he'd ever known, he'd come around. Oh, she knew all about what his ex-wife was trying to do; it was in all the magazines, but she was the best thing for him and he'd figure it out and then they'd have their own happily ever after. Just like she deserved.

Just like Bella and Reese and little Sophia deserved. And Staci was in the position to make it happen.

"All right, Mother. I'll see what I can do."

***

Oh no she would *not*.

Jonathan almost fell out of the hanging basket on the front porch. True, it might have something to do with the yellow jacket that decided to give him a sniff, but Staci's agreement bowled him over as well. This would not do. He'd had such high hopes for the girl.

Jonathan adjusted his fedora, shook his head one more time at Staci's duplicity and Madeleine's utter lack of compassion, and whisked himself back to Home Base. He was going to have to get other Guardians involved.

# Chapter Twenty-Two

"Look, Bella, there's Aunt Staci." Sophia ran across the crowded cobblestone plaza near the primate enclosure by the zoo's entrance gates. "Hi, Aunt Staci!"

Staci had managed, yet again, to surprise her because Bella would have bet that the only time her stepsister had been this close to a monkey was on a date with the gangly and extremely hairy Mark Kurter in tenth grade.

Bella caught up to Sophia just as Staci handed her a few dollars she'd fished out of her teeny tiny candy apple red clutch. Madeleine might have toned down the clothing and hair color, but she still had her work cut out for her with the accessories.

"Thanks." Sophia turned those Casteleoni blues that could melt glaciers Bella's way. "Can I feed the baby monkeys?"

"Sure thing, Sprite. Just be careful, okay?"

" 'Kay!" Sophia skipped over to the vendor to buy the approved treats.

Bella let Staci follow her to a bench that was close enough to keep an eye on Sophia, but far enough that her sister wouldn't overhear their conversation.

"Why are you here, Staci?"

"I was hoping to run into you. Or Reese."

"Reese?" Bella refused to notice the little leap her heart made. It was probably that cold soft pretzel she'd eaten.

"He called your phone. I saw it was him and told him you'd brought Sophia here."

Staci held out Bella's phone, the one Bella had purposely left behind so Madeleine couldn't track her down. She'd never imagined Reese would try to.

"So if you told him where to find me, what are you doing here?"

"Well, Mother happened to overhear that conversation and she—"

"Sent you to run interference."

"Something like that." Staci looked at her fingernails. It was a nice manicure, but Staci was more prone to showing them off than studying them.

"What aren't you telling me?"

Staci grimaced. "She doesn't want you to be alone with Reese."

"Why on earth not? Please don't tell me she wants him for herself."

Staci laughed. "No, I can safely say that that is definitely not what she wants." She looked at Bella. "She's counting on me to ruin the auction."

"How?"

"Sabotage."

"That makes no sense."

'It does if you're Mother."

Bella pinched the bridge of her nose. "I don't understand any of this. Why would she want to sabotage the auction?"

Staci took a deep breath. "Carolyn Charmant is up for Mother's position on the stupid Board. Mother thinks that if the auction's a fiasco, Reese's mom will stay on the sidelines instead of dragging his name through the papers. Or that she'll be guilty by association and the Board won't want her." Staci held up her hands. "Hey, it's my mother's reasoning, not mine."

Bella's mind was reeling. Madeleine wanted to sabotage Bella's best chance at making a name for herself and the restaurant just so she *might* win a Board position? "Why are you telling me this?"

Staci bit her lip. "I'm sick of Mother's manipulations. She doesn't think of anyone but herself. She never has. Not really. She can say she's done what she's done for me and Drew, but it's always been about her. As for her plan, I don't know all the specifics. She just dumped the whole thing on me before I left to come here. Apparently, she was expecting my natural ineptitude to handle it for her." She turned on the bench and looked at Bella with a tear in her eye. "She doesn't even see how insulting that is, can you believe it?"

Bella felt sorry for her. At least *she* knew why Madeleine didn't like her; it must be really tough for Staci when her own mother had no faith in her.

"Well now that we know, we can make sure it doesn't happen."

"Yeah, but she can't know that we know or she'll start with the threats to send Sophia away again."

"So you have to let her think you're on her side, then tell me what she's planning and we'll make sure it doesn't happen. We're only two weeks' out. We can do it."

Staci sniffed. "How do you do it, Bella? How do you deal with her like this day after day, year after year?"

Bella patted Staci's hand. Finally, someone on her side. "I keep my eye on the prize, Staci." She just wasn't going to trust Staci with what that prize was at the moment. Sure, Staci seemed to have had a change of heart, and Bella really hoped she had, but the custody battle for Sophia had to remain a secret until she could finance it.

"Reese!" Sophia's shriek startled Bella for a moment until the word registered.

"I better go." Staci gathered her clutch and shot to her feet. "You have a nice time with him, Bella. Don't let my mother get in the way of your happiness. I'm not going to."

Before Bella could answer, Staci headed off in the opposite direction.

It was a nice thought, but there was so much more involved with her happiness than just Reese. If only it were that easy.

"Hey, Sophia!" Reese said, looking really good in a pair of khakis and red golf shirt. "How are you? How's Willow?"

"Fat and happy. That's what Giac says." Sophia dragged Reese by the hand back to the bench. "Look who I found, Bella."

"I see, Sprite." She looked at Reese. "What are you doing here?"

"I needed to see you."

"Why?"

To kiss her senseless. It'd been his only objective on the ride over here after he'd reconciled it with his no fraternization rule. The problem with Devin had been that they'd wanted different things. He hadn't wanted to settle down. But with Bella, he did. And with her sense of family, she had to want the same thing.

"Will you feed the monkeys with me, Reese?" Sophia tugged on his hand.

"Hey, Soph." Bella pulled money from her shorts pocket. "Reese and I have some business to discuss. Why don't you do it and we'll join you when we're finished."

Sophia pouted. The kid was going to be a knockout when she grew up. Just like her sister.

*Sister.*

He still couldn't get over the flood of relief at the news. He *wasn't* a lowlife scum-bucket for wanting her.

"Okay, but you better hurry. They're going to be full soon."

He watched her skip away. "Your sister is adorable."

"Yeah, and she knows it. Gets away with way too much."

"I bet you were the same way." He shoved his hands into his pockets because they were itching to show her just how adorable he thought she was.

"Me? Hardly."

"Not true. I've seen the way Gus and Giac dote on you."

"Yeah, well, they're like family."

"What was your family like? Your parents?"

The effect of his question on her was stunning. Well, *she* was stunning, but the sheer happiness that lit up her face at that question made her even more stunning. Breath-taking, and he was more than willing to let her steal his. Especially since it proved him right. She loved family as much as he did.

"My parents were wonderful."

As was the smile on her face.

Oh, hell. He was going to start spouting Shakespearean sonnets at any moment.

"They were best friends and business partners. Everyone loved to be around them. It was like one big party in our house with neighbors coming and going all the time. They loved to be with people and wanted a big family. It was such a disappointment to them to have had only one child for so many years."

"Must have been tough on you."

"No really. I was their only child. They showered me with attention and love. I wasn't even aware of what they were going through. But I do remember how happy they were when my mother got pregnant with Sophia. Dad threw open Casteleoni's for free for a whole weekend and set Mom up in one of the booths like a queen. He had Giac and Gus run themselves ragged to keep everyone fed as our friends came to celebrate." Bella laughed and Reese could see the scene. "It was even a bigger celebration when Sophia was born. You might've thought no one had ever given birth before—-my mother included—-with the way Dad treated her and fussed over her." She twirled a lock of hair around her finger. "I'm glad they're together now. It was really tough for my dad after Mom died."

"But that left you with Madeleine and her daughters."

Bella sighed and dropped the hair. "True. But it could have been worse."

He glanced at the path Staci had taken as she'd left. "How?"

"They could have had another sister."

Reese laughed at her make-lemonade take on her stepsisters, but his mind was replaying what she'd said about her parents. *Business partners.* It wasn't a new idea, certainly. Many people worked with their spouse and had thriving businesses.

"Did your parents start Casteleoni's?"

Bella smiled and, again, Reese felt as if the sun had dipped from the sky to sit beside him.

Oh, man. He needed to go see a horror flick or something. Sit through a ball game. Go off-roading. Watch a wrestling match. A marathon of them. Cage fighting. *Any*thing to retain his man-card.

"My grandparents did. It was the only way they could get married."

"What do you mean?"

"They were engaged to a brother and sister. That's how they met, and during their courtships, they fell in love with each other. They couldn't bear the thought of marrying the one they were supposed to, so they had to find a way to buy out the dowries and keep the family honor. But they were immigrant kids—the only jobs they could get back then were in factories. That kind of work wouldn't give them enough, so they came up with the idea of opening their own business. With my grandfather's gift of gab and my grandmother's cooking expertise, they started Casteleoni's out of my great-grandmother's kitchen. It wasn't long before they were able to buy out the contracts and get married."

So her family business had started *because* of a relationship. "That's a great story."

"I know. That's why Casteleoni's means so much to me. It's not just a business; it's my family's history. Sophia's and mine. Part of who we are."

And who she was was so very special. Reese fingered a coin in his pocket. God, he wanted to kiss her.

"So why are you here, Reese? I thought we covered everything last night."

"We did."

Well, not everything…

He kissed her. Took her beautiful face in his hands, tilted her chin up, and claimed her sweet soft lips in the way he'd wanted to since the kiss in the kitchen had whetted his appetite.

God, she tasted good. Better than he remembered. He traced the seam of her lips with his tongue, wanting entrance—

*What* was he doing?

Reese pulled away from the kiss. They were in a zoo, of all places, her impressionable little sister—sister!—was five feet away, and he had a plane to catch. Not optimal circumstances for making out with her, never mind the fact that he shouldn't just walk up and maul her.

"What was that for?" Her gorgeous blue eyes blinked at him and Reese prayed that was desire he saw in them, not disgust.

He shoved his hands back into his pockets, out of temptation's way.

But then she said, "I thought you didn't like kissing me."

"Where did you get that idea?"

"You apologized. In the kitchen."

Hell. *Utter lack of finesse, Charmant.* "I thought you were married."

Her eyes widened and whatever desire he'd thought he'd seen disappeared. "You thought I was *married* and you still kissed me?"

He was botching this. "No, not then. Not when I apologized. I didn't want my attraction to you to interfere with our business relationship yet I'd just kissed you and, well, it wasn't a good idea."

"So where does the married part come in and how on earth did you come to that conclusion? I live with my stepmother, for Pete's sake."

"I thought you lived with Vincent. And that Sophia was your daughter."

It took her two heart-wrenching seconds to react. Two seconds for Reese to wonder if he'd blown it even before kissing her just now.

And then she laughed. Full-on, belly-clutching, bending-over laughter.

"Are you kidding me? You thought I was married to Uncle Vinny? What kind of woman do you think I am? And him? Oh my God. What does that say about him?"

He grimaced. "I'm not saying I'm proud of it, I just put one and one together and—"

"And came up with four thousand nine hundred and eight-seven." She bit her bottom lip. "God, Reese, you couldn't be more wrong."

"I know that now." He wanted to run his thumb over that bottom lip.

"So why is it okay for you to kiss me now? We're still working together—you're not firing me, are you?"

"No, Bella, it's just…" God, he was really screwing this up. He should have stuck to his rule, but Bella made him forget the rules. Made him want to make up new ones. "I've been attracted to you from the moment we met and, well, you're not married."

"So you kiss all the unmarried girls you're attracted to?"

"Usually."

He winced when she laughed.

"At least you're honest."

"That came out wrong. What I meant was, before. Back in my playing days. There were women. But not recently. I haven't kissed anyone recently." God, he was babbling. Make him stop.

Bella touched Reese's arm. "Reese, I'm flattered. Thank you. And I think you're pretty wonderful, too, but it's not a good idea."

"Yeah, I know." Didn't mean he had to like it. Especially when the woman was the one doing the turning down.

"I mean, we have a good working relationship and I need this job. I don't want to jeopardize it."

"It wouldn't have to be an either/or thing, Bella." He listened to himself rationalize and wondered what he was doing. He'd never had to beg a woman to go out with him before.

He'd beg Bella for so much if she wanted him to…

That thought knocked him back on his ass. Good thing he was sitting.

Bella, however, was not. She stood. "It *is* an either/or thing, actually. I just can't. This is business. I hope you understand."

For two more weeks it was. He could last two more weeks. "Okay, I hear you. We'll get through the auction."

"And after, Reese. It won't be a good idea then, either."

"Why the hell not?"

She wrapped her arms around her waist. "I just can't. Right now, the only relationships I need in my life are professional ones, okay?"

No it wasn't, but what was he going to do about it? Knocking her over the head with a club went out a few thousand years ago.

And since when had he felt caveman about any woman?

"Reese!" Sophia came skipping over. "Come see the babies! You can talk to Bella anytime."

No, apparently, he couldn't. Not unless it had to do with set-ups or invoicing.

Man, the painful irony of having his own rule tossed in his face after he'd made his peace with tossing it aside… God, his arrogance. His ego.

Bella jerked her head. "Go ahead, Reese. Make Sophia happy. We're still on for the auction. Anything else, well, it just can't be."

He let Sophia tug him toward the monkeys. He owed Devin a huge apology because he now knew exactly how she'd felt.

And, man, did it suck.

# Chapter Twenty-Three

So where's that Prince Charming guy?" asked Drew a few days later, sashaying in on six-inch heels. Madeleine's next make-over victim perhaps?

Bella steered her stepsister to an unoccupied booth, the gray day outside now matching her mood. "What can I get for you today, Drew?

"How 'bout tall, dark, and hunky?"

Yeah, that wasn't happening. "All out of tall, dark, and hunky. How about a chicken cutlet sandwich instead?"

"I guess." Drew clicked her nails on the table. "Staci says you're pulling a fast one on Mother."

Bella looked around again. Half the regulars would love to put one over on Madeleine and if word got out before Bella actually managed to do it, the plan would be over before it began. "Not really. Staci and I just decided it'd be better to let Madeleine think we're going along with her plan."

"She's going to be pissed when she doesn't get on that stupid committee of hers."

"Nothing I say is going to put her on that committee, no matter what she thinks. It's up to her and, really, it's none of my business."

"Try telling *her* that." Drew nodded to something behind Bella. Some*one*.

Bella groaned. Madeleine, in another one of her Hell-Froze-Over visits, was dressed in her country club uniform that consisted of a lime-and-white striped golf shirt, lime green pencil skirt, and the requisite string of pearls, with her hair smoothed back into one of those ladies-who-lunch matching headbands, and was dragging a little man in a business suit along behind her.

"Lucinda." Madeleine had perfected the queen-for-a-lifetime haughtiness. "Andrew."

Bella cringed along with her stepsister. Drew's father, wanting a boy, had chosen her name, and the only reason she hadn't changed it was because of Drew Barrymore.

"Allow me to introduce Mr. Giovanni Fiorello." Madeleine, as usual, was oblivious to Drew's cringing. "He's interested in buying the establishment and has a few questions."

A stripe of white in Madeleine's black hair would make her look more like the badger she was. Or a snarling wolverine. Or a skunk. Yeah, definitely a skunk; she was a stinky human being. And those eyes were definitely weasely. Just like her personality. No way was Bella going to let the woman sell the restaurant.

Bella smiled at the man; after all, the situation wasn't his fault. And answering his questions could buy her some time and goodwill with Madeleine. "Mr. Fiorello, why don't you have a seat and I'll be back as soon as I put Drew's order in. Can I get you something to eat or drink?"

"Lemonade would be nice," he answered, fingering the collar of a shirt that looked about two sizes too big for him. As did his suit.

Hmmm… How much money could he offer for the restaurant if he couldn't afford to outfit himself properly?

Bella smelled a rat. One that could pass for a skunk.

But she wasn't going to call Madeleine's bluff. As long as Madeleine was occupied with fake buyers, she'd stay away from real ones, and that'd be one less thing for Bella to worry about.

Bella flashed a false smile at her stepmother and turned to leave, but Madeleine was like a leech—yet another animal comparison that was spot on.

Bella added *snake* to that list when Madeleine slithered next to her.

"What did you mean when you told Andrew that it wasn't your business?" Madeleine even hissed the *esses* at the end of her question.

Bella added *bat* to the comparison list because the woman obviously had the ears of one.

"Something Drew was talking about." She walked behind the counter and opened the small fridge for the lemonade.

Madeleine, of course, didn't dare follow. She waited on the other side, tapping a designer shoe. "I hope you weren't referring to my Board activities. They most certainly *are* your business. Because—" Now Bella could swear she heard the soft ripple of a purr in

Madeleine's throat. "Any hopes you have of keeping this place are linked to me having a position on the Board. If that opportunity disappears, there's no reason for me to stay in town, so you can kiss this place and that home of yours goodbye."

Bella counted to ten. "Madeleine, I don't have anything to do with you getting on the Board. I've given your teas, I've done a good job for Connie DeLeo. I've associated our name with a charity auction; what more do you want me to do?"

Madeleine wrapped her bony fingers around Bella's bicep. "I want you to stay far away from Reese Charmant."

Yeah, no kidding. Madeleine would want that even if his mother wasn't up for "her" Board position. But Bella wasn't supposed to know about that.

She tugged her arm free. "That'll be kind of hard since we're working together."

"Quit."

"What? I can't quit. It's too late. We're too close."

"Let him find someone else."

"No one is going to come on board at this late date, Madeleine. Plus, if I did quit, I'd never get another catering job in this town." And she'd never find a way to save enough extra cash to wage a custody battle. It was as if the woman were picking her dreams apart one by one.

"I don't care, Lucinda. I don't want you working for him."

"You can't stop me."

Madeleine's feral grin slithered across her face. "Yes I can."

Oh, hell. She shouldn't have challenged her.

Madeleine straightened her shoulders and crossed her arms, the fingers of one hand strumming on her elbow. "Quit working for Reese immediately or Sophia will be on the first bus out of town. And Mr. Fiorello will be able to name his price for this place."

"Why would you do that? This is our livelihood."

"Because everyone knows I want to be on the Board and if I don't get the position, I'll never be able to hold my head up in this town again. Especially if *she*—" Madeleine shook her head. "I can't live like that, Lucinda. I'll cut my losses and leave. The house, the restaurant, your sister… all of it will be gone." The finger-strumming stopped. "So do we have a deal?"

Bella wanted to claw her eyes out. Wanted to toss a few hundred grand in her face and buy the place out from under her. Wanted to lock Sophia in a room where Madeleine couldn't touch her.

But she couldn't do any of those things. The only thing she *could* do was give in.

Bella exhaled. She should have taken Reese up on that kiss. At least she'd have had something great to remember him by other than two quick stolen ones and the absolute derision and loathing she'd see when she did as Madeleine asked.

And if this wasn't nightmare enough, another shouting match erupted from the kitchen.

Although, it could actually be a good thing and put Mr. Fiorello off the thought of buying the place.

Bella hurried through the swinging saloon doors into the kitchen to find Bruno wringing the threads out of a dishtowel and Gus flailing his arms, bellowing in Italian.

"What's going on?"

"He—" Gus yanked a rag from his apron pocket and mopped his face while Bruno slumped against the countertop, cringing. "Again, with the big noise! It is ruined!"

Today's Special. "What was it, Gus?" Not that she really wanted to know—one more payment to make to Perla and Harry—but if Gus cared, so did she.

He sank onto the stool at the prep table. "A soufflé. A pumpkin soufflé. I make it to practice for the auction."

She didn't have the heart to tell him they wouldn't need it. Especially when this was something that people might actually want to order. "What happened, Bruno?"

"Well, Ms. C, I had a bit of an accident."

"Are you okay?"

"Well, um, yeah, but, um, I did some damage to the van."

"Our van?" Gus threw his rag at Bruno.

It hit him in the chest and caught on his belt buckle as it fell.

"Gus, I'm sure Bruno didn't do it on purpose."

Bruno shook his head. "I think the van will be okay. I can work on it for you. I know about engines and stuff."

"Well that's good." Bella smiled at him, then turned to Gus, trying to placate him, because once the issue with the van was finished, he'd be back to the ruined soufflé. "Why were you working on a soufflé, Gus? We were doing Baked Alaska for dessert." *Were* being the operative word. God, that was a phone call she did *not* want to make.

"It is not for dessert." Gus pulled his bulk up a little straighter on the stool. "I, Giuseppe Sorcio, will donate my expertise to the highest bidder at the auction. The soufflé is but a taste of what I will create for the winner."

Except that Reese wouldn't want to have anything to do with this place once she told him.

She pinched the bridge of her nose, hoping to stave off both the headache and the tears. But what else could she do? Madeleine held all the cards.

Bella sucked in a breath. She'd deal with Madeleine later. "Okay, then let's get this cleaned up. Come on, I'll help you. Bruno, why don't you take the rest of the day off? Get to work on the van. I can handle the restaurant until Aunt Theresa comes in. Her daughter is helping out today, anyway so she can bus the tables."

"Thanks, Ms. C. I will." Bruno slunk out the door, avoiding Gus like the plague.

Giac poked his head in the back. "Is Drew's order ready? And what about this guy's lemonade? Madeleine looks sour enough to provide the lemon."

If he only knew how true that statement actually was.

Bella poured the lemonade and took Drew's plate from Gus. "I'll be back in a jiffy to help you clean up."

Gus shook his head. "No, you have enough to do with that woman. Just go be your charming self and I'll handle this."

Frankly, she'd rather scrape the pumpkin off the oven door than deal with Madeleine, but she also didn't want to leave her alone with Mr. Fiorello too long. Lord only knew what she'd tell him.

Except when she went back out, Mr. Fiorello was nowhere to be found.

"Where'd he go?"

Madeleine whipped around so fast, the air buzzed. "You and your… your… *heathens* chased him off. Do you know how long it's taken me to get him here? He's been dangling on my real estate agent's hook for months now and I finally manage to reel him in and you and that… that… *beast* back there have undone everything I've worked for.

Don't think it'll save you, Lucinda. I meant it: get rid of Reese or I get rid of Sophia."

"I heard you, Madel—"

"Pardon me, madam." Mr. Griff seemed to materialize out of nowhere and tapped her stepmother on the shoulder.

Poor guy probably had no idea how dangerous an action that was.

Madeleine glared at him. "I don't believe this concerns you, sir." Ice could have formed with her tone.

"But you'd be wrong, madam."

Hmm, the little guy had a backbone—one Madeleine would make it her business to sever if he hung around much longer.

"Hi, Mr. Griff." Bella stepped in to ward off the eruption simmering beneath Madeleine's surface. "I see you've met my stepmother, Madeleine Fontaine Casteleoni. Madeleine, this is Mr. Griff. He's opened a shoe store in the old Colantonio place." She wrapped her arm around the man's shoulders to steer him toward a booth. "What can I get for you today, Mr. Griff?"

Mr. Griff wasn't budging. "Actually, Bella, I'm in the mood to celebrate. I've been awarded a seat on the City Council as the merchant liaison to the Chamber of Commerce."

"Congratulations. You'll be representing all of the business on Main Street, then." She cleaned off one of the tables, sticking a discarded napkin into her apron pocket. A couple of coins fell out. She wished he'd sit down so he'd be away from Madeleine.

He slid into the booth. "And I'll have the ear of all the town dignitaries."

"Dignitaries?" Madeleine leaned onto the edge of the booth, all traces of her earlier disdain and condescension gone.

Bella should have guessed that would be a subject near and dear to Madeleine's cold, dead, calculating heart.

Her stepmother slid into the booth. "Do tell me all about it."

The poor guy did not deserve this. Bella set the lemonade down. "Madeleine, perhaps you should——"

"You know, I wouldn't mind one of Gus's specials if you have it, Bella," said Mr. Griff.

"Sorry, but there's no special today." Unless he wanted to scrape it out of the oven.

"Well then, I'd love a cup of your potato soup, if you wouldn't mind."

If Bella didn't know better, she'd think Mr. Griff was trying to get rid of *her*.

"Yes, Lucinda dear, why don't you bring this nice gentleman a cup of soup?"

Madeleine, on the other hand, *definitely* was.

Mr. Griff smiled at her and nodded back toward the kitchen. Bella hung out for another few seconds, fingering the coins in her apron. Either Mr. Griff was utterly clueless, or he had more grit than she gave him credit for.

She just prayed he knew what he was doing.

# Chapter Twenty-Four

Jonathan Griff held back his smile as he watched Madeleine try to reign in her social aspirations. She was far too self-involved to pull off the sycophantic façade she was attempting. Even without his Guardian insight, he could see right through her.

If it were up to him, he'd *poof* her off to some little deserted island with a palm tree, three coconuts, and an army of angry sand crabs, and make his job that much easier. But that went against every tenet in the Guardian handbook and The Boss had ingrained in him the belief that there was goodness to be found in everyone if one looked hard enough.

Well, he was looking, but he'd yet to find Madeleine's. So, he let her say her piece and contemplated what role her absolution would play in the Grand Scheme.

"I utterly adore the patrons of our establishment," Madeleine cooed as she fiddled with the pearls around her neck.

One of the first lessons of Guardian training: nervous twitching usually signified the beginnings of a lie. Madeleine was a textbook example.

"They are part of the family." Madeleine waved at Rosa Angelelli with a smile faker than a two dollar bill. "Hello, Mrs. Andretti."

Jonathan bit his lip and shook his head when Rosa raised her eyebrows.

Ah, Rosa… She'd been a challenge in her youth, but, Lord love her——and He did——the dear girl never forgot a face. Or how to keep a secret. Her nephew, bless him, was turning out to be as much of a challenge as his aunt. But Joey was a project for another time.

"How is it that you were chosen to represent the merchants?" The slit of white between her lips was Madeleine's newest attempt at sincerity. "I thought you were new to our community."

"New? No, I'm afraid not. I've been coming here a lot longer than you've been around, my dear woman."

Sure enough, Madeleine preened. Ah, vanity. It ought to be the eighth deadly sin.

"But why I haven't seen you?"

Because she never saw past the end of her nose. "Well, I've been travelling for a bit, and I did just open the shop."

"I'm just surprised that they've elected someone so newly arrived to such a prestigious post. Why, you'll be meeting with every decision-maker in the city, and at some rather impressive gatherings. I can't imagine that you'll be able to remember everyone's names and positions so quickly. Are you certain you'll be able to represent our merchants adequately?"

Her fake smile wasn't a buffer for the sentiment behind her oh-so-innocuous words. Jonathan had to reach deep within his heart to locate the forgiveness he knew The Boss would want him to find.

He also had to find some forgiveness for Giovanni for bugging out early. Not everyone liked every Charge, but it was still a Guardian's duty to work on their behalf.

"My dear lady, I've always found people to be quite generous. Haven't you? Until someone removes the reason for that trust, that is." Jonathan sat up straighter. Thank heavens the words he needed were coming to him. Wasn't it always the way? About the time he didn't know what to say, he'd think about The Boss and then he'd come up with just the thing. "I gave the folks here my word that I'd do my best by them and they put their faith in me. Now all I have to do is make sure that trust isn't misplaced."

"Well, yes, of course, but I still am surprised that the guild has trusted you with this responsibility when I've—I mean, *Casteleoni's* has been such a predominant part of this neighborhood for so many years."

There was a reason Pride was on that deadly sins list.

"Perhaps, it's not the length of one's service that counts, but the quality of it."

Madeleine fell against the back of the booth, her *hauteur* finally knocked sideways.

Jonathan resisted the urge to grin. Guardians didn't gloat. But he was rather pleased that he'd given her something to think about other than her favorite topic—herself. Madeleine always forgot to take into account the other lives she was affecting and it was time she was reminded of them.

Just then, Bella swung through the saloon doors carrying his soup. Jonathan smiled at Madeleine; nothing killed like kindness. "Would you like to join me, madam?"

Madeleine scrambled from his booth as he'd known she would. She'd never eat "peasant" food again; she'd worked too hard to settle for that. Which was fine with him—and the very reason he'd offered.

"Er, thank you, no." It took her all of two seconds to remember who she was pretending to be. Then one hand slicked back the hair and the other went straight for the pearls. He'd always found the amount of atonement one needed was directly proportional to the fidgeting one did. Madeleine's fidget was off the charts. "Perhaps another time."

Jonathan inclined his head, willing to let her stew on his words. Maybe he'd done some good with them. One never knew.

But then she blew it when Bella set his soup down.

"Don't forget to make that phone call, Lucinda." Her tone could have frosted his glass of lemonade.

Bella's lips clamped shut and if he weren't mistaken she had to blink back a few tears. "Don't worry, Madeleine. There's no way in the world I'll ever forget it."

"See that you don't."

With a last-minute almost-gracious smile tossed his way, Madeleine sashayed out of the restaurant.

"Don't let her get to you, Bella."

Okay, perhaps that was overstepping his bounds as a neighborhood shopkeeper, but as her Guardian, Jonathan couldn't stand to see Bella lose that sparkle in her eye.

"Madeleine wants to sell the restaurant."

"No!" The woman couldn't give up that easily; it wasn't in her character. At least, not unless someone with a big bank account came along—and Giovanni definitely wasn't that someone.

"She's been threatening to, and now she actually brought someone, a Mr. Fiorello, in to look at the place."

"Ah." Jonathan would love to tell her the truth, but Guardians weren't permitted to reveal either the Grand Scheme or another Guardian's identity. Still, he tried to do the best he could within the confines of his position. "I'm sure it's nothing, Bella. She likes her position as the Widow Casteleoni. She's not going to sell out." At least, not to Giovanni. Which was the reason he was pretending to be so interested; if Madeleine thought he was on the hook, she wouldn't be looking for another buyer. Jonathan just hoped another buyer didn't come along. That pesky Free Will The Boss was such a big proponent of could screw up many a plan.

She cleared her throat. "I hope you're right, Mr. Griff."

"I am. You'll see. Everything will be all right in the end."

It was the getting there that was going to be the problem.

Still, he was glad to see the light return to her eyes.

The Boss knew, she and Reese were going to need that light because it was always darkest just before the dawn.

# Chapter Twenty-Five

Bella's finger hovered over Reese's number. She didn't want to make this call. She ought to stand up to Madeleine. Tell her no.

If it weren't for Sophia, she would. She would cut her losses and start over somewhere new, out from under the woman's tyrannical thumb. But she just couldn't leave her sister.

She took a deep breath. This wasn't going to be as bad as she was imagining. As long as Reese had a caterer, he'd be happy, right? And Jolie had worked for her; it wasn't as if Bella was leaving him in a lurch.

But what was she going to tell him? He'd want to know why.

She couldn't tell him the truth. That her stepmother wanted to ruin his event so his mother wouldn't get on the Board and Madeleine could.

It was all so pathetic. *Madeleine* was pathetic. But what did that make *her* for going along with it?

Desperate.

Out of options.

God, Bella hated this feeling. She'd been drowning in it for the past ten years and it wasn't showing any signs of going away. And, now, by cancelling the job, she was guaranteeing it never would because no one would ever hire Casteleoni's for an event like this once word got out.

Which meant she was going to have to put up with Madeleine's machinations until Sophia came of age.

Ah, well, she'd been dealing with it for ten years, what was another eight?

A lifetime, that's what.

Hers.

***

Reese was having a devil of a time. The destination management company he'd hired for the conference had sent incompetents. Two of the Meet-and-Greet staff looked like they were just out of high school and the woman running registration had left her alphabetical knowledge at home that morning. Consequently, the conference attendees were five deep in the registration lines and backing up quickly. To top it all off, the civic association's president, the man who'd hired him, was a huge football fan and kept demanding Reese's presence at one gathering or another.

It was an odd time to think of Bella.

Or maybe not. The hotel conference planner *did* have the same shade of hair. That the planner was a guy was irrelevant. And he'd swear the maitre d's name was Isabella. It didn't matter that the woman was fifty years old, African-American, and shorter than that little old man who's spilled his money at the park. She made him think of Bella. *Everything* made him think of Bella.

And the fact that she'd turned him down.

He looked around at the chaos he was managing in the "war room" at the hotel, where the members of his temporary staff gathered to get their assignments, check in, drop off supplies, and generally touch base with him and each other. Where everything was coming together without his client being aware of any glitches. At least something in his life was working out.

"Matt got the VIPs in," Debra, the tour operator, informed him as she ran into the room.

Reese checked that item off his list. He'd had his doubts about Matt—especially when he'd seen Jennifer hopping into the limo to "assist" with the pick-up. But a last-minute switch in the reception venue required everyone to pitch in and re-do the set-up in the new location, so he'd had to put that one in the hands of Fate and pray for the best.

From the little smile on Jennifer's face, it looked as if it'd worked out... for her.

He just hoped it did for him because he knew all about on-location romances. They didn't always work out for the best.

Okay, so maybe Bella had been smart to put an end to whatever he'd wanted to start between them before it'd begun. But they were going to talk when this auction was over. He hadn't gotten to where he'd been in his career by letting other people decide his life for him and even though he was seriously thinking about wanting to share his life with her, he wasn't going to sit back now. She better have a damn good reason for calling it quits between them.

His phone rang. "Charmant."

"Reese? It's Bella."

Talk about serendipity.

"Hang on a sec." He gave Debra a few last minute instructions, then headed out to the hallway to take the call. "Hey, what's up? Everything on target for next week?"

"About that."

Her tone caused his stomach to bottom out. "What?"

"There's been… That is, there's a problem."

His stomach headed to his knees. "What kind of problem?"

"I… That is, Casteleoni's… We…"

"What, Bella? What's going on? Did the place burn down? Are you injured? What?" He could only imagine what'd put that defeatist tone in her voice, and he had a vivid imagination.

"We can't do the event."

But he hadn't imagined *that*.

"What do you mean you *can't*? We're a week and a half out. The food's ordered. Why can't you?"

"There's a conflict."

There sure was. "What is it? How can we resolve it?"

"We can't. I have to back out of the event. I'm sorry. I know it's not the best timing, but I've got someone else lined up for you. She used to work with me. She's good. Everything will be fine. I promise."

"You also promised to handle the event, so excuse me if I'm not all that excited about your promise." He bit back a curse. "Does this have anything to do with me kissing you?" He should have stuck to his fucking rule and kept his goddamn paws—and lips—to himself. "Because, seriously, I promise it won't happen again. You were right; I was wrong. Can't we just go forward?"

"Reese, it doesn't have anything to do with that. It's just… I just can't. Like I said, there's a conflict and this is the best way I know to resolve it."

"Tell me what that conflict is. I can help."

"I'm sorry. In this, you really can't."

She took a breath and Reese could swear it quivered. If that were the case, what in the hell was so wrong that she couldn't do the job? That she couldn't even tell him?

"I'll have Jolie get in touch with you soon. She's really good, Reese. You won't even know the difference."

The hell he wouldn't.

# Chapter Twenty-Six

I still don't understand why you're letting Madeleine get away with this." Jolie Gardener took the menu cards Bella had set on the bar top and stacked them neatly on the spot she'd just wiped down on her latest clients' pool bar. "You have to take a stand."

Bella slid onto the stool. It'd been less than twelve hours since she'd quit and her stomach was in knots. Quitting went against every professional ethic she had, not to mention every grain of hope in her soul. "Don't you think I know that? But she's serious about Sophia this time. I can't risk it."

"That's why you should. Can't you see? She does this to you all the time. If there's something she wants or doesn't like or needs, she threatens Sophia and you jump. What if, just once, you didn't?" Jolie stopped wiping the granite and pointed her cloth-covered finger at her. "What if she actually had to go through with it? Do you really think she will? She'll lose her bargaining chip."

"There's no bargaining going on."

"Exactly my point. She's got you running scared. But now you have something she wants. You have the opportunity to help out a charity, do a good job for an up-and-coming firm in the city, and make a name for yourself. Not to mention his name. Does she really think Reese isn't going to do whatever it takes to get someone to pull this off? She's delusional if she thinks he's going to let it fail just because you back out. He's got too much to lose, and I don't mean his mother getting the Board position." She tucked her cloth into her chef coat and took the crystal glasses out of the box on the bar and began washing them for the afternoon luncheon Mrs. Kellan was hosting. "No, whatever Madeleine's convoluted rationalization for her idiotic demand, *you're* the one in control now."

Bella grabbed a dishtowel and started drying. "Don't you think

I've run this through my mind a zillion times? It's all I can think about." Well, that and Reese. There was something between them and, dammit, she wanted to explore it.

So did he, but because of Madeleine, they couldn't. It was so tempting to listen to Jolie and throw Madeleine's plan back in her face. If it were just the bakery at stake, maybe she would. But they were bargaining with Sophia. She couldn't take that risk.

*Or maybe she could...*

She set a champagne flute down. "Okay, how about this? What if I tell Madeleine you're handling it, but I still do it? I'll take Casteleoni's name off everything so she won't know, but behind the scenes, I'll still be working the event. That way I won't have to let Reese down and I can buy myself more time."

Jolie took the flute and put it in the glass-fronted cabinets on the wall behind her. "I guess, but you have to take credit the night of the event. You want to get your name out, this is *the* event of the season, and seriously... Does she *really* think that Reese's event is going to seal the deal as far as his mother getting that Board position is concerned? I mean, there's already talk of naming a park after the woman. She *is* Hollywood royalty after all. Local girl done really really good. The whole world's in love with Carolyn Charmant. The only place Madeleine is any competition to her is in her own mind."

"You know that and I know that, but Madeleine will never admit it. She'll take it out on Sophia. That's why I have to be discreet."

"She's not going to do anything to Sophia, Bella. Think about it." Jolie wagged one of the wine glasses at her. "There's no way Madeleine's going to get the Board position. None. No matter what you do. Everyone can see through her and even if Carolyn weren't in the running, do you really think those people couldn't find someone else to offer that position to? Madeleine's deluding herself."

"But she'll blame it on me and Sophia will suffer."

"For how long? She said herself that she won't be able to hold her head up in this town. That she'll move away. She's not going to want to drag a stepdaughter along with her. My money's on you getting custody of Sophia without a battle."

"You think so?"

"Trust me. I've been through the court system. With you, Sophia has a family member who loves her, wants her, and with all the jobs you'll get from the auction, will able to afford her. The courts will never deny you custody." Jolie scooped up the menu cards and handed them back to Bella. "I can guarantee it."

***

"What do you mean, you don't want to see me anymore?" Luke stared at Staci. They'd spent every night since dinner together—though not in the way he'd wanted to. Staci had said they'd had to talk. To get to know each other. It'd shocked the shit out of him that he'd actually enjoyed it. "What's going on, Stace?"

Staci's eyes flickered to a spot somewhere on the wall to his left.

Luke grabbed her chin and forced her to face him. Oh, no, she did not get to do this. Not when he'd finally found someone who wanted more from him than his celebrity and a roll in the hay. Or, at least, he thought she had. Now, he wasn't so certain.

But, dammit! He was a man with more than a little experience with women. He knew when one was interested. She had been—and if the pulse fluttering in her throat was any indication, she still was. Her announcement just didn't make sense.

"Tell me what's going on."

She looked up at him and he groaned. Somewhere along the line in her makeover, she'd gone from hard and tacky to luscious and desirable. And those eyes, swirls of smokey gray/green with gold flecks near the pupils, did him in. "Tell me where I screwed up."

"You didn't do anything, Luke." She smiled, but there was no happiness in it. "It's something I have to do. I can't tell you why, but you need to trust me and let it go. I can't see you anymore. It's over."

He yanked his hand from her skin and raked it through his hair. "Just like that? You're willing to walk away from whatever it is that's kept us from pulling each other's clothes off and rolling around like a pair of horny teenagers to spend time talking and getting to know each other? Staci, we both know there's nothing either of us would rather do than get naked together, but we've taken our time here. We've had hours of conversation and really gotten to know each other. There's something more than just physical attraction between us. I know it and I know you know it. How can you let it go?"

To his utter surprise, tears filled her eyes. Why was she crying?

163

She was the one breaking up with him. He would expect tears if he were doing the breaking up. God knows, he was the authority on women's break-up tears.

"What is it?" For once in his life he was actually concerned about a woman's thoughts, her feelings. A totally foreign concept.

"I have to or someone's going to get hurt."

Ah… *That*, he was familiar with.

He slid his hands up her arms. "Staci, I'll try not to hurt you, I promise. I realize I don't have the best track record, but I'll try not to hurt you."

He could fix this. She just wanted out before her heart got battered. It was a good strategy on her part, 'cause like he'd said, he didn't have the best rep with women. But then, he'd never met one he liked as much as Staci. He'd even thought about introducing her to Jared.

"It's not me, Luc," she explained. "It's a little girl. You need to trust me and let it go. Maybe later, in a few months perhaps, we can try this again, but, for now, you just need to let go."

"What little girl? Who are you talking about? I don't even know a little girl."

Staci pulled away from his grip then touching his cheek and gently stroked through his hair, her smile bittersweet. "I know you don't. But I do. And I can't hurt her more than I already have. So we have to let it go." Then she twisted his heart. "Please."

He knew the value of that word. Knew, too, the strength of love one could feel for a child. Hadn't he uttered that very same word for the very same reason to Reese not that long ago?

He'd have to do as she asked. But he didn't have to like it.

# Chapter Twenty-Seven

R eese hung up the phone and kneaded the back of his neck as Jake entered his office. It'd been one thing after another during the last meeting and it hadn't stopped since he'd gotten back.

"Trouble?" Jake asked, dropping into the chair in front of his desk.

"I hope not." Yeah, he had troubles, but not the kind Jake was asking about. He was still trying to come to terms with Bella quitting on him. It'd been an intrusion he hadn't needed on his trip and he had yet to come up with a solution. She'd said she had someone for him; he hoped to God whoever it was was good. And that it wasn't Staci.

"What does that mean?"

He'd save the new caterer discussion for later. "I got Coach Meade to agree to participate in the auction."

"You're shitting me."

It wasn't often Reese could surprise Jake and if it weren't for the other little "bomb" he had to drop on him, he'd enjoy the moment. "I played up the charity angle. The goodwill for the team."

Jake's eyes narrowed. "Shrewd. But why? You want that pressure? Everyone's going to be watching the two of you. Especially after what happened at Connie's."

Reese shrugged, the knot still tight in his neck. He was living with pressure these days. Of all kinds. "I'm a professional and so's Coach. Speculation has died down."

He hoped. But it was time to fix the relationship, if at least publicly. Reese hoped it would be privately, too. He'd moved on; Devin had, too. Now Coach needed to as well. They'd had a lot of great times before he'd dated Devin, made a lot of memories, great highlights-reel-type stuff. Their names and careers were forever linked and it'd be nice to hear that collaboration mentioned without the inevitable "before things soured between them" rhetoric every single damn time. Plus, it was for a good cause.

"Okay, so since you're in a fence-mending mood," said Jake, "what about asking our caterer's husband to participate? He *is* a local-boy-made-good after all, and a hell of a draw. Whatever your personal feelings, it'd be a great coup for the hospital and sure to bring in more money."

"Actually," Reese stepped around his desk, "he's not her husband."

"What?"

That made it twice today he'd shocked Jake. One for the history books. "He's her uncle."

"So why did you think he was her husband?"

"Long story. Full of misunderstandings."

"Not her husband…" Jake stroked his jaw. "Please tell me you're not thinking of hitting on her."

Reese checked the fist he'd unconsciously formed before it connected with Jake's jaw. "*Hit on*? What are we, sixteen?" He didn't want to *hit on* Bella; he wanted to spend time with her, get to know her. Take it to a new level. One he hadn't with Devin.

She, however, didn't.

"You can't fault me for asking, Reese. I've got a lot invested in this business."

Reese took his time with his answer because he wanted to punch the shit out of Jake.

After spending years being an *investment* by the team's owner, Reese hated being reminded that he was where he was due to someone else's backing. Sure, he'd performed for the team, but when the Devin situation had erupted on the PR end, he'd gotten hauled into the front office and called for it.

Jake's argument wasn't the same, but the fact that he'd felt the need to go there pissed Reese off. He had just as invested as Jake. More, with his name splashed all over the place, a conscious marketing decision the two of them had decided together.

And then there was the matter of the other part of him that was invested. Bella had touched his heart—and squeezed.

Kelly buzzed him on the intercom. "Bella Casteleoni to see you, Reese."

And there went the squeezing all over again. What the hell was she doing here?

Reese exhaled, getting his emotions under control; he'd need them to be to talk with Bella. "Send her in, Kelly."

Jake arched an eyebrow.

"You can stay and watch your *investment* in action if you'd like."

Jake stood and headed for the door. "Not necessary. I trust you to do the right thing."

That was the problem. What was right for Reese might not be right for their company. It wouldn't have been a problem given that she'd quit on him, but now that she was here…

When this auction was over, they were going to have a nice long talk.

Then she walked in, casual in jeans and a t-shirt that hugged her body like he wanted to, and talking was the last thing he wanted to do.

Reese cleared his throat, pushed off the desk, and stuck out his hand at an attempt at normalcy. "Bella."

In that attempt, however, he'd made no preparation for the feel of her skin on his and her touch sparked a fire that made him burn.

"Hi, Reese." She gnawed on her bottom lip and that action alone made him burn even more.

"What are you doing here? I thought you quit."

She winced. "I deserve that."

He didn't answer. She did.

"I wanted to apologize."

"An apology isn't going to fix it. You said you had someone in mind? She's good, I take it?"

"She is, but she's…"

Great. Something else to stress him out. "She's what?"

"She's me."

"Come again?"

Bella nibbled her bottom lip again and this time it had no effect on Reese whatsoever. The woman had him so tied up he couldn't react because every reaction he had seemed to be the wrong one.

"I'd like to come back. Do the auction."

Music to his ears, but suspicious nonetheless. "Why?"

"Because I said I'd do the job."

"What about your conflict?"

"It's not the conflict I thought it was."

She'd turned him inside out for *not a conflict*? Hell, he was right: stay away from people he worked with. Period.

But then she tilted her head and a sheaf of corn silk hair slid over her shoulder and down her arm, caressing her skin like he wanted to—

*Mind on the job, Charmant.* "There's a little over a week left. Am I going to have to worry about you doing this again? Right now I might be able to find someone. Three days out, I'll be stuck."

She winced again. "I deserve that, I know. But no, I promise I will not back out on you. And I'm sorry for doing it in the first place." She held out her hand. "Okay?"

He shouldn't take it. He shouldn't touch her. Hell, he shouldn't even be in the same room with her.

But he took her hand and shook it.

And then he went and made matters worse.

It was just supposed to be a little kiss. Just a nibble, really.

Her hand had slid into his, he'd felt the sizzle rocket through his veins, and he'd tugged her against him.

In his defense, she'd gone willingly.

She'd even tilted her head up willingly.

And when he'd covered her lips with his, she'd clenched his side *very* willingly.

After that, he'd been lost.

It didn't matter that this wasn't a good idea. It didn't matter that she'd quit on him. It didn't matter that they had a tenuous working relationship and both of them had their reasons for keeping their distance.

Right now, none of that mattered because she tasted even better than she looked. And she felt… There were no words for the feeling of her curves plastered against him, soft where he was hard—so very hard—her body yielding against his, the sound of her groan almost undoing him.

He absorbed it as he tried to absorb every part of her, as unable to stop kissing her as he was to stop breathing.

And when she parted her lips to let him in, he couldn't *not* sweep in and taste her. Reality would come later; right now, this was a dream. A moment out of time.

He cupped her head with one hand, held her against him with the other. Met her tongue when it stroked his and danced with it. She tasted of mint and buttery croissants and something solely her own.

He tilted her jaw with his thumb then, his fingers spanning her neck. Her pulse jumped against it in rhythm with his. Her hair skimmed the back of his hand, as soft and silky as he'd imagined, and he ran his fingers through the strands, imagining it streaming over his chest, his stomach…

Desire, fierce and hot, slammed through him, and he wrapped his arms around her, turning to back her up against his desk.

But then Kelly buzzed him on the intercom. "Reese, Coach is on line three."

Coach. Devin. The mess he'd made of things…

Sanity wiggled its way into their kiss and Reese ended it. Reluctantly.

He did take great satisfaction in the shudder that rippled through her, but it took her less than ten seconds to shut down. He didn't want to take the damn call.

"You should answer that." She turned to leave, but he grabbed her arm.

"Coach can wait. Talk to me, Bella."

"It's nothing, Reese." She wouldn't look at him.

"I'm not going to apologize for kissing you."

She looked at him then, and man, he wished she hadn't. There was such sadness in her eyes.

"It was a mistake."

Kelly buzzed him again.

Reese jabbed the button. "Kel, tell Coach I'll call him back." Then he shut the damn thing off. "Like hell it was a mistake. You can't tell me you don't feel what's between us, Bella."

"It doesn't matter. It *can't* matter." She wrapped her arms around herself and turned away again. "I should have just called you and told you instead of coming over here. There can't be anything between us."

His knees hadn't given way during that kiss, but her words threatened to take them out from under him, so he leaned against his desk. "There already is something, Bella. You were as involved in that kiss as I was."

"Okay, so, maybe there's an attraction—"

"There's no maybe about it." He refrained from proving it to her. Barely. "Is there someone else?"

She started to shake her head, then stopped. Her blue eyes flickered toward him, then away. "Yes. There's someone else."

"I don't believe you."

She straightened her shoulders and smoothed her hands over her shorts. "You don't have to believe me. Not about this. All you have to believe is that I'll prepare the best food for your event to make it a success. But anything else is out of the question."

# Chapter Twenty-Eight

ella shut her bedroom door behind her, seeking a few moments of peace before Sophia would be home. With Madeleine around, there was rarely any.

She leaned against her pink fluffy robe, trying to recapture the serenity she always found in her room. The decor hadn't changed much since she and Mom had chosen the sunshine yellow paint on the walls and the rainbow patchwork quilt that summer before Sophia had been born. They'd had the most wonderful few weeks selecting paint and accessories for this room and the nursery. Everything had been right with her world.

Then.

Bella flopped onto the bed. Everything since? Definitely not right.

And now there was Reese to complicate matters.

She put her fingers on her lips, still able to feel him there. If it hadn't been for that phone call, God knew how long they would have continued.

He'd looked surprised when she'd pulled away. He'd also looked delicious, but she had to forget that and everything else she found appealing about him.

She'd tried the relationship thing a few times, once even talking about moving in with her boyfriend. That had been when boarding school brochures had begun appearing on the coffee tables.

The woman would have a fit if she actually got involved with Reese.

Madeleine was going to be unbearable when his mother got the Board position. Jolie was absolutely right on that front. The best Bella could do was be as innocent as possible when the fall-out hit.

But here, in her room, she could allow herself to imagine that things were different. That she and Reese could examine their attraction without threats or manipulations hovering over their heads.

She stared at the ceiling and tossed her hands back over her head. Something clinked. Mr. Griff's coins. Sophia must have left them there.

She sifted through them, letting them fall onto her chest, each one like a tear falling onto her heart. Other people worked and raised children as single parents; if only she could.

She closed her fist over the coins. But other people weren't fighting Madeleine.

She softly thumped her fist against her chest. No. Such. Thing. As. Fairy. Tales.

Or Prince Charming.

***

Jonathan Griff sat on the park bench outside Reese's office building and tapped the iTouch screen to close out the image of Bella in her room. Just a little longer then Bella could have her happily ever after.

# Chapter Twenty-Nine

O h, let's see, Gus! Don't be such a spoilsport!" Perla teetered on her high-heeled sandals and ran to Casteleoni's lunch counter, her bangle bracelets clanging like a drunken percussion section after he'd made the mistake of telling her that Gus had made something special for Bella. He should have known the woman would hound his partner until Gus gave in.

Unfortunately for Perla, Gus had no intention. Giac had tried it himself.

"This gift is for my Bella, Perla." Gus tapped her on the nose. "Not you. Only she can open it."

"He won't even show me," said Giac. "Says Bella's the one who gets to see it first."

Perla harrumphed and settled on a stool next to him. Giac covered his laugh with his hand. She acted like she was six instead of sixty. But she was a good woman and really cared for their Bella.

As did the rest of their regular customers. Giac surveyed the restaurant as nostalgia swept over him. They'd watched Bella grow up here, from a happy-go-lucky cherished little princess to an overworked, overly responsible serving girl.

Which was not what Sal and Ana had envisioned for her. But Giac could think of no way to alter the status quo.

The door chimes tinkled as Reese walked in.

Hmmm...perhaps there *was* a way to change Bella's situation. Maybe, if they played their cards right, Bella just might end up with the winning hand. *And* Prince Charming.

Giac slid off the stool and walked over to the newest player in the Casteleoni saga.

"Hello, Reese. Bella's not in yet today. Last minute details, I'm sure." Giac guided Reese further into the restaurant. He didn't want the guy to bolt before he had a chance to work on him, er, talk to him. "Why don't you have a seat over here and I'll get you an early lunch."

"Thanks, Giac, but I'm meeting someone. She should be here any minute." Reese helped himself to a table.

*Meeting someone?* Well, that threw Giac for a loop. He shoved his hands to his hips and felt his mouth fall open. Was the man completely blind to Bella's feelings?

*Meeting someone?* The nerve of that no-good, two-timing, stuck-on-himself, son-of-a-gun! And to bring her around *here!* Why, Giac'd show him! When he was through with Reese, the man would be squeaking like a mouse in a trap. Who did he think he could get that was better than their Bella? Probably some high-maintenance, Miss Richie Rich Pants with more money than sense who—

"Reese, darling."

Giac spun around. *Oh.*

"Hi, Mom," said Reese.

Giac closed his mouth, dropped his fists, and plastered the most welcoming smile on his face he could muster.

The guy took his mother to lunch. Sheesh! He just flew to the top of Giac's list as Most Eligible Man for Bella.

"Giac, this is my mother, Carolyn—"

"Carolyn Charmant, yes I know." Giac swept into a bow over the movie star's hand, placing a reverent kiss upon the back of it. "Welcome to Casteleoni's. It is such a pleasure to have you join us. I've seen every one of your films. I must say, my particular favorite was your first Camelot film. That dress you wore in the coronation scene was to die for! It must have weighed a ton! And you looked so regal in it. So effortless. Truly a wonderful piece of work."

Carolyn laughed and extricated her hand. "Why, thank you. It's always nice to meet a fan."

"See, Mom? I told you you wouldn't have to worry about being embarrassed."

Giac shut down the gushing. "Oh, my apologies. I'm so sorry. I'll just seat you right over there where you'll be out of the—"

"Oh, no. You misunderstood." Carolyn patted his arm and Giac decided he was not going to let Gus wash his sleeve ever. This shirt would be framed and hung next to the autographed program from Tony Orlando's last dinner theater show. "My son has talked me into donating something for the hospital event. He seems to think there's a great demand, but I wasn't sure."

"I'm sure it will be one of the most bid-upon items at the auction." Giac would make sure of it. *And* that he won it.

"See, Mom?" Reese said as Giac headed back into the kitchen. "You still have that star quality. I tell you, your donation is going to be a big hit."

His mother laughed. "I'm glad you still think of me as a star, but I'm afraid that shine has dimmed somewhat. I'm sure there'd be much more interest if you were donating something. Dinner and dancing? Or maybe just a kiss." She patted his hand. "The winner might be able to take your mind off that other man's wife."

Reese stared at his mother's hand on his, trying not to stare out the window for a glimpse of Bella. Why had he thought bringing his mom here would be a good idea? Getting shot down by Bella yesterday hadn't done enough damage to his ego? And his heart? But he wanted to see her again and this lunch was the perfect excuse. "She's not his wife."

"What?"

Reese glanced up to see his mother's surprised expression. "I guess I forgot to mention that. Bella's his niece, not his wife."

"His niece. Hmm. Interesting little tidbit to forget to tell me. I've been so worried about you, about how you would be dealing with your feelings and all the last-minute arrangements, but you forget to tell me this? You do know I had the Arts Center Board members rearrange their schedule to accommodate my visit today just for you, don't you?"

"Arts Center?"

She arched an eyebrow at him. "Don't try to change the subject, Reese. The Arts Center Board is considering asking me to be a member and we're going to discuss it this afternoon. But first, I want to find out about Bella."

"Mom." Reese sighed. "I'm a grown man. I don't need you to worry about my love life."

"Nonsense. You're my son. I'll worry about you forever. Especially your love life. And somebody has to worry about it or how will I get grandchildren?"

Worrying did not make babies. Reese knew *exactly* what did and for the first time in his life, he was actually thinking about it as a reality not an abstract. Which only added to the pain of Bella pulling away from him. "You already have six grandkids, Mom."

"I mean yours, dear."

"They're going to be a ways off. Right now, I've got this business to run. That's enough of a child for me at the moment."

His mother cocked her head and just looked at him. Reese started to squirm. Big words coming from him when he'd gone running to her with his doomed feelings for Bella. He rubbed the back of his neck.

"So, if she's his niece, why haven't you called her? Why the long face? I'd think you'd be jumping for joy that she's free."

Reese looked up. "It's complicated."

"Oh, honey. Now what?"

"Mom, you're talking to me like I'm ten."

His mother sat back, her lips pinched.

Reese sighed. "I'm sorry. This is more than some crush that a soda and a double scoop of ice cream can cure."

"I can see that. And I want to help in any way I can. I'm your mother; your happiness is important to me. It's one of the cardinal rules of parenting. We never outgrow it."

"I'm glad you're my mom." He meant the words. His was a close family, normal sibling spats aside, and they all knew they could count on each other. Which is why he'd shared his feelings for Bella with her. "But I have to handle this myself. There's nothing you can do."

"If you say so." She tapped the fork tines on her napkin.

"Mom, don't."

"Don't what?"

She could still guilt him into confessing his secrets even at his age. "Like I said, it's complicated. I can't risk my business by starting a relationship with someone who works for me. And Bella says the same thing." And that was the story he was sticking with. Not the fact that even though he'd kissed her, even though there was major chemistry between them, he apparently wasn't worth the risk.

First his heart, then his ego. Bella had shredded both of them. Yet still he couldn't get her out of his mind.

His phone vibrated in his pocket. Reese grabbed it, glad of the distraction, and his fingers brushed against some change he'd forgotten he had.

"So you've talked about a relationship?" Mom just wouldn't let up. "And you're both on the same page? Then it can work, Reese."

If only that were true.

# Chapter Thirty

Bella never did put in an appearance. Reese was on the fence about whether or not that was a good thing, but in the end, it didn't matter. The auction was tomorrow night; he'd see her then.

And afterwards… Afterwards was a whole other story.

He'd put his mother in a cab after lunch for her board meeting, then headed over to Luke's condo to "remind" him where he'd better be tomorrow night. He wasn't taking any chances with this event.

Luke opened the door beer in hand. And a couple more under his belt if the smell was any indication. "I'll be there tomorrow, Reese. Don't worry. You don't have to check up on me."

"Let me in." Reese pushed by Luke. "How many have you had?"

"Not enough."

From the looks of the place, Luke had had *more* than enough. Gym clothes flung over the sofa, empty beer cans tossed—and missed—at the trashcan, newspapers chucked onto the floor. "Something wrong?"

"Nah." Luke swayed around him, kicking at a beer can, then caught his balance with a hand on the flatscreen.

"Is it Tanya?"

"Hah!" Luke swung his foot again and would have fallen if Reese hadn't caught his arm. "No way could Tanya do this to me. Uh, uh." He shook his head like a dog after a walk in the rain.

Reese took the beer from Luke's hand and led him to the sofa, shoving the laundry onto the floor as they both sat.

"Thanks." Luke's cockeyed smile was as empty as the six-pack on the floor.

"What's going on, Luke? Is Jared okay?"

Luke waved the air as if he were swatting flies. "Sure. Fine. Never been better."

"Then what is it?"

Luke's sigh could probably be heard clear across the state. He closed his eyes and when he opened them, they were much clearer than they usually were after a six-pack and a half.

"Woman."

One word, so much angst. Reese could relate. "Staci?"

Another shuddering breath. "Yeah." Luke grimaced. "She broke it off."

"Oh."

"Yeah, 'oh.'" Luke sat forward, his elbows on his knees. "Who would've thought I could fall so fast? Not me, that's for sure. Love-'Em-and-Leave-'Em-Luke—that's me." This grin wasn't empty; it was full of self-derision. "Now I know what it feels like on the other side. And it stinks."

"I know what you mean."

Luke swung his head around to face Reese. "You, too?"

"Me, too."

"God, man, that's rough. I knew you had it bad for her, but I could have sworn she felt the same way about you."

"I was hoping the same thing, but she's throwing my own rule in my face. Keeping our professional relationship professional."

"And you've changed your mind?" That seemed to sober Luke up.

"The auction will be over after tomorrow." "

Luke shook his head. "Look at us. What a pair. Two of the most chased after guys in the NFL, sitting on my sofa, pining after two women." He flopped back next to Reese and flung his hands over his head, *thonking* against the wall. "I don't get it. Where'd we go wrong? Why is it that the ones who matter are the ones who won't fall all over us?"

"Beats me."

They sat there, silent.

"Bella said there's someone else."

"Ouch." Luke looked at him. "Staci said the same thing, only it's some kid."

"A *kid*?"

"Yeah, I know. Makes no sense to me."

But it might to Reese. With both Bella and Staci backing away from them, it might have something to do with Sophia. But what? And what the hell did he and Luke have to do with it?

"Do you think she meant Sophia?"

"Bella's sister?" Luke shrugged. "Beats me. I mean, yeah, Stace has been hanging with her, but what would dating me have to do with the kid?"

"Unless her mother thinks you're a bad influence."

Luke shrugged. "Anything's possible, I guess. But from what Staci's said, the woman doesn't have anything to do with the kid. Pawns her off on Bella or Staci and Drew all the time. She's got some big agenda to get on the Arts Center Board and is sashaying all over the place to get in people's good graces. Staci said it's kinda nauseating to watch her mother sucking up to the board members."

"The Arts Center Board?" Reese had barely heard of the organization yet today he'd heard about it twice.

"Apparently the woman thinks it's the height of society to be on the Board and now that there's an opening, she's lobbying for it."

The spot his mother was probably discussing right now with those very same members.

And suddenly everything fell into place. Bella quitting the event. Demanding that there be nothing between them.

"Madeleine's put them up to it." And the woman was using Sophia as a pawn.

"Why would she do that? It makes no sense."

"I'm not sure why, but it's got something to do with the Board." Reese's instincts on the playing field had never let him down and this felt like one big Hail Mary play on Madeleine's part. "She wants to be on it and my mother's getting an invitation to become a member as we speak. There's some connection, I'm just not sure what."

"From what Stace has said, the woman *is* a manipulative son of a bitch." Luke kicked a can out from under the sofa. "You know they call Bella Cindabella, don't you? Madeleine's taken her stepmother role to heart for years."

"I've heard that nickname." He smiled inwardly as he remembered the first time they'd met.

"You know what that means, don't you?"

That he was going to have some well-placed words with Madeleine Casteleoni. "What?"

"It means you get to play Prince Charming and ride in on your white horse to save the damsel in distress."

For once, Reese didn't mind the poking fun at his nickname—because that's exactly what he felt like doing as he got off Luke's sofa and headed out the door. If Madeleine was bullying Bella, he was going to put a stop to it.

Halfway down Luke's front path, Reese's cell phone rang. "What's up, Kelly?"

"There's a problem over at the hotel with the VIP suites. Jake's in a meeting with the NBA people, so I can't interrupt him. You might want to head over there."

Damn. Reese sighed and kneaded the muscles of his neck. "Right. I'll get on it." He snapped the phone shut and cursed. If this truly were a fairy tale, he'd have a fairy godmother swoop in and handle it so he could take care of Bella.

But it wasn't and this was his job. The situation with Bella would have to wait.

***

Mr. Griff popped out of his office in the shoe store and told the new girl to take the rest of the day off. After she left, Jonathan Griff pulled a long gold chain from beneath his shirt. Dangling at the end next to his St. Michael's medal was a key.

Chuckling, he approached the glass case at the front of the store and turned the lock. A small door levered open.

"It's about time to deliver these."

# Chapter Thirty-One

J ust an eensy weensy peek, Gus?" Perla looked like a just-coiffed Pomeranian begging for a doggy treat as she hung onto the pass-through window into Gus' kitchen. "I won't tell, I promise."

"No, no, *e* no." Gus slammed a pot with each word.

"What won't you tell, Perla?" Bella tapped the woman on the shoulder, apparently surprising them all with her arrival.

Perla spun around, her guilty grimace quickly replaced with a bright—fake—smile. "Oh, nothing, love. Absolutely nothing." Perla patted her teased hair and did a quick little two-step around Bella, back through the counter opening.

Bella looked from Perla to Gus. What were they up to?

"Hey, Gus. Everything you asked me to get is in my car. Someone parked in our spot and I had to park down the street. Please send Bruno out when he's free to bring it all in." Bella slipped an apron over her head.

"*Si,* but first you must come." Gus grabbed a brightly wrapped package from beneath his prep table and shrugged through the saloon-doors. His grin was as wide as his girth.

"What's that?" She smiled. This was what Perla was talking about. The woman liked to be the first to know.

Gus waved a finger. "Tomorrow you will make us proud. All of us. Your mama and papa, too, God rest their souls. You will make the *festa magnifica* and help the hospital. For this, I make you look *magnifica,* too." He clutched her chin and smacked a wet kiss on both cheeks. "This is for you."

Bella had a hard time undoing the bow as she struggled with the lump in her throat. The customers' applause wasn't helping matters.

"Hurry up, honey." Perla rushed back through the counter to her side.

Bella held up the package with the industrial-strength ribbon. "You want to help, Perla?"

"Love to, doll." Perla pushed past Mr. Campanale, and with one flick of a tangerine talon, removed the ribbon.

"The woman can get through any gift wrap in under twenty seconds," mumbled Harry.

Perla glared at him as she handed over the gift.

Bella lifted the lid and pulled back layers of rustling tissue paper. "Oh, Gus," she breathed, "it's beautiful."

Shimmering seafoam green fabric whispered along the tissue paper as she lifted a long dress from the box. The criss-cross bodice was sleeveless and the skirt had a long slit up the back. She'd have to rethink her shoe choice for tomorrow night because there would be no black waitress shoes for this masterpiece.

"Thank you, Gus." She kissed his cheek. "It's absolutely beautiful."

Gus patted her hand and, behind him, Giac wiped a tear "You'll look like a princess," he said.

"In this dress, I'll feel like one."

Gus seemed to be having a hard time putting his emotions into words. Perla, however, had no such problem. She petted Bella's skirt as if it were made of mink, and a calculating look came into her eye. She lunged at Gus, attaching herself to his arm.

"Gus, you've certainly outdone yourself with this. Simply extraordinary. Which is why I'd like to talk to you about a little outfit or two I could use for my trip to the beach this summer. You see, Francesca and I..." Perla led Gus into the kitchen to finagle a new summer line.

Bella laughed as she repacked the gown in its box. The downtown department stores would reap the benefits once Francesca got wind of Perla's plan because the sisters were in a constant battle to out-do each other.

Bella put the dress under the counter, away from ketchup bottles and salt shakers. When she stood, Mr. Griff was at the counter.

"Good afternoon, Bella."

"Hi, Mr. Griff. What can I get you?"

Jonathan smiled. This was the fun part of his job. "Actually, my dear, it's what *I* can get for *you*." He set the burgundy velvet box on the countertop. Raphael's golden bow shimmered in the sunlight streaming through the windows. "I have a gift for you. It's only a loan, and you'll understand why when you see what's inside, but—" He put his hand on hers when she went to open the box. "You have to wait until at least noon tomorrow to open it or I'll have to take it back. No earlier. Can you do that?"

There'd been a few over the years who hadn't been able to wait, but he was always pleased when his Charges proved him a good judge of character.

"I don't understand."

They rarely did. "I know, lass. And I can't explain it now. But what's inside this box is yours for only twelve hours, so you don't want to waste any time by opening it too soon. Trust me on this, okay?"

"Okay, Mr. Griff, I can do that."

He'd known her character was good. Just like he'd known it about Reese. He was definitely improving his Guardian skills.

"But on one condition," she said.

Or maybe not. "Condition? That's not how—er, that is, it's highly irregular."

"So is teasing me with a present I can't open until tomorrow." Her smile took the sting out of the admonition just as he would expect from someone of her character.

"Touché, my dear. All right, what's your condition?"

"That you don't leave me any more tips. You've overpaid enough to last the rest of our lives. If you want me to accept your gift you'll have to accept my condition."

Now that was a condition he could live with since Bella would no longer need his "tips." "Very well. I agree.

"Great. Then we're even." Bella held out her hand.

He shook it. *Even*? She didn't know the half of it. And that's how it should be for mortals. His job was to not let them suspect a thing about what he really was.

"Here, Bella." Mr. Campanale walked up to the counter and slid four quarters toward her. "I was a little short yesterday for your tip."

She captured his hand before he could move it away. "You don't need to do this, Mr. Campanale. Please, keep your quarters. Buy some flowers for Mrs. Campanale's resting place, and the next time you visit her, tell her they're from me, okay?"

Mr. Campanale had a tell-tale drop at the corner of his eye. "God bless you, my dear. God bless you."

Jonathan slid from his stool and glided toward the door, Mr. Campanale's benediction following him into the sunshine. "Not to worry, dear man," he whispered. "He already has."

***

"Your *mother* is the reason you broke up with me?" Luke stomped through Staci's kitchen after her. "Are we living in the Dark Ages? Your mother isn't some all-powerful ogre, Stace. She can't harm Sophia and get away with it. She can't control your life." Luke sighed. This, he could deal with.

Staci *shhhh*-ed him and pulled the patio door closed behind them. "I didn't mean she'll abuse her, Luke. Mother's not like that. But she will send the poor kid away. Raising another woman's child is definitely not something my out-for-number-one mother is capable of. And if I mess up what she's got going on, Sophia's the one who'll be most hurt. I can't do that to the sweet kid. She's lost so much already."

"You like kids?" Luke put his hands on her shoulders and squeezed. Dare he hope?

Staci shrugged, her laugh self-conscious. "Who'd have thought, right?" She shrugged out of his hold and walked to the edge of the patio where she toyed with a holly branch. "I've been spending some time with her and I really like her. The way she sees the world. Her trust." Staci shrugged. "It's refreshing and, in a way, makes me feel good about myself."

Luke tucked that little tidbit away for another time. "So, if we can somehow manage to get Madeleine on the Board, Sophia—and you— would be in the clear, right?"

Staci shook her head. "Only until next time, Luke. With Mother controlling two-thirds of Sal's estate, she's pulling the strings. She can make Bella dance to whatever tune she's playing. Me, too, if she ever finds out I care about Sophia."

Luke tapped his lip. He knew all about strategy—and that experience was about to come into play. "What if someone else were to pull *her* strings? Then *she'd* be the one dancing."

Staci finally smiled the first smile since she'd opened the front door. "What do you have in mind?"

"Why don't we get out of here and I'll fill you in?" Now that that misunderstanding was cleared up, Luke was ready to move in and stake his claim. Staci liked kids, had an unexpected altruistic side, and turned him on, along with having some depth and some smarts. And, oh yeah, cleavage. He *was* still a guy, after all.

"Okay, Luke. I'm all ears."

***

Staci tried to keep her hopefulness in check as Luke drove down by the riverfront. It wasn't fair that her mother had control of so many lives all by playing on people's emotions—emotions she obviously didn't have.

Luke pulled into his driveway in one of the high-end condo complexes and killed the engine. But he didn't open the door. Nor did he say anything. He just looked at her.

"What?" She fiddled with the hem of her shirt and glanced away.

Luke turned her to face him with a finger under her jaw. He traced it around to her chin then drifted it softly across her lips. "We can beat her, Stace." He brushed some hair from her face. "That is, if you want me to help."

She wanted so much more. But this was a start. "But Mother doesn't make idle threats, Luke. You don't know her."

"And she doesn't know me. You, however." He leaned closer. "I want *you* to know me very well."

The look he was giving her let her know *exactly* how he wanted to know her now, and oh, she wanted that, too. And if he could make Mother's threats disappear, she could.

Luke dropped his hand. "You're not another conquest for me, Staci."

"I sure as hell hope not." She deserved better. For the first time in her life, she finally realized—and believed—that she deserved better.

He slid his hand to her cheek and her heart skipped a beat as he looked deeply into her eyes just like she'd always wanted a man to do. But other men had only rarely taken the time to look higher than her collarbone.

"No. You're not. I like you, Stace. I really like you, and it's been a long time since I've liked a woman for who she is instead of what she looks like. Oh, don't get me wrong, I like how you look—hell, I love that—but this caring, nurturing, unselfish part of you… it… I…" He turned away.

This wasn't Luke, the arrogant, cocky football player. This was a vulnerable side Staci had only glimpsed when he'd mentioned his son. This was Luke who *wanted* her. Who *liked* her. Who saw something in her she needed desperately to believe was there.

"I need you, Stace," he whispered, his gaze burning into hers.

So much need; Staci knew it intimately.

"Let's go inside Luke," she whispered back.

"You're… you're sure?" Luke looked as if he'd just been given a gift but was afraid it was going to be snatched away.

She smiled and stroked his cheek. Gotta love the guy for giving her an out.

Her hand stilled. *Gotta love…*

Holy—

Staci swallowed. "Yes, Luke. I'm sure."

He recovered quickly after that. He was out the door, around to hers, and had it open before she could find the handle.

*Not* that she would have known what to do with it if she had… She loved him.

As if she were a fairytale princess, Luke offered her a hand out of the carriage, but when their fingers touched, it was so very real that Staci couldn't have let go even if she'd wanted to.

And, oh, she didn't.

Luke didn't either. Intertwining their fingers, he fumbled with his house key with his free hand while she held the screen door with hers. He finally turned the lock, shoved the door open, then kicked it shut behind them, tossing his keys onto the table with a clatter while tugging her toward the stairs on the far side of the living room.

Staci stumbled on something, their joined hands the only thing keeping her from going down.

She looked at what she'd tripped on. A crumpled t-shirt and a bag of chips. She looked around the room. Oh, man. He was a slob.

"Uh, sorry about the mess." A sheepish Luke was an endearing Luke. "I got upset when you broke it off and went into a bit of a tailspin." He kicked an empty beer can into a pile of dirty laundry. "Luckily, I never made it past this floor." He slid his palms to her cheeks and touched his nose to hers. "The upstairs is clean. Do you… would you like to see it?"

Staci felt herself melt under the heat in his gaze. That desire was for her and it fed an empty place in her soul. "Yes." Her voice was so choked she could barely get the words out. "I would."

A stairway had never seemed so steep, the climb never so long, as Luke led her up to the second floor, each step laden with a significance Staci had never felt before.

But then, none of this felt like anything she'd felt before. Not how she behaved with Luke, not who she'd become, and not the way her knees were practically shaking with nerves.

And all of it was marvelous.

As he led her toward his bedroom, Staci realized why it all felt different: *she* was different.

She was finally herself. Not a daughter who had to act out to get her mother's attention, not the sister of someone she'd related to through the actions of their mother, not the stepsister who'd been jealous of a girl who'd lost everything. Staci hadn't known who she was, but now, with her decision to help Sophia, the effort she was putting into both her working and personal relationships with Bella, and Luke looking at her as if she were everything he'd ever wanted, she finally did. And she liked who she'd become.

Luke led her into the master suite, the tan walls as warm as cappuccino, and closed the doors behind him with a soft click. The bed, with its black-and-tan-striped comforter, stood on the far wall between two mahogany nightstands and Staci couldn't take her eyes from it. Everything else faded from but the thought of her and Luke and the sharing of their souls and bodies they would do on that king-sized bed.

Luke came up behind her, his hands sliding around her waist and she could feel how much he wanted her. "You sure about this?"

More sure than anything before in her life. She turned in his arms, pressing her lips to his. "Take me to bed, Luke."

"Ah, Staci," he murmured against her mouth, "I've dreamt of you saying that." Luke slid his hands low, cupping her, his erection pressed between them as he kissed her.

And kissed her.

Long, drugging kisses that fired her blood even as a sweet heaviness swam through her limbs. Hot, heavy breaths caressed her cheek as his tongue slid between her lips to turn her insides to mush.

Staci grasped the strong, broad shoulders of an athlete, his muscles clenching beneath her fingertips as she slipped them beneath his collar, needing to feel his skin.

He pulled her to him, her aching breasts relishing the pressure, her nipples peaked and tingling at the contact, and she groaned into his mouth. He slid his lips from hers and dotted kisses along her jaw to find the hollow beneath her ear as shivers followed in their wake.

Her head fell back and she groaned. "Please... Luke. I... I can't stand."

Luke laughed softly and kissed her again. His hands threaded through her hair, and it was amazing she remained upright. "Stace."

One word, one syllable. Staci's knees gave out at the longing in it and it was only Luke swinging her up in his arms that saved her, both literally and figuratively, from falling at his feet. He made feel special. Cherished, and utterly feminine. All Eve, sensuous and desirable.

She reached up to stroke his cheek, the desire in his gaze giving her the confidence to make the move and know that this would be more than just a one-night stand. For both of them.

Her fingers trembled against his skin. "Luke." The husky voice didn't even sound like hers.

Luke carried her to the bed, kneeling to place her in the center. He wanted her. It was there in his gaze, in the slight tremble of *his* fingers as they trailed over her arm, the soft kiss he brushed to the back of her hand when he raised it almost reverently to his lips, and the beat of his heart when he placed her hand there. "See what you do to me?"

Rising from the mattress, Staci kissed him. Then she slid her hand from beneath his and ran it down along his abdomen, tugging his shirt from his jeans.

Luke braced himself on one hand and yanked the rest of the shirt free. "Touch me."

She didn't need to be asked twice.

She shoved the shirt up his chest, reveling in the play of muscles beneath his sleek skin. As he reached behind his neck and drew the shirt off, she took the opportunity to taste him, licking along his abs as her fingers played with his taut nipples.

"*Stace.*" He exhaled as he sank against her so she knew just how much he wanted her. "You're killing me."

"What a way to go, huh?" She slid her hands inside his waistband. "These need to come off."

Luke caught her words with his mouth, drowning her moan as his tongue did wicked things to hers while his lower half ground against her.

Staci gripped his two firm, tight cheeks, her fingers tracing the seam between them, and it was Luke's turn to groan. Then he wrenched himself off her, lying beside her and fumbling with his fly.

Staci brushed his hands away and maneuvered into a half-sitting position. "Let me."

Luke laid back, a hell of a sexy smile on his face. "I'm all yours, babe."

He *was* all hers. And if he didn't know it yet, he would.

Staci slid his zipper down inch by maddeningly slow inch. And if it was this torturous for her, she could only imagine what it was like for him.

She smiled. Good.

She slid her palms along the line of his hips, and shoved his jeans down a few inches, but not enough to free him.

"Babe." His hips flexed upward as he groaned.

Staci stilled her hands. "Say my name, Luke."

His eyes opened. He blinked. Then he licked his lips and a smile curved the corners of his sexy mouth upward. He hiked himself onto an elbow and cupped her cheek with his other hand. "Why? You think I don't know who I'm with?"

He tugged her to meet him as he sat up, capturing her lips in a hot, open-mouthed kiss that put to rest her doubts. Almost. Because this was too important to her; it meant too much. "Do you, Luke? Do you really?"

He took the time to search her eyes. To travel over her nose, linger on her lips. To thread his fingers through her hair and stroke the ends across his cheek. "Staci Fontaine. The sexiest woman I've ever seen. The woman who hasn't been off my mind since the moment we met. The woman I don't know if I'll ever get enough of. That's who I'm with. That's who I want."

Staci trembled with the passion in his words. Passion for what he was saying, for what those words meant, and… for her.

"Show me, Luke. Show me how you feel."

*Show me what it's like to be wanted for myself, to have someone care for me. For me, the person. Not me, the body.*

She didn't utter the rest; she couldn't. But the words hovered there, in her subconscious, where they'd taunted her for years. How she wanted him to be the one to make them go away.

And he did, slipping the clothes from her body with murmured words and hot kisses, a nip here, a lick there, stoking a fire deep inside her, tendrils licking through her veins.

He laid on top of her, pressing her into the soft mattress with his strong, hard body, every point of contact sending shivers racing through her. Somehow he managed to get out of his jeans, and the pressure of his thigh sliding between her legs had her moving against him.

He kissed her, their tongues dueling and tasting, sucking and stroking. He tasted of coffee and sugar and heat and him. "You taste so good." He stole the words from her as his tongue dragged along her collarbone. "I could do this for the rest of my life."

His confession sliced through the haze of desire between them. Staci opened her eyes, seeing puzzlement in his. "*What?*" she asked, not sure she'd heard right.

A smile replaced the puzzlement. Then a cocky grin. "Yeah. That's right. You heard me." He framed her face with his hands. "The rest of my life, Staci. The rest of *our* lives."

"But—"

"Shut up, woman, and let me show you what I mean."

He reached into a nightstand drawer, ripped apart a foil package, and rolled the condom in place. One more scorching look, the grin back, then Luke bent his head to feast on her neck, sending shivers down her spine and out through every limb as his fingers danced upon her skin as they slid lower, brushing the last scrap of material she wore.

"Lift up for me, babe." He ran his fingers along the crease of her thigh, stroking just under the edge of her thong.

Staci obliged him and he hooked his fingers under the band and drew it down her leg. He repositioned himself on the other side and repeated the action, this time, though, moving down her body.

"Oh, man. What's this?"

He kissed the spot she knew he would. The one only she and one other person knew about.

The spot with the tattoo of a pink rosebud unfurling into bloom.

She'd gotten it four months ago after Mother had mortified her by flourishing her date's rap sheet during their first—and last—date, condemning the man in front of the entire place.

It'd been Staci's private rebellion—Mother found tattoos distasteful—but Staci hadn't yet worked up the nerve to show her. She'd sworn the tattoo artist to secrecy.

Luke looked up at her, laughter dancing with desire in his eyes. "I'm guessing Madeleine knows nothing about this."

She laughed. How freeing it was to laugh at this moment. To share something so intimate and personal with someone who understood. "You guess right."

"I'd love to tell her about it." He kissed the pink petals again. "But this is our secret. I'm not sharing such a precious memory with anyone else, especially not that woman."

Those were the last words they said for a while as the feelings and emotions overtook them, sending her heart racing and her mind into a thousand sparkling, shattering pieces as he drove her over the edge of completion. But those words were the ones that kept repeating themselves in her mind. Luke had created a special memory between them. One just for them. Their own little inside joke and every time he kissed that rose, that one small, should-be-insignificant piece of artwork, Staci felt her heart belong a little bit more to him.

# Chapter Thirty-Two

hat's the present for, Bella?" Sophia bounced into Bella's bedroom the next morning, almost knocking the box to the floor.

"It's a gift from Mr. Griff." Bella ran her fingers once more along the gown Gus had made her. It was utterly beautiful and for the first time, she knew she was going to feel like her namesake.

"Can I open it?"

"Not yet, honey. Mr. Griff said I can't open it until noon."

Just then, the bells of St. Gabriel's and the grandfather clock in the living room rang in the lunch hour.

Sophia grinned. "It's noon."

"So it is," Bella laughed. "Okay, let's open it." Like two kids on Christmas morning, Bella and Sophia untied the gold voile ribbon and lifted the lid.

"Oooh!" Sophia clapped. "Look!"

Bella looked. She couldn't *not* look. Inside the box on a velvet pillow were… the Lucite shoes from Mr. Griff's store.

"Can I try them on, Bella?"

Bella shook the shock from her muddled mind. "Sure. Like I said when we saw these in the store, every little girl should feel like a princess at least once in her life."

"And big girls too?"

Bella smiled. "Yes, big girls can, too, I suppose."

"Like you tonight with that pretty dress and these Cinderella shoes." Sophia waltzed around the room, humming the movie theme song Bella had grown to hate over the years. "I bet you'll meet a handsome prince and fall in love and live happily ever after."

And mice would turn into horses and a pumpkin into a carriage and she'd rush off at midnight—

Wait. Hadn't Mr. Griff said she had twelve hours with the shoes and then she had to give them back?

She smiled. Ah, if only tonight *were* going to be a fairytale…

Still, she hesitated before lifting one of the shoes from of the box. *What if—*

Oh for heaven's sake. She was being irrational. It wasn't as if Mr. Griff was her own special fairy godfather.

"This dress makes Gus your fairy godmother, you know," said Sophia, draping the gown across the front of her. "Just like the one in the movie."

Who'd been an older female, but, yes, the comparison was there. There were a lot of comparisons all of a sudden.

It'd be so nice to believe that it was true. That at the stroke of midnight she'd run off and leave her shoe and Prince Charmant would come after her.

And Madeleine wouldn't interfere.

She handed the shoes to Sophia. Let her little sister believe in magic and fairy tales for now; reality would come soon enough.

***

"Uh oh, Giac." Perla scooted onto one of the stools at the counter at. "Hurricane Staci at two o'clock."

Giac looked over her retro-eighties, Snookie-*pouf*. Perla was right. Staci and her take-no-prisoners attitude were storming the gates of Casteleoni's. Just what he didn't need at this eleventh hour when he and Gus were putting the final touches on Bella's presentation before they loaded everything into the van. He scrambled out of his apron and intercepted Staci before she made it past the counter.

"Giac." Staci gripped his arms, the first touch the woman had ever willingly given him. And Giac had been okay with the status quo. "We need your help."

Of *course* there'd be a reason for her to be nice to him; she needed something. "I'm kind of busy right now, Staci. And shouldn't you be? The auction's in a few hours."

"I know. That's why we have to move fast. My mother is making everyone's life a living hell and she's threatening to send Sophia off to boarding school."

So what else was new? What Giac wanted to know was why it had suddenly become a soapbox for Staci.

He was saved from answering by the door bells jingling again.

A man Luke had never seen before—because he would have remembered *him*—strode through the door and—

Put his hands on Staci's shoulders? What was happening in the universe?

"Hi. I'm Luke." The guy extended a hand. The other never left Staci.

Giac shook Luke's hand automatically because he was still processing why the guy was touching Staci. Surely someone of his obvious good taste wouldn't fall prey to the likes of her?

"Has Staci brought you up to speed?"

"Speed?" Giac felt as if he were moving in slow motion through molasses. And he didn't have time for it. They had to get everything loaded. He shook his head, trying to clear the confusion. "I'm sorry, but I have to get moving. Perhaps we could discuss this some other time, you two—"

"Oh but Giac, you have to listen." Staci put a hand on his chest.

Giac looked down at it, waiting to feel the pain of the knife she probably stabbed him with… but couldn't. He looked back at her.

She plucked her hand away. "Sorry, but we really do need your help. It's for Bella."

"Bella?" That cleared his head somewhat. More when he started to worry that Staci was planning a minefield for her nemesis. "What do you want with Bella?"

"We want to help her." Luke stepped around Staci and clasped Giac on the shoulder. "Look, we all know that Madeleine wants one thing and one thing only."

Giac nodded. "World domination." He wasn't kidding, but Luke laughed anyway.

"Besides that. She wants respectability. To be one of the 'in' crowd. And she thinks becoming a Board member is her ticket to the cool crowd. Problem is, she's aware that she's going to need something extra to get herself invited in."

"But they've spoken to Carolyn Charmant about the position. I heard her mention it myself when she was in for lunch."

"But Mother doesn't know that and we have to make sure she doesn't until this auction is over," said Staci.

"How?" Regardless of her improved taste in men, Staci could be just as conniving as the witch who'd given birth to her.

"She thinks Bella isn't working the auction."

"Why on earth would she think that? It was a coup in the Casteleoni cap she's counting on to improve our standing in the community."

"Because she thinks if Reese fails, his mother will never get the position and she'll have a shot at it."

"You're kidding."

"Unfortunately, no. But that's the way Mother's mind works."

"Well, obviously we're not going to let tonight turn into a fiasco, so what are you proposing?"

Luke and Staci wore identical Cheshire-cat smiles. The same ones Giac had learned to be wary of.

"What's said to be the best revenge?" Luke asked.

"Duh. Living well. Why?"

"Exactly." Luke leaned on the counter conspiratorially. "We all know that Reese is head over heels for Bella. What do you think would happen if Bella ends up with a better social standing than Madeleine?"

Ah, for a moment, Gus had reveled in the hope that their plan had a prayer of succeeding. And while it was the same one he had for Bella, the reality was, it couldn't happen if Madeleine was against it. "You're forgetting one thing: Sophia. Bella will never do anything to jeopardize her sister. Plus, there's this place to consider. It's almost as important to Bella, and Madeleine can wreak havoc and revenge here, as well." Giac sighed. "Sorry, you two. It's a nice idea, but it'll never work. Madeleine's got the law on her side."

Luke's grin got even bigger. "I think I've got that part figured out. Casteleoni's is going to take some more effort, though. That's where I'm hoping you'll come in."

Staci nodded and grabbed his arm. "Please help, Giac."

*Staci* was asking for his help? Weird had just gotten weirder. And maybe, just maybe, that meant this could work.

"What do you need me to do?"

Luke jerked his head to bring the conspirators together. Even Perla leaned in to listen. "So first I'm going to talk to Reese's mom...

## Chapter Thirty-Three

W here's that boy?" Gus stormed around the kitchen, but was careful to avoid knocking any of the trays now lining the kitchen counters.

He hefted himself onto a stool and stared at the alley entrance, as if that would make Bruno arrive earlier. The boy was supposed to help him load the van before they picked up Bella for the drive to the riverfront.

Suddenly, there was a loud squeal of tires, followed by a screech, then the sound of an aluminum trashcan meeting a brick wall.

Gus groaned. At least he wasn't baking the soufflé here. That noise would have deflated it.

The steel door creaked open and Bruno stood there with a kicked-puppy expression on his face. "I'm here, Gus."

Gus sighed. "I hear." He walked toward him, waving away the stammering apology Bruno was in the process of forming. It didn't matter now. "We must get the trays loaded. The sternos are packed and the utensils ready." He lifted one of the boxes and headed outside. "You put the boxes on the van floor, then the food, she will go on top—-"

Gus slammed to a halt in the alleyway and stared. *That* was not the catering van. That was… that was…

He didn't even bother to turn around. "Where is the van?"

Bruno cleared his throat. "Ah, the van. Yes. Well..." He shuffled his feet. "Well, um. I... um... was going to fix it after that mishap with the door a few weeks ago?"

"What fix?" Gus spun around, his temper beginning to boil. "The van, she no need a fix. She runs fine."

Bruno shook his head and the ear flaps of his cap waggled like dog ears. "Yes, well, there was this little clicking noise and I thought I could, you know, take care of it."

"So?" The boil was about to steam.

"Well... um... here's where it gets a little tricky—"

"Tricky? *Tricky?*" The pot boiled over. "We don't *need* tricky. We don't *need* little click fixed. We *need* the van to get to the auction. Now how we do this?"

Bruno cringed as Gus came toward him. Gus knew he was being unreasonable, because clearly, the van was not coming. But they could not show up at this high-society event in that... that... "It's an abomination." He had Giac to thank for that useful word.

"No, it's a *station wagon.*"

"It's an *orange* station wagon."

Bruno hung his head and the ear flaps on his cap drooped. "It was supposed to be a rust color, but I guess when my buddy mixed the paint he added a little too much orange—"

"A little!" Gus didn't care that his shout echoed along the walls of the alley. Everyone would see it soon enough and they'd be a laughing stock showing up in this... this... *zucca* on four wheels.

"Well, okay, maybe a lot. But it's all we have now, Gus. It'll carry all the food and I rented a tux to wear, so I'll look professional when I unload it at the boat."

Gus exhaled every bit of air in his lungs and threw up his arms before spinning around to head back into his sanctuary. "Fine. Giac and I will go in his car." It was a compact, already a tight fit on a good day. With serving trays and mixing bowls and what-not, it would probably end up looking like a clown car. "At least I will not have to arrive in that pumpkin."

***

"You look beautiful, Bella. Just like a princess," Sophia said just before the doorbell rang. "I'll get it!" she bellowed, galloping from the room.

Sophia's adoration went a long way toward calming Bella's nerves. She put the rhinestone drop earring in her other ear and smoothed the front of dress. Gus had done a magnificent job and he'd made her feel beautiful.

Would Reese think so?

Bella sat on the edge of her bed. Those kinds of thoughts were best forgotten. Tonight was not the night to go there. She had to make

197

sure everything ran smoothly because once Madeleine found out she was still on the job, that pumpkin soufflé mess would be nothing compared to her stepmother's ire.

She slipped on one of Mr. Griff's pumps, readying herself for the cool hard feel of the Lucite, but instead, found her foot cushioned as if there were a pillow inside the shoe. She picked up the one on the bed and looked at it. No cushioned sole. Odd. Very odd.

She thought back to Sophia's fairy tale prattling this morning. If only Gus *were* her fairy godmother. Or maybe Mr. Griff was.

Yeah, and she was off to the ball where her ride home would turn into a pumpkin at midnight.

A shaft of sunlight slid through the blinds and glinted off the last of Mr. Griff's coins as if it were winking at her.

"Bruno's here, Bella!" Sophia hollered from downstairs just in time to save Bella from listening for singing mice… Bella picked up her purse and headed out the bedroom door.

Thank God Madeleine was at a hair appointment getting all done up for the event. Bella had had to time this precisely.

"Thanks, Soph. Do you have your bag? Bruno and I will take you to Aunt Theresa's." Bella ushered her sister out the door.

But she came to a dead stop on the front path.

"Bruno, *what* is that?"

Bruno wrung his hands. "It's my car."

"It's *orange*."

Poor Bruno flushed almost the same shade. His eyes shifted and he stared at his feet. "I know," he mumbled.

"But where's the van? All the food? Giac and Gus?"

At last the poor guy looked up. "I got it all taken care of, Ms. C." He swept a hand to the back of the car as if he were a game show host. "All the food's in the back and Gus and Giac are driving over with everything else. I even rented a tux so I'd look real professional tonight. I want to help you make this a success."

She couldn't be angry. He really had gone to a lot of trouble to make it right. And she wanted tonight to be a success also.

"Here you go, Ms. C." Bruno held the door open like a royal footman. "Your carriage awaits."

Sophia was already in the middle of the front seat. She patted the passenger side. "Come on, Bella. I want to hear the mice."

"Mice?" Bella looked at Bruno who, once again, hung his head and shuffled his feet.

"The breaks squeal."

"Squeak," Sophia corrected. "You said they squeak just like mice do." The little girl pounded the seat again. "Come on, Bella. I want to ride with the mice and you don't want to be late for the party."

***

"You think this will work?"

Giac held his breath as Carolyn Charmant considered what Luke had just proposed. Everything hinged on her agreeing to do this. It's why he'd grabbed the jar from under the front counter and why he'd let Gus drive *his* car to the riverfront, something that would normally require a presidential order and motorcade. But there was a time and place for everything and tonight, *The Midnight Maiden* was it.

"You really think so?" she asked again.

He, Luke, and Staci nodded.

The movie star didn't answer. This was, after all, her son they were talking about.

But then the award-winning star of stage and screen smiled and put a hand to her forehead. "All right, then." She cleared her throat and her voice lowered. "You know? I do believe I feel a migraine coming on."

199

# Chapter Thirty-Four

Reese was directing the drayage company at Community Hospital for the Meet-and-Greet, when he felt a tap on his shoulder.

"Hey, Charmant."

"Coach. What are you doing here? We weren't expecting you for another two hours."

Randy Meade took off his cap and rubbed his thinning hair. "I know, but I got something to say to you and I thought it'd be better before the auction than during."

*What about after?* Reese really didn't have the time for a heart-to-heart at the moment. Especially with the condition of his heart right now. He'd put it on the injured reserves list and was looking forward to rehabbing it once this event was over.

"Can it wait, Coach? I'm pretty busy."

Randy grabbed his shoulder. "No, it can't. I got a plane to catch tonight and you owe me, son. At least a bit of your time. I won't take up too much."

Reese gave a last look around, barked an order at Kelly, and then faced Coach. "Okay. What is it?"

Suddenly, Randy didn't look like the awe-inspiring coach who'd led a team of men and a grateful city to a Super Bowl victory. "I want to apologize."

An apology was the last thing Reese had expected.

"I know I should have said something before, but until little Maggie was born, I just didn't have it in me to blame my daughter. I made you out to be the big bad wolf taking advantage of my little girl, and, well, I did you a disservice." Randy looked him in the eye. "And I'm damn sorry about the ending of your career. You were one hell of a football player and deserved to go out better."

Reese swallowed the lump in his throat. "Thanks, Coach. That means a lot. But our argument didn't end my career—my injury did."

The "Coach" was back. "Maybe. But if it hadn't, you would have had the job to come back to. But I made it personal and I'm damn sorry I did. It cost you."

"How could it not have been personal? I was dating your daughter. I wish to God I'd stayed away from her."

Randy actually smiled. "Yeah, at the time I did, too. But I had a nice talk with Devin after Maggie was born. Just the two of us, watching that little baby sleep in her crib. And you know what my daughter said?"

Reese shook his head.

Randy cleared his throat. "She said she was sorry for causing the disagreement between us, but she'll never regret going out with you. Even though her heart broke when you ended it, she said you did something good for her. If you hadn't ended it when you did, she never would have met her husband and our little Maggie wouldn't have been in that crib." Randy cleared his throat again and looked away. "You know the baby was named after my late wife?"

Reese nodded. "I'd guessed as much."

Randy glanced back with a sheen in his eyes. "Yeah. Well, there could have been another baby—a different baby—in that crib, but it wouldn't be my little Maggie. She has my wife's eyes, you know."

The two men were silent for a bit, then Coach coughed and stuck out his hand. "So. I wanted to apologize. Tell you there are no ill feelings on my part. A little late, I guess, but I wanted you to know."

"No, Coach." Reese shook his head. "I should have just stayed away from her. I knew better than to mix business and pleasure. I just forgot to pay attention to my conscience."

"Nonsense, Reese." Randy's old coaching voice rose to the surface. "Nothing would have made me happier than for you and Devin to end up together. But when you ended it, even though it was for the right reasons, I forgot that you were still the same guy I'd always known. I couldn't see beyond the fact that my daughter had gotten her heart broken. I should have." He clasped Reese's hand. "I'm sorry for losing sight of that."

Reese's grin was small. "Well there's a turnaround."

Coach shrugged. "You were—are—a stand-up guy, both on and off the field. There was never any delineation between the two for you. That's why you're doing so well with this new venture. Who you are as a person, not just a celebrity, goes a long way toward driving your business. People know what to expect when they hire you on, Reese, because everything you've ever done, both on and off the field, has been done with integrity. Be you, Reese, who you've always been, and your clients will keep coming back. Be true to yourself—"Coach tapped him in the vicinity of his heart—"and you can't go wrong."

***

Madeleine tapped the driver on the shoulder. "I'd like you to pick up the pace. I'm meeting a very important investor and I do not wish to be late."

The driver glanced in his rear-view mirror. "Ma'am, I am doing the speed limit as per my contract. I can't risk getting a ticket. Don't worry, though. I'll have you both at the party just in time."

Madeleine huffed and slid to the back of the car she'd rented to transport her and Mr. Fiorello to the auction. She must keep up appearances after all, but if that twit in the driver's seat didn't hurry it up, she and Mr. Fiorello wouldn't arrive before the Board members. She wanted to be on hand to welcome them personally.

The driver glanced back again, his green eyes twinkling behind his spectacles, a black beret pulled low. He shifted on the phone books he'd piled to make himself taller. There hadn't been enough time to arrange for a different, "special" car, so he'd had to make do.

Improvisation was his best trait, anyway. And once he'd gotten wind of what Luke and Staci were up to, he'd scrapped part of his old plan and was hastily trying to put together a new one. Keeping Bella's stepmother from arriving too early was part of it.

It was all Jonathan Griff could do not to laugh aloud at what the rest of the evening held for Madeleine.

Including the flat tire that happened just as planned.

"A flat tire?" Madeleine shrieked at him when he lowered the partition separating the driver's quarters from the rest of the limousine to give her the bad news. "What kind of incompetent fool are you? Do you understand how important it is that I'm not late? I told you I *must* be on time."

Such an unbecoming and unnecessary reaction, but then, Jonathan had expected no less from the woman. Giovanni Fiorello really had his hands full with this one.

202

Madeleine threw her head against the headrest and exhaled. Loudly. "It's as if the gods are against me."

"Oh, no, ma'am. He wouldn't do something like this." No, only desperate Guardians in training would. His poor Boss, though; always getting blamed for things He hadn't done.

"Did you say something?" Madeleine arched her eyebrow and glared at him out the corner of her eye, an effective move if executed properly.

Madeleine had perfected it.

"I said I'll change the tire as fast as I can, ma'am." Jonathan slid from his stack of phonebooks and walked around to the trunk. A raised lid, a few thumps and bumps, a clang or two, and Jonathan walked over to the tire in question. He took a quick survey of the street before bending down to examine the "flat." He wiggled his finger and the back end of the car hovered a good six inches off the ground. The shriek from inside assured him the lift had been noticed.

Jonathan sat on the curb, whistling. Every so often he'd twiddle his fingers and the sound of a lug wrench hitting the pavement would emanate from beneath the car. There were perks to this Guardian business. Faking a flat tire and its tiresome fix were one of them.

"Can you hurry it up?" Madeleine raged through the lowered window. Heaven forbid she actually deigned to look out at him—but that served his purpose well. He didn't need her to see what he was— or, rather, *wasn't*—doing. "What's taking so long? Don't you have a cell phone? Why don't you call your company and have them get another car here? I don't have all night for this nonsense."

Jonathan lowered the car a little more forcefully than necessary. Praise be, it shut the woman up.

Thank God—and Jonathan did, often-—that Madeleine wasn't his Charge. Poor Giovanni deserved some divine sympathy.

"It's about time," the woman snarled when he opened the driver's door after "depositing" his supposed tools back in the trunk. "You better hurry. We've already lost too much time as it is."

A *thank you* went a long way with people, but Madeleine, apparently, had never learned that lesson.

Jonathan tipped his hat to the woman, feeling sorrier for Giovanni by the minute. The woman needed a good lesson in manners. "We'll be off now, ma'am. No time flat, just like I said. No pun intended, though."

Madeleine didn't even crack a smile. She huffed and threw herself back into her seat, her arms crossing into a pretzel across her chest. "Just get going. I have half a mind to call another driver."

Jonathan bit back the comment about half her mind. It wouldn't be very angelic of him.

"You're certainly welcome to, ma'am, but with this big shindig at the hospital, I'm pretty sure all the car agencies and taxicab companies have their hands full. I doubt you'll be able to find another car at this late hour." He really had to struggle to keep his grin from slipping out.

Madeleine sucked her cheeks in so hard they almost popped out the other side. She looked at the ceiling. "Can anything else possibly go wrong?"

If she only knew.

# Chapter Thirty-Five

S taci. You're here." Bella heard the disbelief in her voice but couldn't help it. She truly hadn't expected to see Staci at all during set-up.

"Of course I am. I told you I would be."

Staci looked indignant. Not that Bella could blame her. Her stepsister had been rather amazing recently—as compared to her earlier lazy, selfish, gluttonous, blob-like self.

"Your outfit is very nice."

"You like it?" Staci smoothed the coral skirt over her hips. The cream blouse was demure enough to be respectable, but sassy enough to be fashionable. "Luke said it was the perfect choice for tonight."

"Luke?" Bella stopped construction on the cheese tower to really look at Staci. "I thought it was over between the two of you."

"Just like you weren't going to work this event."

Bella acknowledged that direct hit.

"Besides, I really do like him. We have a lot in common."

No, Bella wasn't going to mention Luke's bank account balance. It seemed as if Staci really had changed more than her appearance.

"I wish you the best of luck."

"Thanks." Staci held up a tray. "So, should the antipasto go on the bar or the food station?"

"Leave it by the cheese. It'll be too big for the bar."

"Okay." Staci did a little hop-skip back to their food cart and grabbed another cheese tray. "I've got this covered, Bella, if you want to see how Giac and Gus are doing on the boat." Staci dismissed her with a flutter of acrylic fingernails.

"Staci, what's going on?"

"I don't know what you mean." Staci's look of wide-eyed innocence was as fake as her fingernails.

"Come on. Even for you, this overacting is a bit much. You're up to something, I can tell. And I want to know what it is. I've got too much invested in this evening for you to ruin it."

"Bella, really. I'm just trying to help out. I have no ulterior motives. I promise."

Then why did her hand slip behind her back? Were her fingers crossed?

Bella tugged Staci's hand out. No crossed fingers. But that didn't mean they hadn't been.

"Seriously, Bella, I wish you'd trust me on this. I have your best interests at heart." Staci smiled and set the cheese down. "Now, go. You know Bruno's in there with Gus so there's sure to be some disagreement going on. I'll be fine."

Torn between a possible future disaster and the imminent one between Gus and Bruno, Bella headed aboard *The Midnight Maiden*. "Call me if you need any help."

"I'll be fine." Staci picked up a few pieces of cheese and balanced them on the top of the pyramid Bella had made, pretending to be busy until Bella disappeared inside the ship. Then she tossed the cheese back onto the tray and whistled.

Luke ran from the car with something cradled in a football hold against his chest.

"This is a lot heavier than a pigskin," he huffed, pulling it from beneath a towel. "Where do you want it?"

Staci motioned to a table draped in layers of pastel chiffon. "Under here. We don't want Bella to see it and start asking questions."

"Right." Luke put it down and stood, brushing his hands. He smiled at Staci and caressed her arms. "Have I ever told you how cute you are when you're planning a coup?"

# Chapter Thirty-Six

ella stood on the deck of *The Midnight Maiden*, awestruck. The drayage company Reese had hired had really outdone itself. Twinkling lights outlined the bow, vined along the mast lines, and wended through the topiaries the florist had supplied, turning the deck of *The Midnight Maiden* into a fairy land. Silver candelabra and utensils gleamed in the reflected light, and glass dishes rimmed in silver prismed rainbows of color onto the shimmering silver satin tablecloths while soft waves lapped against the dock, the motion setting the candle flames dancing in their protective glass surrounds.

"Beautiful," she whispered, trailing her fingertips over the back of the fabric-draped chair.

"Yes." The word was soft and deep from behind her.

Bella spun around.

Reese. Looking breathtakingly handsome in a coal black tuxedo and crisp white shirt, the lights flickering along the strong line of his jaw and the sensuous curve of his lips.

She really didn't need to be thinking about his lips right now. Not when it was all she could do to keep from replaying the feel of them on hers.

"Hi." She fiddled with a strand of hair that had fallen from the knot at her neck and tucked it behind her ear as she looked around. "They really did a great job. This is gorgeous. Everyone's going to be so impressed."

Reese didn't say anything.

"Is something wrong?" She swished the gown, imagining all sorts of awful things that could go wrong tonight. She'd thought about warning him about Madeleine, but was counting on her stepmother's social aspirations as a deterrent to bad behavior.

Later on tonight when they got home, however… She'd deal with that when the time came. She was not going to let her personal business interfere with Reese's professional one.

"Wrong?" Reese coughed. "No. Nothing. You look stunning, Bella. That dress..." He cleared his throat again. "Whoever made that thing is a genius."

"It was Gus."

"Then his talents are wasted in the kitchen, but I'll gladly avail myself of them tonight."

"I'll be sure to tell him. He and Bruno are getting the food set up in the galley. They wouldn't let me in there until everything was settled. Said they didn't want me to get anything on the dress."

"Good idea."

Oh she had plenty of good ideas and one in particular was all about getting the *out* of the dress.

Okay, so maybe that wasn't such a good idea.

"Reese, listen, about tonight. About the reason I quit on you last week."

"It's not important. You're here now and tonight will be perfect."

"But—"

"Reese, I've got to talk to you." Luke ran up the stairs. "Hey, Bella. Staci said everything's ready for you in the galley."

"Oh. Okay." She took one last look at Reese. "I guess we'll talk later."

"Sounds good."

***

"A migraine? You're kidding, right? My mother's never had a migraine in her life." Reese swiped a hand over his face.

With their reestablished friendship, Luke didn't relish lying, or the bleak look on Reese's face, but it was in the guy's best interests. He just hoped Reese would see it that way when it all played out.

Luke shrugged. "That's what she said. Your father helped her back to their car and she asked me to tell you. She seemed pretty worried about you." That, at least, wasn't a lie. But Carolyn had seen the bigger plan and was in full agreement.

"Great. Now what do I do? I've got an open slot on the auction block."

"Well..." And here was where it all began. "Actually, that's not true." Reese looked over at him and Luke had to work hard to keep the look of innocence he'd struggled to put on his face. "It says on my bidding list 'A Charmant Evening.' Your mom's not the only Charmant in your family people would want to spend an evening with, you know."

Reese groaned. "This is what I get for letting Kelly design the program layout. She thought it'd be cute to play off the *charming* angle of my name. Now it's coming back to bite me and I don't have a choice, do I?"

"I could always volunteer."

Reese gave that a half-second's consideration. "No, my name is on the event and the program. I'll do it."

Luke tried not to crow. Phase Two complete.

# Chapter Thirty-Seven

The staff knew the minute Madeleine came aboard. The air shifted and grew tense, as if Nature was warning them.

Bella ducked into the galley and sent Jolie out to "just happen" to pass Madeleine in the dining room and allay any suspicions the woman might have. Now if she could just keep up the pretense for the next four hours, she'd be okay.

The cocktail hour passed without incident, though it'd been a bit tricky to keep Uncle Vinny from spilling the beans. He'd heard why Bella was hanging out in the galley and wanted to speak with Madeleine. Only Bella's insistence that she had it all under control kept him from outing her. But he hadn't liked it.

Luckily, the Board members had reserved seating at the bow of the boat so they were all in one place. A draw too good to resist for Madeleine, who'd been circling their perimeter like a shark the entire time, her laugh just a little too loud, her actions a little too desperate. But Bella had been thankful for them because it'd allowed her to come and go as she'd had to to keep the event running smoothly, though Jolie was a great help in that area. Gus was working his magic in the galley, and Bruno had managed to not drop anything noisy.

But then Reese walked into the galley and *Bella* almost did the dropping.

"There's a change to the program," he announced, not looking happy about it.

"Oh?"

"Yes, so I'm going to be busy during the auction. I'd like you to make sure the staff keeps clearing while the auction is going on."

"Me?" Madeleine wouldn't be able to miss her.

"Kelly's going to be busy with the auction, so yes, you'll need to do it."

"All right. I'll manage." Somehow. But she owed him after all. And surely Madeleine wouldn't make a scene. After all, the Board members were here and she was still toadying up to them. She must not know they'd met with Reese's mom.

And Heaven forefend if she *did* find out before the night was through. Then they'd *all* need some fairy godmothers because all hell would break loose.

***

Smatterings of applause found their way down to the belly of the boat, telling Bella the auction was going well. Reese must be so pleased. The event was a success. Even Madeleine had removed the pinched look from her face and replaced it with something considerably close to a smile, so things must be looking up with her Board member networking.

Bella refused to think it had anything to do with the negotiations with Mr. Fiorello.

Staci popped her head into the galley. "Gus, they're ready for you next."

Gus mopped his brow. "Yes. I come." He stumbled against the counter, catching a spatula before it could hit the floor. Bella and Giac held their breath.

At last, Gus held the soufflé in his hands and beamed. Giac gave him a victory sigh. "Go get 'em, Gus."

Gus bowed slightly. "The winner will be amazed by my creation." He waddled up the stairs.

Staci winked at Giac.

"What was that for?" Bella asked.

"What was what for?" Giac was suddenly very busy cleaning an already spotless countertop.

"That wink." Bella grabbed the rag from Giac's hand. "Why did Staci wink at you?"

Giac shrugged. "I don't know. Maybe she likes soufflés?" He resumed his cleaning.

Bella chewed the inside of her cheek. Something was odd. Since when did Staci and Giac get along, let alone *wink* at each other?

"Come on, Bella." Giac tucked his rag into his apron. Let's go watch the rest of the auction."

***

"Thank you, Belinda for your generous donation of nine holes with our winner. And thank you, Mayor, for your generous donation to the hospital fund. I hope you enjoy your time on the links." The auctioneer shuffled a stack of papers. "Next up is Mr. Gus Sorcio, tonight's chef, who has agreed to donate his time and expertise to cater our winner's party. And he's brought with him this evening one of his original recipes, a pumpkin soufflé."

Polite applause greeted a grinning Gus as he stood beside the podium, his soufflé held high. Bella glanced at Giac and saw tears drizzling down his cheeks. She patted his arm and he closed his hand over hers.

The auctioneer began the bidding. A woman in front signaled. Then another. A hand went up in the back. Bella looked around, pleased for Gus that there was a lot of interest.

Then the bidding slowed and Gus's face fell. The gavel fell once. Twice. Then a bidding card was raised and Gus heaved a sigh of relief. Bella turned to see who had salvaged her friend's ego and, across the room, met Reese's smile.

Warmth spread through her and she couldn't help returning it. He nodded slightly and Bella felt her cheeks warm.

Suddenly, a shrill voice cut into Bella's reverie. Madeleine. It figured.

"I'll bid two thousand dollars," Madeleine said. "There's not a better chef in this town and I would be remiss to let his services go for so little." The crowd was silent as the gavel fell for the third time. Gus was uncertain as he stole a look at Bella.

Bella waved him on. Madeleine had won the soufflé fair and square. But what on earth was she up to?

As the woman left her seat to take Gus's soufflé, Bella had her answer. Mr. Fiorello sat next to her. Madeleine wanted to prove she had the best chef in her restaurant and the money to hold off if Mr. Fiorello's first offer wasn't high enough.

It was a good bluff, Bella had to admit. But would the man call it?

Behind Mr. Fiorello, Bella saw Staci glance their way. And wink again. And this time, Bella caught Giac winking back.

Aha! That's what they'd been up to. Bella felt a surge of gratitude she never would have imagined feeling two months ago toward her stepsister. It seemed the changes in Staci were more than superficial.

"And now," the auctioneer began again, "for our final item of the night. An evening with a Charmant."

Bella's breath caught. She remembered her own evening with a certain Charmant, but doubted the winner of the auction would have anything similar with Reese's mom.

There was a tittering of excitement from the audience. It was no secret Carolyn Charmant was this evening's special guest. The crowd turned in their chairs, looking for the famous actress.

But it was Reese who headed to the podium.

If Bella had been just another member of the crowd, she would have missed the slightly nauseated look on his face right before he leaned over to say something to the auctioneer. But she wasn't just any member of the audience. She was one with a vested interest in anything having to do with Reese Charmant. Whether it was good for her or not.

The auctioneer shook his head. Was he laughing as Reese shrugged those broad shoulders?

"Ladies and gentlemen," the auctioneer spoke into the microphone. "There seems to be a change in plans."

Butterflies opened their wings in Bella's stomach.

"It seems Ms. Charmant has taken ill. Nothing serious, but it does preclude her from attending this evening's event. However..." The man's grin got bigger and he turned to Reese. "I'm sure you're all aware there is more than one celebrity in the Charmant family. Our very own Super Bowl-winning quarterback, Mr. Reese Charmant, has willingly consented to fulfill his mother's obligation. So, ladies." The auctioneer put the microphone back in its holder and gripped both sides of the podium. "Get your checkbooks ready. And all for a good cause. Do I have someone to start the bidding?"

Bella held her breath before it fell out of her shoes. Someone else was going to spend an evening with Reese. She wanted to sink through the floor. Damn. She knew it was completely illogical, but he was hers.

Even though she couldn't have him.

The bidding was fast and furious, keeping time with the sinking of Bella's heart. She couldn't stand there and watch it. Bella pushed behind Giac, sidestepping around other patrons. If she could just get to the galley—

"Nineteen hundred."

Bella's head whipped around. That was Staci's voice. And Madeleine was standing next to her, pleased as punch.

*What about Luke?* Or was it all some sick plan Staci and her mother had concocted to steamroll Bella's spirits even more?

"Two thousand," another woman called out.

"Twenty-one hundred." Staci again.

Another woman, Bella couldn't see who but did catch the snow-white hair, bid twenty-five hundred. Bella found herself hoping that mystery woman would win. She'd feel much better if Reese went out with someone old enough to be his grandmother.

And, yes, she realized the ridiculousness of her wish, but it was what it was.

"Three thousand," said Staci with a Cheshire-cat smile.

Murmurs buzzed around the crowd as everyone looked to the white-haired bidder. The woman shook her head.

Bella's heart sank as the gravel fell for the first time, then the second, and finally the third. She'd been outplayed by her stepsister. God, when would she learn?

She'd almost made it to the stairwell back to the galley where she wouldn't have to watch Staci's triumphant march up to the podium, when a hand gripped her arm. She turned to Staci's smiling face.

"Here." Staci thrust something heavy into her solar plexus. "Go claim your prize."

"What?" Bella looked down. A large mason jar was in her hands. A mason jar filled with Mr. Campanale's tips.

Realization dawned and Bella felt gratitude well up within her—only to come crashing down. "Your mother—"

"Let me deal with my mother. You go on up there and claim your guy."

He *was* her guy, and suddenly, Bella felt as if she was walking on clouds. The sounds around her faded away as she started toward the podium. Reese stood there, smiling. Even Madeleine's hiss didn't stop her as she floated past the woman. She only had eyes, and ears, and every other one of her five senses for Reese. She'd think about Madeleine tomorrow.

"Hi," Reese said softly as she reached him.

"Hi."

He took the mason jar from her with a raised eyebrow.

Bella chuckled. "Mr. Campanale wanted me to use his tips for something special. I believe the hospital fund qualifies."

"It certainly does."

Just the sound of his voice could start her skin humming, her fingers itching to touch him, her heart thudding.

Reese gave the auctioneer the jar and took her hand. He led her through the crowd, past an apoplectic Madeleine, and down the stairs to the gangway.

The band was just striking up as Bella and Reese exited the ship, walking in silence to the near-deserted pavilion.

Candles flickered in the soft breeze while the drayage employees were breaking down the tables. Reese whispered something to one of the men and the pavilion emptied.

They were alone.

Their fingers linked, Reese led Bella to the middle of the pavilion. It was their own private dance floor. The muted music from the band floated to them on the soft evening breeze.

Reese twirled her in front of him and opened his arms. It was the most natural thing in the world for Bella to step into them, her head resting against his chest. Reese circled her waist and pulled her close. They swayed in time to the music.

Bella savored it, pushing out any hint of Madeleine. This was for her. For the rest of her nights without him. She'd won him fair and square. Well, okay, perhaps not fair, but Staci *had* given her the winning bid.

His hand spanned her waist, his fingers skimming the cutouts on the back of the bodice, and Bella forgot all about the restaurant and her stepmother and everything else but Reese. Her skin sparked wherever he touched. Tiny tremors shivered across her back as he pulled her closer, the steady thump of his heart beating beneath her cheek. Her own stammered a reply and her breath hitched as his hand slid up her spine. The intoxicating mix of Reese and his cologne assailed her as the lights twinkled around them.

"Bella." His voice rumbled against her cheek.

She shivered, but not from cold. Bella tilted her head back to find his mouth a mere whisper away.

"I was hoping you'd bid," he murmured just as his mouth captured hers.

Bella stood on her toes, leaning into the embrace. Letting the strength of him support her as their lips met.

This was no tentative first kiss; they'd dispensed with that days ago. This was a kiss of remembrance, yearning for another chance.

Reese's mouth slanted over hers. He nipped at each of her lips before his tongue urgently traced the seam between them. On Bella's groan, he swept in.

He tasted far better than her memories. Better than her dreams. Bella clenched his arms as her knees threatened to buckle. His biceps tightened and one of his hands found her head, caressing her scalp as his kisses claimed her mouth.

His other arm slid beneath her backside, lifting her up to delve so he could kiss her more deeply, and Bella wanted to crawl inside the haven his arms offered, wanted to blot out everything else but what was happening right here and now between them.

She threw her arms around his neck, plunging her hands into the thick chestnut waves brushing his collar. She returned his kisses, her tongue melding with his, and knew this was a night she'd always remember.

The kiss went on and on. Time stopped and Bella was aware of only Reese. He surrounded her. He filled her.

He *ful*filled her.

She wanted it to go on forever.

"Well isn't *this* cozy?"

A tidal wave of cold water crashed over them. Madeleine stood ten feet away, her hands clenching her bony hips.

Bella stumbled away from Reese as if she'd been shot. His arms tightened, but Bella squirmed, yanking herself free.

She could only imagine the ramifications of this nightmare. Madeleine's eyes were *blazing*, her lips clamped together so tightly it looked like she'd swallowed them.

Bella cleared her throat, ran her fingers shakily through her hair, though the effort was futile, she knew. She smoothed her dress and tried to erase the passion from her face.

From the look Madeleine gave her, Bella knew she'd failed miserably.

"Mad—" Bella started.

"I believe we were having a private meeting." Reese sounded more composed than Bella felt.

If she weren't standing right next to him, well, okay, practically on top of him, she wouldn't have realized the angry hold he had on his emotions. His muscles were rigid.

Madeleine didn't appreciate the rebuke. The woman tossed her head, lifted her nose in the air, and turned on her heel. "And I shall have my own private meeting with Mr. Fiorello." She glared back at Bella but kept on walking. "Right now."

Bella started after her, but Reese grabbed her arm. "Let her go."

Bella started to tremble and desire had nothing to do with it. "Oh no oh no oh no." She wrung her hands. "I knew this would happen. I knew it. How could I have let it happen?"

"It's okay, Bella, I can handle Madeleine."

"You don't understand, Reese. No one can handle her. Not when she has the legal right—" Bella pinched the bridge of her nose. "Oh, God. It's all ruined. What have I done?" Her head throbbed. She massaged her temples.

Reese gripped her shoulders, his fingers kneading the flesh above her collarbone. "Sssh, Bella. It's all right. Don't worry."

Her eyes flew open. "Don't *worry*? Worry is about the only thing I can do." She pulled away from him again. "I've got to talk to her. I can still fix it." She looked around, trying to get her bearings. Which way had Madeleine gone?

There. Bella hiked up her long skirt to run past Reese when he grabbed her arm. His voice was urgent.

"Bella, let me—"

Bella squirmed away. "Let you? I can't *let* you. Letting you is why she's so mad in the first place." She started to run. "Oh, God, please don't let me be too late."

She stumbled as she ran over something small and round and shiny on the floor, and tripped out of her shoe. Reese was too close for her to stop and pick it up without having to fight with him again. She had to get to Madeleine before the woman did something irreversible.

Bella gave a last look at her pump lying on its side, irony gnawing at her insides, but she still ran after Madeleine.

Along the way, she pulled off the other shoe, then flew up the gangplank and stairs, ignoring the calls from Jolie, Staci, and Giac. She ran around the ship's bridge to the tables on the back deck.

And there, primly setting a pen down, her back straight, sat

Madeleine. She handed a stack of papers to Mr. Fiorello and turned to Bella.

That feral grin was back in place.

Bella could only stare, horror-stricken. It was gone. All of it.

Oh, God. Please, no.

Before she could stop herself, Bella strode up to her stepmother. "Madeleine—"

"Lucinda." Madeleine's tongue slithered between her teeth. "Where are your manners? Surely you want to congratulate your new boss on his very recent purchase of our restaurant?" Her hand swept toward Mr. Fiorello.

Bella gritted her teeth and tried to smile politely to the man.

"And do be a dear and take Gus's... *thing*...home with you, won't you?" Madeleine pushed back in her chair and held the soufflé out to Bella.

Before Bella could reach it, a blur of something small and bald with wire-rimmed spectacles lurched forward. "Oh, my pardon. I must have had a bit too much of my whiskey." Mr. Griff bumped into Madeleine.

The soufflé teetered for a moment, then fell back as if in slow motion, splattering against the woman's chest, orange and brown globs landing squarely in the middle of Madeleine's stark white sash, the only relief from the absolute black of her dress. Large chunks of the soufflé wavered for a moment from their precarious perch then plopped to the floor beneath—and onto Madeleine's brand new black suede heels.

Madeleine shrieked into the stunned silence, "You careless, little man! Look what you've done!"

Luckily, Mr. Griff moved away or Bella swore Madeleine might have struck him. The woman brushed her sash, but only succeeded in spreading the spongy orange mixture even more. She threw down her hands in disgust. "That's it! I have had it with Gus and the restaurant, and this stupid thi... thing, whatever it is." She snarled at Bella. "I'm glad I sold it!"

That was it, then. Sobs threatened to overwhelm Bella, but she refused to give Madeleine the satisfaction. Or the opportunity to threaten Sophia. It galled Bella that she had to bite back her bile over losing the restaurant, but Sophia was more important. She couldn't risk Madeleine's anger any more. That kiss had done enough damage.

While Madeleine sputtered and cursed Mr. Griff, Bella threw back her shoulders, spun on her shoeless heel and regally walked back to the stairwell, past Reese, down the stairs, took Bruno's keys from him, promised Jolie more money to see to the clean-up, and left just as the church clock chimed midnight.

# Chapter Thirty-Eight

R eese punched Bella's doorbell at an ungodly early hour the next morning. Not that it mattered to him what time it was because he had yet to even glance at a mattress. He'd been up the rest of the night planning how to fix this. Selling the restaurant had caught him completely unawares. God, the woman truly was a monster, threatening Bella with both her sister *and* her legacy.

No wonder Bella had steered clear of him. Well, no more. Madeleine had thought she was cashing in her trump cards, but she hadn't yet dealt with him. Or his parents. Mom, especially. The woman would do anything when her children's happiness was threatened. Even loan him way too much money.

He punched the bell again, not caring if he woke the whole damn household. Someone needed to call the woman on the carpet and he was so going to relish doing it.

He gave up on the bell and pounded the door. The transom above it shook. Good. That's how he felt after spending the rest of the party and what was left of the night worrying about Bella, wracking his brain, then calling his parents, his attorney, and any favor he could think of.

Drew opened the door bleary-eyed. Well, that couldn't be helped. "Where's Bella?"

The girl shook her head and shrugged.

"Then where's Madeleine?" Reese demanded.

Drew stepped aside and waved a hand somewhere past the stairs. Reese took it as an invitation.

He strode into an empty kitchen and saw a set of French doors opened to a patio.

Madeleine, sipping tea from a delicate cup as if she were royalty, sat there on a wicker chair in an austere white dressing gown that made her hair look as insidiously black as her soul.

She sat back calmly, setting the cup in its saucer, its slight rattle the only indication she was not as composed as she affected. She offered him an inquiring smile.

He wanted to slap it right off her face, but as God was his witness, he'd never struck a woman in his life. If Madeleine were a man, however, she'd be eating dirt right now through gaping holes in her gum line.

She rose. "Why, Mr. Charmant, this is an unexpected—"

"Sit down." Reese had no time—nor inclination—for niceties.

She sat.

*Good.* He grabbed one of the other flimsy wicker chairs. It crackled when he half-crushed it beneath his fingers. Again, *good.* He felt like breaking something. He spun the chair around, straddling it.

Madeleine's eyes flickered at the French doors. *Ha. Flicker away, lady, because you've got to get past me to get off this patio.* He wasn't allowing her to go anywhere until he had his say.

And his way.

Madeleine might think she knew what being in control of a situation was, but now, he was in charge.

Because he held something he knew she wanted.

"I'm here for one reason only."

She quirked an eyebrow at him, which simply made her look more like the pointed weasel-faced wretch she was.

"My mother will decline the seat on the Board and recommend you, but I want something in return."

He'd surprised her. *Good.*

"Why?" Her eyes narrowed.

"Because you're going to rescind the sale of the restaurant you made last night."

"I can't. I signed papers."

"State law says that you have three days to change your mind in a business deal. You just changed your mind."

Madeleine tapped her thin, shriveled lips. "But with the restaurant gone, I have no reason to care about being on the Board and since I sold it, I obviously don't care to be on the Board."

Reese stood up and leaned on the table, his face mere inches from hers. "Oh you care. You put this family through hell because you care so much. Last night was just your showboating. Rescind the damn sale."

"And if I refuse?"

*Don't tempt me, lady.* "I'll use the full force of my celebrity to blacken your name not only in town, but across the entire state. Hell, I can call the media and make it nationwide. Toss my mother's cachet in there and this could go worldwide. You won't be able to show your face anywhere with any semblance of dignity, let alone be on *any* Board whatsoever. Everything you've worked for—threatened and blackmailed for—will be gone."

The color drained from her face—not a particularly good look on her—but the woman had chutzpah that was for sure, as she sucked in her panic, slid a calculating grin onto her face, and strummed her claws on the tabletop.

"So I keep the restaurant and you'll ensure me a seat on the Board?"

"No." He pulled an envelope from his back pocket, set it on the table, and slid it across to her. "You'll sell *me* the restaurant and I'll ensure you my mother's backing. I can't speak for the entire Board."

"That's not good enough."

"That's all I've got. Take it or leave town because I guarantee after I get through spilling this whole sordid tale to the media, you're not going to want to be here."

He'd do it, too. It no longer mattered that he was obliterating the line between his personal and professional lives because Bella's happiness was tantamount to everything.

He realized that now. Come hell or high water—or even Madeleine—Reese would use whatever talents, strengths, know-how he had to make Bella happy.

Madeleine took a sip of her tea. Oh, she was trying to be cool, calm, and collected, but Reese could see the flutter at the base of her throat.

He could feel the pounding in his temple. He didn't need this.

"All right. I'll do it."

"And you'll give custody of Sophia to Bella."

The veneer of civility slipped from Madeleine's face and she laughed a cruel, heartless laugh. "Over my cold dead body. That little girl is mine."

"She's not yours. She's Bella's blood, and you care for her as much as you care for Bella. Besides, with your Board activities, you won't have time to care for her." He nodded at the papers. "And with the sale of the restaurant, you'll have more than enough money to live on. You won't need Sophia's money."

"I've never taken a dime of that child's money."

"So you say. But the speculation could ruin your reputation by the time an audit is conducted. Do you really want to have that specter hanging over your head?" He looked at the time on his cell phone. "I've got an appointment with the local news in thirty minutes. Do we have a deal or not?"

Madeleine gnawed on the inside of her cheek—another not-so-good-look on her—and her eyes narrowed to slits. She picked up the papers and nervously unfolded and re-folded them. "Why on earth do you want to tie yourself down to this provincial little town? You could be in Hollywood. New York. And to do it with *Bella* of all people? God, man, have you no taste?"

Reese reigned in his anger. "Just sign the damn papers. The sale and custody."

"What? Did you have your attorney up all night? I hope he charged you through the nose."

"Just sign the papers." His fingers curled into a fist instinctively, but he unfurled them. He would not go to jail for assault; that'd ruin all his plans.

Of which the first half had just been completed. Reese patted his front pocket. Now it was time to go for the touchdown.

***

Luke leaned over and popped a grape into Staci's mouth. Thank goodness he'd planned-—*hoped*—ahead. He had at least four pounds of the fruit to get through.

"You're not sorry about pulling a fast one on your mother last night, then?" he asked gently.

Staci pulled the sheet up and chewed thoughtfully. She swallowed and shook her head. "No. I'm glad I finally defied her. What I didn't count on was what she'd do about it. I'd never thought she'd sell the restaurant. Not in a million years. She liked the income too much. That Mr. Fiorello must be made of money to offer enough for her to say yes." She took the next grape he offered. "Nope, I thought it'd be a way for Bella to get something nice in her life without worrying that my mother would send Sophia away." Staci sat all the way up.

"You know," she brushed a swath of hair off her face. "I never realized how controlling my mother really is. To what lengths she'd go to get her way."

"Really?"

"Really." Staci turned to him and Luke sucked in his breath. Gone was the tacky broad who'd worn the tight clothing. This new Staci, confident and giving, had an inner beauty which radiated out through her skin. "If you knew why she was the way she was, you might understand."

He liked this new Staci. Really liked her. Actually... he even loved her. Imagine that. "Eh hem." He cleared his throat. "So, why *is* she the way she is?"

"She's got entitlement issues. She thinks that—"

Luke's cell phone broke into their conversation. "It's my attorney. It might be about Jared."

Staci nodded. "I understand."

"Hello? What? Uh huh. Yeah. Okay. Sure, sure. What's the address?" Luke reached for a paper and pen. "Yeah, got it." He hung up. Boy, the last twenty-four hours were just full of surprises. "Well, I shouldn't have any problems getting full custody of Jared now that Tanya got arrested last night."

"She did? For what?"

Luke grinned. "You know, sometimes there is justice in this world. She's been arrested for solicitation." He held out a hand to her. "Were you serious when you said you liked kids?" He saw her startle of surprise and the little gnaw on her lip. But then there was a smile as her hand slid into his.

Her eyes sparkled. "Yes. I was. Let's go get your son."

"And maybe make him *our* son?"

Luke smiled as he helped a stunned-silent Staci get dressed and down to his car. This relationship thing was better than he'd ever realized. And good thing, too, because if he'd realized it sooner, he wouldn't be with Staci. And that would be a damn shame.

***

"I don't ever want to go home again, Chloe." Bella wrapped her hands around her coffee mug in her friend's farmhouse kitchen.

Chloe sat beside her and pulled a tray of muffins between them.

"I know, sweetie, but you can't just kidnap Sophia. Sophia's the ace up Madeleine's sleeve to keep you dancing to her tune and she knows it."

Bella sighed. "I know, but I'm just so worried she's going to send Sophia away. You should have seen how angry she was last night over one little kiss."

"Little?"

Bella felt her cheeks warm and not with embarrassment. She could still feel the heat between her and Reese. And wanted to relive it all over again, feel the thrill, the shimmering in her stomach, his body surrounding hers, his incredibly potent maleness overcoming her senses—and obviously, her good sense. "Well, okay, it was more than a little kiss, but I am an adult, for Pete's sake. Can't I kiss a guy without being made to feel like an awkward teenager?

"Apparently not," Chloe answered. "So what are you going to do now that she's sold the restaurant? Have you told Sophia?"

Bella shook her head. "I didn't have the heart to. I just picked her up from Aunt Theresa's house last night and brought her here. I told her Senara wanted to have a sleepover."

Chloe poured another round of coffee. "You know you're welcome to stay here as long as you like. Luckily, this place has plenty of bedrooms, but at some point you're going to have to face your evil stepmother."

Bella dropped her chin into her hand. "Do I have to?"

"Yes. You do. Maybe you should talk to Reese, too. The guy looked pretty bleak when you left."

Bella shook her head again. "What more can I say to him? He heard her, he knows I've got no place to run my catering business from, so he's definitely not going to be interested in hiring me again."

"What if he's interested in something else?"

Bella sighed. "It doesn't matter. Madeleine's proven she'll do whatever's necessary to keep me in line. I can take losing the restaurant, but I can't lose Sophia." Bella sat back, her hands on her thighs. "No, what I've got to do is get started on finding a place to build my catering business. Last night was a success, regardless of Madeleine's theatrics. And there was a huge turnout of this city's top movers and shakers. Hopefully, I'll get referral business." She stood. "I've just got to go back, eat crow around Madeleine, and keep Sophia safe at home. Once my business is established, I'll use my portion of the sale to fight her for custody. It's all I can do."

"And Reese?"

Bella turned from the tenderness in her friend's face. The pain was raw, but she could do nothing about it. "Until I've got custody of Sophia, I can't see him again. Period.

"Uh, Chloe? Bella?" Dakota, Chloe's eldest, called from the front door. "I think you're going to want to see this."

## Chapter Thirty-Nine

Reese was more nervous than he'd ever been in a game, or at any post-game interview. He shouldn't be; he was used to talking to the media, but that'd always been about a game or, of late, his business.

But today was different.

He shrugged into the new shirt and jacket his mom had brought with her. He could use a shower, but time had been his enemy last night so he'd have to make do. Some deodorant, cologne, and toothpaste were going to have to suffice.

"Are you sure you want to do this this way, honey?" His mom brushed some imaginary lint off the black fabric.

"I'm sure, Mom. That way, there's no question in anyone's mind. Especially Bella's."

His mother rolled her eyes. "She's a smart lady. She's not going to question you."

His mother didn't know Bella. But he did. And he knew this was right. For both of them.

"Is it here yet?" He looked at Kelly.

"Just pulled up. As ordered."

Reese ran a finger under his collar. "Good. It has to be perfect."

"Oh, honey, how could it not be with you behind all of this?"

Reese gave his mom a quick peck on the cheek and shook hands with his father. "Wish me luck."

***

Jonathan Griff chuckled and put away his iTouch. "It's not luck you're needing, Reese, my boy."

He picked up the reins, gave them a flick and started off to make the rendezvous.

***

Bella could *not* believe her eyes.

Even with Sophia and Chloe's kids laughing and hollering about it, and Chloe alternating between amusement and amazement, Bella couldn't comprehend what was pulling down the driveway of Chloe's farm.

A carriage.

A glass carriage.

A *round* glass carriage with big wheels, a liveried driver, a pair of footmen, and a bunch of horses.

And Reese riding inside.

"Uh, Bella?" Chloe nudged her. "I think your Prince Charming has just ridden in on his white horse."

"Six white horses," said Senara.

"And television cameras," added Sophia.

Bella tore her gaze away from Reese for a few seconds to see that, yes, there were indeed television cameras in the news vans following the carriage. When they reached the circular part of the driveway, the vans split up, each vying for the perfect angle as the carriage pulled up to the front porch steps.

The footmen—Giac and Gus—jumped off the back and opened the doors.

Mr. Griff, the driver, saluted her from the brim of his hat.

"Good thing you put that dress back on," Chloe muttered.

Bella fiddled with the skirt. She'd come straight here after leaving the boat and while she'd slept in one of Chloe's t-shirts, she'd decided to wear the dress home and change there.

Reese stepped down from the carriage.

Chloe nudged Bella's shoulder. "You might want to meet him halfway."

Bella took a tentative step down, but then stopped. What he was doing... Madeleine wasn't going to like it.

"Bella." Reese held out his hand as he climbed the porch steps to her.

Bella wanted to take it, but there was still Sophia to worry about. "Reese, I can't—"

He ran up the last three steps and put a finger to her lips. "Hear me out first."

Oh how she wanted to nibble on that finger. To suck it into her mouth and do all the stuff her dreams had imagined for her last night.

But she didn't. Because there were kids around. And camera crews.
*Camera crews?*

"What's with the reporters?" she whispered.

"Just pretend they're not there."

She raised her eyebrows. "You might be used to them, but I'm not." And didn't want to be. She wasn't quite sure where he was going with all of this, but she had a feeling he wouldn't want to get shot down on live tv.

Oh, God. *Live* tv…

He reached for her hand. A dozen cameras honed in on her face.

"What are you doing?" she whispered, trying not to enunciate clearly for lip readers watching at their homes.

He smiled at her. "It's all going to be all right, Bella. I spoke to Madeleine this morning."

"You what?" That she said loud and clear for everyone to hear.

Reese smiled and brushed a few strands of hair from her face. "I told you. It's all going to be all right." He reached into his back pocket and pulled out a folded stack of papers bound in blue and handed it to her. "It's all right here."

"I don't understand—"

"Read them."

She bit her lip before taking the papers warily as if they were going to bite her. She didn't like blue-bound papers. Legal papers. She was almost afraid to open them.

"Go ahead. They won't bite."

She cracked a smile at that, but still took her time.

And then she read the words.

And she couldn't read them fast enough.

Now she certainly wasn't a law scholar, but words like *sale of Casteleoni's restaurant to Reese Charmant*, and *full custody of Sophia Analiese Casteleoni to Lucinda Isabella Casteleoni, effective immediately* were easy enough to understand.

It was the idea behind them, however, that still had her stumped.

"What does this mean?" Her voice was a whisper because of the shock.

"They mean just what they say. Madeleine sold me the restaurant and is giving custody of Sophia to you."

"But why?"

Reese glanced behind him at all the news vans. "Let's just say that it's in her best interests, especially if she wants to be on the Arts Center Board."

"But your mother has the last seat."

"No, my mother was *offered* the last seat. She declined—and very generously suggested Madeleine as her replacement."

"But why would the Board want Madeleine? She doesn't have a high profile or any big social or philanthropical connections."

"Ah, well, you see, that's where this gets a bit hazy. It's where you come in."

"Me?"

Reese nodded and pulled something from his jacket pocket as he bent down.

Onto one knee.

And then she saw what he was holding.

Her shoe. The one she'd lost on the boat.

Just like the first time they'd met.

Reese smiled up at her. "The reason you come in here is because Madeleine will have enough cachet for the Board if you would do one little thing." He held out his hand for her to put her foot in it.

Bella bit her lip to keep from laughing out loud. "Oh? And what little thing is that?"

He slid the shoe onto her foot. "That you marry me."

"Marry—?" She hadn't seen *that* coming.

Reese stood up and gripped her arms as she teetered in shock. "Yes, marry me. Be my wife. I love you, Bella, and I want you, me, and Sophia to be a family. Forever."

His gaze was so intense, this had to be real. It wasn't a dream. She glanced around. The cameras were trained on them, Gus, Giac, Mr. Griff, Chloe and all the kids, especially Sophia, were watching, hopeful smiles on everyone's face.

"Marry me, Bella. Make me the happiest man in the world."

She flung her arms around his neck. "Yes! Yes! Of course I will marry you!" she said as she rained kisses all over his face.

Until he gripped her head in his hands and brought her lips to his and sealed their pact for ever.

Bella got her family's legacy, her little sister, her Prince Charming, and her fairy tale all wrapped up in one.

The End

# MEMORANDUM

**TO:**  Raphael, Archangel

**RE:  HEA**, Case #HRHCLICC11134529875004213534.A1A

As follow-up to report A1 concerning Charges, Henry Reese Hapsburg Charmant and Lucinda Isabella Casteleoni Charmant, I have the following additions:

This angel-in-training wishes to acknowledge the exemplary contributions of fellow Guardians, Giovanni Fiorello and Angela Custode for their diligent supervision of their Charges, who were not always the most "suggestible" of individuals.

Angela Custode has affected great change in Anastasia Fontaine and cemented by the bidding process at the hospital auction, bringing about the woman's True Love three years early. As such, Colton Jamison has been granted a life that had not been Foreseen. His big brother Jared is thrilled with the latest addition to the family. Plans are still on track for Olivia Jamison to be born in the normal timeframe.

And to Giovanni Fiorello for diligently directing Madeleine Jean Smith Fontaine's contrary actions down a path that led to the final reconciliation with her objectives and The Grand Plan. Not knowing the final outcome is always tricky with maverick Charges such as Ms. Fontaine, and Giovanni comported himself well and in the best interests of his Charge, The Grand Plan, and our working relationship.

This Guardian-in-training is thankful to have had two such talented Guardians to assist him in this assignment and is happy to report that everyone has attained their prescribed Happily-Ever-After.

Respectfully submitted,
Jonathan Griff, Guardian-in-training

# Thank you!

Thank you for reading *If The Shoe Fits*. If you enjoyed this story, please help others find it by posting a review on Goodreads, Amazon, Apple Books, Barnes & Noble… wherever you bought it. Feel free to share a link, tweet about it, Facebook it… All efforts are greatly appreciated.

I love to hear from my readers so check me out online and feel free to friend me!

www.JudiFennell.com
https://www.facebook.com/JudiFennell.Author/
https://www.goodreads.com/series/list/2778890.Judi_Fennell.html
https://www.bookbub.com/authors/judi-fennell


Sign up for my newsletter at:
http://JudiFennell.com/newsletter-signup/

Keep reading Kate and Alex's story in *Through the Leaded Glass*

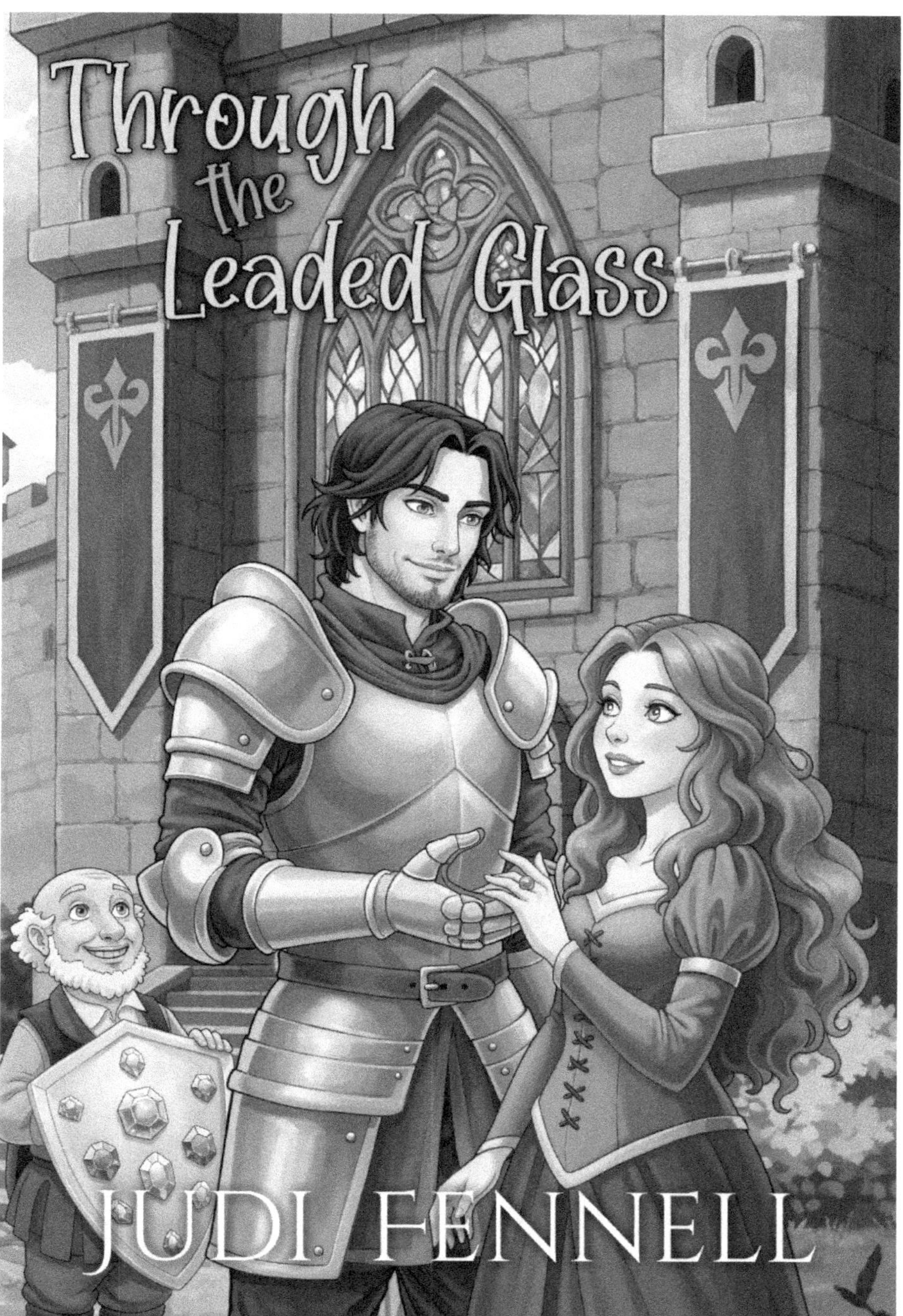

Through
the
Leaded Glass
JUDI FENNELL

*Once upon a time...*

Not so very long ago,
there lived a girl who had it all:
marriage, career, a happily ever after.
She was set for life.

This is not her story.

*This* is the story of a career girl
who didn't need a man—
until a (real) knight in shining armor and a magic ring
Showed her that falling in love is timeless.

# Prologue

*English Countryside, 1487*

The earl of Shelton's day was well on its way to hell.

"God's blood!" Alexander Traverse stormed into his tent and slammed his gauntlets onto the table.

Nicholas, Baron Crawford of Caversham, amiable friend, but more often of late, miserable sot, raised his mug with an "I'll drink to that," before slumping back into his chair.

Alex slammed the gauntlets again. "My pardon for interrupting your rest, Nick."

Nick peeled one eye open. "I'm not resting. I'm toasting your upcoming betrothal." He sloshed some ale over the rim.

Alex grabbed the drink. "You've had enough."

"No." Nick made an ineffectual grab for the mug which almost sent him tumbling to the ground. "I haven't had enough."

"What's gotten into you, Nick?"

"Bout half a cask of ale, I'm guessing."

Alex spilled the remains into a ewer and tossed the mug onto a bench. "I need you sober."

"But *I* need me drunk." Nick looked around. "What'd you do with m'drink?"

"Your drink is the least of my worries when the Shelton betrothal ring has gone missing."

Surprisingly, it only took two bleary-eyed blinks for Nick to understand the implications. "The ring's *gone*? But… but that means…"

"That there is a thief in my home."

Nick managed to sit up. "More than that, it means your luck is gone. You shouldn't joust. And Isobel—oh, no." He crossed himself—

surprising because religion was usually the first thing Nick tossed when he tossed back his drink. "You can't ask for her hand now."

"Of course I can. I just can't use that ring to do so."

"Isobel will never agree, Alex. No woman will. The legend says—"

"I'm more concerned with a thief in my home than an ancient legend, Nick. And, as a God-fearing man, I'd think you'd place no faith in the legend of the ring. You can't possibly believe in it."

"How can you not? Your family's good fortune is said to be tied to the ring."

If it were anyone but his friend questioning him, Alex would thrash him for his insolence. "No more ale, Nick. You sound as mad as that gypsy woman this morn. Though she did say it with sweeter breath."

"The gypsy wasn't Telesa?"

"No. Another. A stranger." Which was the damnable thing. He would not have expected Telesa to allow a stranger into her territory.

"What did she say?" Nick asked, looking more sober by the minute.

"Don't tell me you believe in fortune-telling as well as legends."

"Gypsy women's tales—especially *strange* gypsy women's tales—are not to be dismissed. You of all people should know. What'd she say?"

Alex knew all about gypsy fortune-telling thanks to Telesa and her band. They'd camped on his family lands in his youth and he'd seen how they used their so-called fortunes as mere ploys for trinkets and gold from the *gadje*.

He pulled on his gambeson. With his squire off to replace the bridle Alex now believed had been ruined on purpose, Nick was the only aid he'd have to arm himself for today's joust—hence the reason he was doing it himself.

"The gypsy was spouting dire warnings of death and destruction unless I aid the woman who finds what I've lost." He picked up his cuirass. "Help me with this."

"No." Nick sat back in his chair. "Dire warnings, Alex. This could be the day you finally lose. You shouldn't joust."

"Dear God, Nick, what's wrong with you? It's a story. A legend. And I didn't *lose* it; it was stolen." Of that he was certain; he'd hidden the ring with the rest of the keep's valuables after his wife's death.

He sucked in the pain that still had the power to steal his breath a year later. *Jeanne.* And the baby she'd died birthing. Only young William was left.

Alex closed his eyes. Damn fate for taking them from him. And damn the king for requiring him to marry again.

But such was his duty. His dammed duty.

He shoved the gauntlets aside as he set the cuirass on the table. "There's no truth to the legend, Nick. I'll beat Farley, ring or no. I haven't lost to him yet."

"*Yet.* The ring's never been gone before."

"You want me to forfeit over a legend?"

"It's not as if you need the gold."

"True. But what of honor? How well do you think Isobel would regard my suit if I bow out of the joust like a coward?" Nick knew nothing of honor anymore. He was drunk more often than not. But then, he could be for he didn't stand to lose what Alex would if he didn't follow the king's edict. "No, Nick, I must meet Farley. As I need Isobel's birthing ability to ensure the Traverse lineage, she needs my reputation to save her family land."

"Her *birthing ability*?" Nick picked up a gauntlet and flung it at him, his aim on point, surprisingly. "God's teeth, Alex, you reduce her to a brood mare? What about her status as your *wife*?"

"Jeanne was my wife."

"It'll be difficult to beget legitimate heirs from Isobel without marriage."

"Of course I'll offer Isobel marriage. But I don't have to like it."

"Then why do it?"

"'*La grandeur d'un homme se mesure à la parole tenue.*'" The measure of a man is but the strength of his words. The Shelton motto had been ingrained in him since youth. Unfortunately, the same couldn't be said for his older brother. Alex wouldn't be in the position he was in if Frederick had sired his sons on the right side of the blanket. "I gave my word to King Henry that I'd marry within thirty days."

"But what about love?"

What did Nick know of love? The man flitted from intrigue to intrigue like a butterfly among flowers. Alex, however, was all too familiar with the concept. Which was why that emotion would never again enter into his marriage. It had hurt too much when he'd lost it.

"Help me prepare for the joust, Nick. I'll make swift work of Farley, then return to my keep to discover who has stolen the ring, and Isobel will never be the wiser."

About many things, actually. Other items had gone missing over the months. A hawk, a horse, provisions from the pantry... The girth on his saddle had been loosed on three occasions, as well, and now there was the frayed bridle. And the ring.

Something was very wrong at Shelton and Alex was determined to find out who was behind it.

'Twas bad enough he had to dance to the king's tune; he wouldn't dance to a thief's.

# Chapter One



*Pennsylvania Countryside, Present Day*

*O*h lord, get me out of this mess.

Kate Lawton untangled her curls from the grommet holes of her green brocade surcoat and surveyed the area around her. *Ready or not.*

*Not.*

She adjusted the neckline of the gold shirt and tossed an over-sized sleeve off her wrist. Her watch snagged on the lining. Great. Alicia would kill her if she wore a twenty-first century item with her so-called authentic medieval costume where anyone could see.

She flung the watch into the back of her Beamer with the rest of her modern day trappings. Well, except for the credit card, cash, and ever-present cell phone she shoved into her pocket. Those she couldn't do without. And she was keeping her running shoes on. They'd be hidden beneath the burgundy taffeta skirt.

*Jolly old England, here I come.* She made sure she had her ticket, then headed to the castle gate of the Pennsylvania Renaissance Faire, passing a King Arthur wannabe and his two goth-Guineveres. Merlin stood by a fountain in the market square speaking to a courtier, a hunchback chatted with a fairy, and a tavern wench practically spilled out of her costume welcoming people to the "shire." People really did this on their days off? Fun, she guessed. If it were your cup of tea. If Alicia weren't her oldest and dearest friend…

Kate dug her cell phone out of her pocket and called her.

"Good day to you, fair lords and ladies." For all Alicia's Anglophilia, she sure could butcher an English accent. "I'm off to the shire and unavailable 'til Monday. Please leave a message at the chime."

Kate tapped the phone off and sighed. Technology was a wonderful thing—why the hell couldn't her friend have decided to abandon this century *after* Kate had caught up with her? She was already thirty minutes late.

Shaking her head, Kate pulled out the map Alicia had e-mailed her and looked for the route to the jousting field along Guildsman's Way. Alicia had marked a blue banner as their meet-up spot.

Following the signs, Kate passed minstrels, a street juggler or two, and more than a few knights in shining armor, along with hundreds of others in period costume. Any period, it seemed, that suggested England of yore. Young and old, even babies, were done up in the spirit of the faire. Kate smiled when a little girl of about two jumped around waving a pirate's hook and grabbing at the plumed hat on her head.

Soon, very soon, that would be her and Emma. One more office visit to complete the adoption agency's paperwork and then she'd be all set for the trip to China next month to get her daughter.

She took a deep breath and continued down the road, determined to enjoy today and not live in the future, though it couldn't come quick enough.

Guildsman's Way was filled with all sorts of shops. Mostly kitschy, but then, what would one want after a day spent in old time England but a bunch of shields and swords and… were those lizards? She looked at the sign. Ah, baby dragons. That was actually a great marketing idea.

The jester juggling medieval cookware through this crowd, however, wasn't. He was a disaster waiting to happen.

Which, of course, was what happened. Kate almost got conked on the head with a cast iron skillet when the breeze blew his silver and purple ruff into his face and his figurative house of cards came tumbling down.

As it was, she half-fell onto a table outside one of the shops, then almost skewered her palm when it landed on a bunch of metal-worked jewelry. Rings, circlets, costume pieces in tarnished brass with bad fake jewels—even a tacky dog collar choker.

She was about to turn away when she saw an interesting ring. The dingy brass band was more polished than the others near it, though the fan of metal behind the stone was banged and dull. Grime covered the glass emerald and she was surprised by its weight. If she didn't know any better—and the price weren't so low—she'd swear that enormous gemstone was real.

She slid it onto her finger. It was the right size. Maybe...

*Nah.* Like she'd have any place to wear a banged-up piece of costume jewelry. She removed it and set it down, only to plant her palm on top of it when the jester knocked into her again.

She looked at the ring. It looked... odd. As if the surface was rippling with different shades of green.

It had to be a trick of the light. She picked it up, turning it to so the facets caught the sunlight. There was an engraving inside the band. "*La* something something, *à la*, something." Illuminating.

She was about to put it back when the merchant bowed to her from behind the table. He was dressed head to toe in orange and brown, complete with an bit ol' feather in his hat that brushed across her face.

"May I help you, my lady? I have a goodly assortment—"

The clang of the jester's cookware as he walked away and the wail of a fire engine drowned out the rest of the man's words.

"Shall I wrap that for you or will you wear it?"

"What?" She looked at the ring. "Oh, no, I don't want—"

"Nonsense, my lady. Of course you do. Why the stone matches your surcoat. It's one of the finest specimens I have from the late medieval period." He took the ring from her and slid it back onto her finger. "And perhaps I could interest you in a matching necklace and ear bobs?"

The guy was slick, and what the hell... It'd make a good story. "Earbobs sound painful, but I will take the ring." She gave him his five bucks; he'd earned it.

"Pray, do not miss Captain Drake's *Golden Hinde*, my lady, on your way to the joust. I'm certain you shall find other items of interest there. "

"Uh, sure. Thanks." Kate doubted it. One banged up piece of fake jewelry was enough. So was all the "my lady"ing. Kate Lawton, Assistant Vice President for McGoldrick Advertising, was through being "*my lady*"ed. That had been the sarcastic term Jay, her ex-husband, had used every time she'd wanted to get a job or start a family. Since the divorce, she'd worked too hard to earn her title and the respect of her colleagues to be addressed in such an archaic, sexist way. It was her personal measure of success that she'd earned the career and respect she'd sought. And now, she was just a few signatures and a plane ride away from the family part.

Still, when she saw the ship—a *pirate* ship—complete with mast, bow, and gangplank, she decided to stop. Alicia loved all things pirate and a bribe, er, gift might mitigate any anger for being late.

Kate crossed the "gangplank," passing a "pirate" the size of a refrigerator who would have had no trouble making someone walk the plank. Sawdust and leather tickled her nose as she headed toward the bow where a thin, bald man shuffled some items on a gnarled wood table. He turned at her approach, smoothing a silver shirt down over purple pants and did the bowing bit everyone here was so fond of.

"Good day, m' lady." A smile lit his lined face as he tied a purple bandana over his head. "I am Master Griff. What can I get for you?"

Another "m' lady." Kate stifled a snort. And what was with all the purple? Official faire colors? "Hello, Master Griff."

His weathered skin, with the deep creases at his mouth, looked as if he really had spent time on the open sea. The glasses he wore could only be called spectacles, but the astonishing green eyes that twinkled behind those spectacles were completely out of character, glittering as if they held the knowledge of the ages.

"I'll bet you want a special item and I have just the thing." His gaze raked her from head to toe, stopping on her new ring. "Yes, just the thing."

He took a shield from one of the bins behind him. A dented, tarnished shield, faintly etched around the perimeter with cloudy glass jewels barely fastened to the surface. The leather straps on the back had seen better days.

"I was thinking of something in better condition," Kate said.

"I'm sure you were. But—" He jerked his head and lowered his voice, reeling her in as if he were about to share the secrets of the universe with her. "Then you wouldn't have something special. You'd have just another common shield. This has some character. It has—" His gaze darted around the dim interior of the ship as he whispered— "a history."

Of course it did. "Really."

He leaned in closer, his voice lower. "This was a nobleman's ceremonial shield. The etchings were inlaid with gold and it was covered in sapphires and rubies." He slid the shield across the table, dust bunnies leaping like lemmings over the edge.

"Legend says that on the day the nobleman was to propose to his second wife, the family betrothal ring was stolen." He ran a finger along the shield's rough edge, his watch band scraping on the metal.

Oh sure, *he* got to wear his watch.

"The ring was the family's good luck charm, and from the moment it went missing, it was the beginning of the end for the poor man." Master Griff rubbed his chin. "There was a jousting tournament that day. The man competed. He'd always led a charmed life..."

"And?" Kate leaned her hip against the table and crossed her arms, her new ring snagging on a loose thread.

"Well, the nobleman didn't believe all that nonsense about the ring being a good luck charm, so even though it'd been stolen, he went ahead with the joust. 'Course he'd never lost before, so he wasn't worried at all."

"Let me guess. He lost."

Master Griff's smile disappeared. "Yes. To his sworn enemy. And not only was he defeated, but gravely injured as well."

"Then what?" Despite herself, Kate wanted to know where this was leading. The guy was good.

"His injuries ended his jousting career and his ability to defend the king."

"But why lose everything just because he couldn't joust anymore? If he was a nobleman, he should've had lands and other means of income."

"Ah." Master Griff wagged his finger in her face. "I said *he* didn't believe the legend, but his people and the lady he planned to marry did. When the ring went missing, she knew the good fortune was over and distanced herself from him." He sighed. "When that happened, others saw the beginning of the end and abandoned him as well."

"Like rats leaving a sinking ship."

Master Griff nodded. "And so, with rumors abounding, they shunned him and his people. The coffers ran dry, supplies low, and, as a final blow, his young son was found murdered within the castle walls. The man was left alone, without income, save a few possessions." Master Griff pointed to the shield. "One that you see before you, much the worse for wear."

Kate tapped her lips. She'd bet the twenty bucks this thing cost that there was an identical one beneath the counter, but what the hell. Alicia loved stuff like this and she'd get a kick out of the story.

She smiled. "I'll take it. If the shield isn't worth your price, the story certainly is."

"And now you have a very special item. One no one else has."

"And no one probably wants, judging from the looks of it," she added as she handed over the cash. How many times a day did he tell this same story?

"Oh, trust me, there's not another one like it anywhere." He patted her hand. "Have a wonderful adventure here today. And be sure to visit the glass blower's shop. It's on your way to the joust."

Kate slid her arm through the leather straps as she left the ship, praying they'd hold together for the rest of the day, but she wasn't holding out much hope.

She felt the heat from the glass blower's ovens before she saw the shop, but the tinkling butterfly wind chimes were what got her to stop. They'd look pretty outside Emma's bedroom window.

She followed the cobblestone pathway lined with garden sculptures past the *Enchanted Forest Gifts* sign. A fountain gurgled beneath pergolas overflowing with flowering vines, silk butterflies, and twisting iridescent glass objects, like something you'd find in a fairy forest. Unfortunately the sounds of an airplane overhead and the trucks rumbling by on the Pennsylvania Turnpike just beyond the faire walls stole a little of the magic.

Lord. Now she was sounding like Alicia.

An alcove held more glass objects amid scented sachets, potpourri, and candles. She ran a finger lightly over a delicate blown-glass tulip's petals that appeared to be covered in dew, and a ceramic frog peeked out from under a bundle of cinnamon sticks beside a green-horned glass unicorn.

Out of the corner of her eye, she caught a flash of purple and silver as someone darted out from behind a statue at the end of the shop.

Had Master Griff *followed* her?

She went after him, peering around the corner where he'd run, but what she saw there stopped her cold.

A two-foot tall stained glass window, arched like something from a gothic church, leaned against the wall, with a design…

It was a picture of a woman. A woman with long auburn curls, and a green and burgundy dress just like *she* was wearing.

*Exactly* like she was wearing.

Kate walked toward the window. She wasn't a fan of coincidences, so either Alicia had had this outfit specially made or—

*Or what?* Kate shook her head. This place was getting to her, what with tales of magical rings and fairy forests.

But then a fairy *did* approach her. Or, rather, a teenager dressed as a fairy. Which was so much more normal than the road she'd started going down, thankfully.

"May I help you, my lady?" asked the sales clerk.

"That." Kate ignored the "my lady" and handed her some cash. "I'd like to buy it." Well, not really *like* to buy it; more like *compelled* to. She wanted to get to the bottom of the coincidence.

"Okay," said the clerk. "I'll be right back with some tissue paper to wrap it up."

Kate nodded absently, her attention caught by the vibrant colors of the piece. The green was so brilliant it looked like what the emerald on her ring ought to, and the woman's auburn hair gleamed like sherry when the sun hit it. The resemblance was amazing.

Kate brushed the long sleeves of her surcoat up her arms, hiked the shield higher, and reached for the window.

All of a sudden, the air around her stilled.

Then it began to shimmer.

Then, with a heart-thudding *whoosh*, it spiraled around her like a cocoon, blocking out every sound but her heartbeat. A brilliant burst of color whirled around her like a tornado, her world tilted, and…

…she started to fall.

# Books by Judi Fennell

**ROYALLY SUNK SERIES**

*Mermen and mermaids are just mythology, right?*

*Try telling that to the unsuspecting humans who fall head-over-heels for those who don't always have heels...*

### In Over Her Head

Reel's a merman without a tail, and Erica's terrified of the ocean. Only one thing could get her into the water: a gun. And only one thing could keep her there: the sexy merman who saves her life, only to risk his own.

### Wild Blue Under

Valerie's a mer princess landlocked in the middle of the country. Rod is the prince who sets out to rescue her. But can they dodge a usurper's plot and make it back to the ocean before his tail—and his claim to the throne—disappear forever?

### Catch of a Lifetime

Logan ran *away* from the circus; all he wants is for his life to be normal. The naked woman who shows up on his boat is anything *but* normal. Especially when Angel turns out to be a mermaid—with an angry sea monstress after her.

### Love on the Rocks

Princess Mariana isn't a poser; she really *is* an artist which she's about to prove with the statue she's carving on a deserted island. Problem is, Jace is hiding out there so the one thing that will set Mariana free from her royal prison is the one thing that will get Jace killed. Romance is rough enough, but when there's a tsunami in the weather forecast, love is on the rocks.

*Once Upon A Time sounds good in a fairy tale, but real life isn't like that.
Or... is it?
With the help of a guardian-angel-in-training, these lucky couples will find that
falling in love is the greatest tale of all!*

### *Beauty and The Best*

Jolie is a personal chef by day and a romance writer by night. So when she gets a gig for the hot reclusive artist, Todd, she has the perfect hero for her book. Until Todd finds out and kicks her out of his kitchen, his home, *and* his heart.

### *If The Shoe Fits*

Once upon a time, a long time ago, in a land far, far away, there lived a girl by the name of Cinderella. This is not her story. *This* is the story of Lucinda Isabella Casteleoni, who, like her namesake, has a wicked stepmother, two tacky stepsisters, and countless hours of hard work to (not) look forward to. But unlike that fairy tale princess, Bella's Prince Charming is nowhere to be found. Until a little old man with sparkling green eyes opens a shoe store down the street. Then the magic begins...

### *Through The Leaded Glass (prequel)*

An accidental trip to medieval England has ad exec Kate scrambling for a way home… But can she bring the hot knight in shining armor she's fallen in love with back with her?

~~~



*Girls' Night Out never tasted so good! Magic Mike has nothing on these guys.
Sit back and enjoy the show as the guys of BeefCake, Inc. show you how it's
done...*

### *Beefcake & Cupcakes*

Lara wants her cupcakes to be a success. Exotic dancer Gage wouldn't mind sampling them, but his work schedule to pay off his nephew's hospital bills doesn't leave him time to do so. Until a party where beefcake meets cupcakes and, *oh*, is it delicious!
~~~

*Beefcake & Mistakes*

When Bryan mistakes Jenna for a hooker and she realizes he's her adopted son's father, the mistakes and misunderstandings start to grow. But something else is growing between them, too. Sometimes, one wrong turn can be oh so right…

*Beefcake & Retakes*

Tanner wants his ex-wife to be out of his life forever, but when her grandmother has a stroke and he has to pretend to still be in love with Juliet, can he risk a retake on the one woman who never stopped loving him?

*Beefcake & Snowflakes*

Gina's had a crush on Darien since forever—until the day he humiliated her in school. Fifteen years later, he leaves her cold. Exotic dancer Darien has come back to town to set a few things to rights. One is the mess he made for Gina years ago… and *maybe* rekindle the flames they'd once had. But the only way to melt the snow around Gina's heart is to turn up the heat, both on the job… and off.

<div align="center">~~~</div>

## MANLEY MAIDS SERIES

*What happens when three irresistibly sexy brothers lose a poker bet to their enterprising sister? They get hired out for her housecleaning venture. Now, the Manley Maids are at your service. Satisfaction guaranteed.*

*What A Woman Wants*

Resort owner Sean plans to buy an historic estate, making a name for himself and making millions, so he moves in under the guise of cleaning the place to thwart the one condition of the inheritance. But heir Olivia and her menagerie get under his skin, and he finds that the poker bet that got him into this mess isn't the only game-changer.

*What A Woman Needs*

Movie star Bryan wants fame and fortune, not a repeat of his penny-pinching "normal" childhood. After the publicity surrounding of her husband's death, Beth needs is a normal life for herself and her children, and the movie star who lost a bet to clean her house—with paparazzi in tow—isn't it. But as flirtation turns into seduction, Bryan needs to convince Beth he's more man than a maid. Or actor. Because he's playing the lead in a reverse Cinderella story, and it might just be the role of a lifetime.

### *What A Woman Gets*

Liam has no patience for women who spend a man's money without giving a thought to any actual work. But to make good on his bet, Liam must not only tolerate socialite, Cassidy, he'll have to clean up after her when her father cuts her off. With no money and no home for Liam to clean, Cassidy has no choice but to accept a job offer— as Liam's new maid. But when sparks fly between them, will it be true love or just another messy affair?

### *What A Woman*

MaryAlice Catherine is all set to clean her grandmother's friend's house, only to find the woman's cocky grandson whom she'd had a crush on growing up—and he'd known all along—is living there and she's mortified. Jared remembers it differently; Mac was always a bossy little thing, but he's not going to let her call the shots now. But with the two of them living in one house, there's no telling who's going to come out swinging.

### *What A Guy Wants*

Beckett is ready to pay up for his lost poker bet. He just didn't realize he'd have to do it with his heart. Jennifer is the one who got away and now she's right here in front of him. In her house. That he's here to clean. Jennifer can't believe the bad boy from high school she'd had a major crush on is in her home, but if there's one thing her ex-husband taught her, it's that she can't count on the bad boy. Until Beckett lays all his cards on the table and he turns out to be someone Jennifer can bet on after all.

www.JudiFennell.com

# Here's Judi!

Award-winning, best-selling author Judi Fennell loves to laugh and loves love, so it's no surprise there's a little bit of each in every book she writes. Check out her fairy tales with a twist for a taste of her light-hearted, tongue-in-cheek paranormal and romantic comedies. From mermen off the coast of the Jersey Shore, to genies with magic carpets, to male strippers à la Magic Mike, and manly maids whose motto is *Satisfaction Guaranteed*, there's always a laugh and love to be had.

And, in her copious (?) amounts of spare time, she helps authors with all aspects of writing and indie-publishing with her formatting, cover and promotional design, editorial, consultation, and audiobook company, www.formatting4U.com.

Judi lives in suburban Philadelphia with a menagerie of four-legged friends, and the minute those creatures start A) singing, B) sewing clothing, or C) cleaning the house will be the day she retires from writing…!

www.ingramcontent.com/pod-product-compliance
Lightning Source LLC
Chambersburg PA
CBHW071754190726
48292CB00003B/975